Thursday's Child

Published by Brolga Publishing Pty Ltd
ABN 46 063 962 443
PO Box 12544
A'Beckett St
Melbourne, VIC, 8006
Australia

email: markzocchi@brolgapublishing.com.au

National Library of Australia
Cataloguing-in-Publication data
Tracey Friday, author.
ISBN 9780987639004 (paperback)

A catalogue record for this book is available from the National Library of Australia

Printed in Australia
Cover design and Typesetting by Elly Cridland

Thursday's Child

Tracey Friday

Dedication

In memory of much loved Nan Finch,
forever an inspiration.

Chapter One

Iris was enjoying her stroll as she made her way back from the village store. It was a perfect spring afternoon and the air was pleasantly scented with the heady aroma of honeysuckle. Savouring the moment, she tilted her head back and closed her eyes as she faced the warmth of the sun. Her curly brunette hair cascaded over her shoulders as she smiled and breathed in deeply.

"Honeysuckle, my favourite," she said, now facing the abundant hedgerow. "I'll pick a bunch for the kitchen window sill, what do you think?"

There was no reply from her daughter Maggie. She was searching for a four-leafed clover within a tuft of grass in the middle of the lane.

"Mind you," Iris continued, "we'll have to make sure there are no white fly or other bugs, don't want them crawling all over the kitchen, do we?"

Again, there was no reply.

Iris reached over to the hedgerow, mindful of not standing too close to the deep ditch. Being only five-foot-three inches tall, she needed to stand on tiptoe to reach a good-sized stem at the base and flicked it over. The stem made a satisfying popping sound as she pierced it with her thumbnail and felt the cool juice splash under her nail and trickle down to her palm.

Suddenly, the peace and tranquillity turned to sheer panic.

From all around the country lane flocks of birds, that had just seconds ago been snoozing, instantly catapulted skywards in unison. Their collective flapping and squawking was drummed out by the roar of the village air raid siren.

Iris immediately tossed the honeysuckle aside and sprinted the short distance to reach her daughter. As she passed her bicycle, her foot collided with the stand and the bicycle toppled over causing her to stumble, but thankfully, remain upright. "Maggie, quick," she said, as she grabbed her daughter's arm and they ran together to the ditch.

The bicycle wheels rotated horizontally at tremendous speed from the impact and the few groceries that were in the basket scattered from the force. The bag of flour, that had cost precious ration stamps, burst open and sent a small white cloud upwards. This was closely followed by a red ball of yarn that un-rolled itself as it sped down the lane as if to say, 'it's okay, follow me', before coming to a stop.

Even though Maggie was familiar with the siren's shrill tone, at five years old, it was still terrifying. She covered her ears trying to block out the deafening noise as hordes of planes flew overhead on their way to London. The vibration alone felt like the village brass band and drums were playing inside her chest and the ground seemed to jump under her feet.

Iris quickly assessed the groups of stinging nettles in the ditch. Cradling Maggie in her arms she hoisted her skirt up and over, encasing Maggie entirely. Her petticoat would offer some protection from the nettles as she jumped in. They landed, miraculously without injury, with Iris still shielding Maggie from possible bomb debris. For Maggie, jumping into ditches was the fun part, the vibration and thunderous noise was not.

The spring had been relatively dry, so there was no water awaiting them at the base. Even though the stench was initially stifling from the damp vegetation closest to the soil, that was not Iris's main concern right now. Still holding Maggie in her skirt cocoon, she crouched and tried to sit as comfortably and carefully as she could in the confined space. She lent backwards slightly with her back supported against the far side of the ditch and her feet wedged against the other side. Maggie was crying from the over-head noise more than the restraint.

"For goodness sake Maggie, stop crying," Iris shouted over the roaring noise, "we're safe here," although she wasn't too sure.

Being where she was made Iris recall another time when she had un-expectantly landed at the bottom of a ditch. As a young child she had one day leaned a little too far over the side to pick some wild strawberries. Even though her reach was stretched to the limit, she frustratingly found the tempting cluster was still a whisker away. But, holding her breath she was able to lean a touch more…

That touch more caused her to over-balance and tumble down the side, landing tummy down in shallow putrid water. Not only was she facing a clump of slimy frogspawn, but she had nearly swallowed a water-boatman bug when she suddenly gasped in, realising that the shallow water was home to hundreds of tadpoles swimming all around her. It gave the illusion that her lovely white Sunday dress had pulsating polka dots.

She had managed to grab a handful of wild strawberries as she tumbled, but they had been crushed from the impact. Her heart skipped a beat when she saw deep red oozing from her hand and as she slowly unclenched her fist she realised it was not blood but the once succulent fruits were now a messy pulp.

Coming back to the moment it suddenly occurred to Iris that she always seemed to want things out of arm's reach. And she wasn't talking wild strawberries or honeysuckle here. She thought of the man she truly wanted but couldn't have, however much she tried to ignore her feelings and desires as she continued to battle her wayward morals that bubbled below the surface.

Maggie gave another cry.

"Shhh, hush," Iris said impatiently, trying to settle her own frantic breathing, she was scared too. Why did the child have to fuss all the time? As she tried to concentrate on possible impact if the Germans decided to offload any bombs on the way to the capital. She waited and prayed for the by-pass to be over and prayed for an end to this awful bloody war.

"Keep going, please keep going," she whispered over and over as she rocked Maggie gently from side to side. Soon the roars of the engines faded, and Iris continued to strain her hearing until she could hear them no more. The all-clear siren came a few moments later.

Her immense relief quickly turned to stabbing pain as she realised that she had brushed against the stinging nettles. The tell-tale signs of large white bumps appeared on her forearms and lower legs. She was no stranger to being stung, the pain was bearable under the circumstances but finding some doc leaves would alleviate the stings.

She spotted a cluster a few feet away to her side. When she sat up straighter to try and peer over the top of the ditch she found that she was still too far down to see the lane but was just able to see the tops of the bicycle wheels that were still spinning. The spokes caught the sunlight and cast small shooting lights upwards.

"Nothing like announcing we're here, Mr Jenkins of the Home

Guard will have something to say about that," she said, as she uncovered and boosted Maggie up onto the lane then reached out grasping a handful of doc leaves as she climbed up and out.

"Hey Maggie, it's alright now," Iris said calmly as the leaves instantly soothed her stings.

"You've been stung," said Maggie, "does it hurt much?" She sniffed and brushed her long brown hair away from her face. "Do you want more doc leaves?"

"No, it's all right now." Iris reached into her skirt pocket and replaced the doc leaves for her handkerchief positioning it over Maggie's nose. "Blow Maggie, come on, but not too hard, you don't want to pop your ears." She then gathered the end of her skirt and dabbed her daughter's teary eyes.

Trial and error had proved that in the long run it was better to placate rather than shout and scald as it tended to stop Maggie's snivelling much quicker.

"What a kerfuffle," she said tickling Maggie's tummy causing the youngster to giggle. A quick glance told her that the bicycle was not too damaged as she retrieved the now half empty bag of flour.

Maggie, ever resilient and realising the danger had passed, skipped after the ball of wool. "That was scary, but not as big as last time," she announced, rolling the wool up as they made their way home. "The last one was really big."

"You mean when we were at grandma's?"

"Yes."

They both looked at one another and burst out laughing at the memory of when they had cycled up to grandma's house for tea. Iris hated her interfering mother-in-law but tolerated the odd afternoon there to keep the peace and it was during the last visit that the air-raid siren had sounded.

Iris had quickly ushered Maggie and her mother-in-law out of the kitchen and through the small door under the stairs. The three of them sat under the narrow staircase in silence on old creaky apple boxes, there for that very purpose. Their knees huddled together in the cramped space being mindful not to fidget too much to get any splinters from their makeshift seats.

Maggie knew that the raid was big because she could feel the vibration intensify. It seemed that hundreds of planes were continually flying overhead. She imagined that a huge monster had stomped into her grandma's garden and was roaring down on the house to scare the people inside.

Afternoon sunlight had seeped underneath the little door because it was at least three inches short of the floor. From those shards of light all that Maggie could focus on was her grandma's hair. The sheer vibration from the overhead had caused some plaster dust from the stair slats to land on top of her grandma's bun and over her shoulders. Even though Maggie was terrified by the noise she was more mesmerised by her grandma who looked like she had been sprinkled with snow. Maggie had tugged lightly on her mother's apron to bring it to her attention. Her mother didn't say anything but nudged Maggie's leg with hers and giggle-coughed a couple of times.

The reference to that afternoon was just the ticket Iris and Maggie needed to deal with today's raid.

"Come on Maggie, let's go home and find your father." Iris suddenly felt the need to see William. Even though the air raid today was relatively small, compared to some, it still unnerved her. This had been the first time she had been out in the open, without the security of the Anderson shelter. She was also frightened because she wasn't with William, and this made her realise that she didn't want to die without him. So many confusing thoughts entered her head as she lay with Maggie waiting for the danger to pass. She honestly and truly believed that she would die today.

It suddenly dawned on Iris how much she took William for granted and how heavily she depended on him. She had never told him she loved him. Perhaps she did in her own way, but it was always conveniently avoided. Whenever William told her he loved her, she either smiled or said she knew or changed the subject completely. It was the way she had been brought up, as her parents had never told her they loved her, always stating that showing emotion was showing weakness.

Iris knew William, who was five years older than she was, had almost given up hope of them ever having a child. She had begrudgingly endured years of trying for a family until William had finally conceded that some things were just not meant to be. Iris knew as she got older that the chances were slimmer than slim and that made her inwardly jubilant. She welcomed her monthlies with open arms, however painful they were.

Then at forty-one years of age, the worst day of all happened when Iris discovered she was pregnant. Maggie arrived just three years before the start of the Second World War. Iris felt there was not a person on earth who she could share her deepest secret with.

Iris had married William for an escape; it was as simple as that. She had purposely omitted to tell him that she never wanted children in case he wouldn't marry her. She believed children were too demanding and that she wouldn't be able to do what she wanted. They seemed too much trouble and bloody hard work. But when she realised she was pregnant she knew she had to get on with it. She had considered an abortion but living in a small village where everyone knew everyone's business she had decided it wasn't worth the risk of being ostracised.

Life was damn cruel and unfair sometimes.

After so many years of trying for a family, she was unsure whether it had been a natural thing that she had taken so long to conceive with William or the likely possibility that her lover had fathered her unfortunate child.

She and William had been married for twenty years and lived in a tied cottage owned by the Squire of Primrose Farm Estate. William had come from generations of Kentish farm workers where, more often than not, the tied cottages stayed within the workers' family and were passed down from generation to generation. Fifteen cottages were tied in with the estate and Iris and William lived at number 1 Primrose Cottage. William was the farm manager who took over the role upon his father's death some years before.

Iris tolerated farm life. It was boring, hard work and rough on the hands, but she had to chip in and make the best of it. By nature, she was a lazy creature but accepted this was the life she had chosen. Given the alternative, Iris knew deep down that she was onto a good thing here although it didn't stop her wanting more.

Tongues wagged, so to avoid unnecessary attention she excelled at putting on an act and became so good that at times she almost believed herself. Whenever she was particularly melancholy she admonished herself wishing that she had waited a little longer to capture a more upmarket man with better prospects then she wouldn't have had to work at all.

In the beginning, she would have done anything to escape her childhood home. Home? It wasn't a home, just four walls.

The crux was that an abusive upbringing had disintegrated her heart and soul. As soon as she laid eyes on William she put her plan for freedom in place. It was all about freedom and escape, nothing more.

She had never felt love so wasn't totally sure what it really was, although her lover made her feel alive and desirable. Over the years, she had grown fond of William and they did have some good times and outwardly they seemed relatively compatible.

They were married within five months of meeting much to William's mother's doubt of Iris's intentions. Iris alienated William's friends and pushed him to assist more in his father's role while she waited patiently for his father to turn up his toes.

In the meantime, while his parents were out at work all day it sometimes enabled her to lie in bed until way after ten. Yes, she had to work a little on the farm as well but there were ways, means, and the odd liaison to skip the boring routine. In the early days, it was heaven. It was the freedom and easy life she sought.

Despite William's parents, she had her own little home and most importantly she was out from under the roof of her bastard father who had always been cold towards her but warm to her bitch of a sister. He had used his fists all too often where her mother had been too cowardly and weak to intervene. God, how she hated her mother for it and this was the reason she hadn't seen her in years.

Chapter Two

When Iris had realised she was pregnant she had thought that perhaps having a baby might not be all that bad. She decided to try and make the best out of a bad situation and avoiding the chores was a little incentive that helped. No matter how much Iris tried, she felt she wasn't able to love Maggie as she deserved. Iris couldn't overcome the fact that Maggie, despite being a good, happy child who gave unconditional love to her parents, was an extra person she had to care for. It was just so inconvenient.

As they approached Primrose Cottage they spotted William running towards them. Iris watched him, it seemed, with new eyes as this strong handsome man with short blond hair, pleasant face and dazzling blue eyes bounded up to them knowing they were safe. This was the man she felt safe with, the man who had never raised his fists to her and the man she depended on. Also, this was the man she cheated on, the man she manipulated and the man with the natural abilities and morals she envied, even begrudged, but knew she would never have.

His quiet placid nature with a genuine respect for people was why the farm workers valued him as a boss. He was able to get the best out of people, was fair but could also get furious if a job was not done properly.

"Thank the Lord, Iris," exclaimed William breathlessly, "you're both safe, I was so worried." He swept Iris up, off her feet, and swung her around.

"Me too," laughed Maggie, holding up her arms for her father to pick her up.

"Of course, freckles," he said, with watery eyes. "My girls." They embraced each other.

"I was so scared, William," cried Iris, "Hadn't had a daylight air-raid for a while, and to top it all we've little flour for the rabbit pie and I've used up all the rations."

"Bugger the pie, love," he laughed, "you're both safe that's the main thing. Hey Maggie, eggs for tea? I think Betsy Chicken might give up her lovely eggs for this occasion, what do you think?" The three of them made their way back to the cottage. William and Iris held hands whilst Maggie ran alongside trying to steer her mother's bicycle in a straight line.

That evening, after William had read Maggie a bedtime story and tucked her in for the night, he and Iris sat down at the kitchen table to talk about the day's events.

"Right love," he said, reaching across to cup Iris's hands in his. "How are you really? Maggie's asleep, so no more pretence my girl."

"A little shaken," she said, pulling out her hands from under his. "But I'll be back to normal in no time, you'll see, now don't fuss." As she got up she placed her hand gently on William's shoulder. This motion in itself was as close to a loving gesture as Iris could manage and in that moment they both appreciated the meaning for what it was. She made her way over to the stone sink to fill the kettle. "Want a cuppa before we turn in?"

"That's my girl, tough as old boots and yes please, perhaps with a teaspoon of honey?"

"Don't push your luck, Mr Harris," she laughed, as she put the heavy kettle onto the range plate. She checked to see if the fire was reasonably stoked. "You're in luck, the fire's up enough for that cuppa and I'll even boil you an egg for your pack up tomorrow."

"Goodness me Iris, the royal treatment no less. Two fresh eggs in two days, there'll be none to sell to the village shop," he mocked. "Look," he said, turning serious, "would you feel safer if we bundled up Maggie and slept in the Anderson shelter tonight? It wouldn't be too bad as it isn't a cold night."

"No, Maggie's well asleep now and I don't want to disturb her. Let her be, I'll be all right, we'll laugh at this in the morning no doubt. Don't want Jerry to get one over on us anymore today. Wait a minute, what was I thinking?" she said, turning to look at William. "Eggs for tea and a boiled egg for tomorrow's lunch? That's too grand. You'll have a tomato sandwich and be done with it."

"Yes, you're right, love. How about we take our cuppas up to bed?" he smiled. "What are you laughing at?"

"You're funny, William, the thought of taking up a cup of tea in one hand whilst holding the chamber pot in the other? Very romantic I must say."

Chapter Three

It was late August and the cuckoos, woodpigeons and sparrows were in direct competition with one another. The painted lady butterflies gathered in abundance around the 'pop pop' shrubs as Maggie called them and the clucking from the chicken pen said it was breakfast time.

Maggie threw back the covers and jumped out of bed. She was wearing a pink-striped cotton nightie that came down to her ankles and her long hair was a complete unruly mess. 'The untidy fairies have visited during the night' her father often said. Maggie stepped onto her rug, as it was warmer than the floorboards, then she sprinted through her door to the thin-carpeted stairs on the landing. This was one of Maggie's favourite times of day when her parents weren't around to tell her off as she sat on the top stair and bounced on her bottom all the way down.

Once she reached the last step, she got up and ran into the living room and stopped by the polished chestnut sideboard and jumped. This caused her mother's ornamental cuckoo clock atop the sideboard to 'cuckoo' out of sequence from the movement and the loose floorboard underneath to leap. Maggie giggled every time she did this then she continued passed the two-seater sofa with the lumpy cushions and through the open doorway into the kitchen.

"Morning," she shouted, as she quickly ran through the kitchen on her way to the porch.

"Good morning Maggie, don't forget your wellingtons," said her mother.

As Maggie sat on the back doormat the hessian prickled her bottom and the backs of her legs like tiny hedgehog spikes. She reached for her mud splashed wellie boots. They were well worn as the mothers in the village often pooled shoes and clothes to get the maximum wear when their children had outgrown them.

"There's a war on Maggie and we mustn't waste anything." Maggie often heard her mother say this. It seemed to Maggie that there was always a war on, but that didn't stop her mother or any grown up from saying this regularly.

With wellies on, she ran down the garden pathway, passing 'the girls shed' with the checked curtains, passed the washing line and chicken run then veered to the left onto the stepping stones leading to the outside lavatory. Iris had, over time, trained climbing roses to grow over the lavatory roof so it would be nicer to look at.

Although the outside was nice, Maggie didn't like the inside of the lavatory. There were lots of cobwebs, despite her mother cleaning regularly, and big spiders. When it rained the water often trickled under the wooden door making small puddles on the ground. At twilight you could hear the frogs croaking and because the walls and roof were made of corrugated iron it enhanced the croaking and scared her. Once, Mr Tomkin's cat had leapt up onto the roof while she was inside and she had screamed at the sound of the thump and its scratching claws.

In Maggie's mind, the lavatory was definitely not a nice place to be. Her father always cut up pieces of newspaper to use as toilet paper and she used to sift through to find pieces with words as she didn't think it was right to use pieces with pictures of people.

For some time she had persevered with the lavatory chain. She was very independent and had wanted to do this for herself but it was a tricky piece of equipment and you were not guaranteed a successful flush every time. Maggie had eventually worked out that if she grasped the end of the rope with both hands and gently lowered it halfway then released it immediately and pulled it down quickly and as vigorously as she could it would work. A smile of satisfaction appeared as once again her system had worked and the clunking of the chain and the whooshing of the water was music to her ears.

Next, Maggie continued to the 'girls shed' as her father jokingly called it. Iris had put up blue and white cotton check curtains made from a worn tablecloth and had finished the look with an old dark blue ribbon for tiebacks. Over time the curtains that touched the glass had sun-bleached but the inside had remained the original blue. The shed carried an earthy smell of gardening tools and pellets of chicken feed.

An established spider web that looked like fine cotton wool was housed in the top corner of the window.

"We all have to live somewhere," her mother would say as an excuse not to get rid of it. Maggie sometimes stared at the web for a long time hoping to catch a glimpse of the occupant, wondering just how big it was. Once, when Maggie wasn't feeling overly brave but was overcome with the urge to see the spider, placed an apple box upside down over the garden bed, careful not to disturb her mother's forget-me-nots. She stood on the box and lightly tapped her fingernail on the window hoping to provoke the spider into action. Either the spider was in a deep sleep or just couldn't be bothered with the antics of a small child.

On another occasion, she picked up one of her mother's gardening sticks used to prop up new plants and slowly positioned the thin stick at the brink of the web. She quickly looked to her left to double check the door was still open just in case she had to make a hasty retreat if the giant spider suddenly leapt out to grab her for its dinner. She then prodded the web gently. All Maggie could hear was the rapid beating of her heart.

As the stick lightly touched the web, a tiny piece of old window putty fell making a clicking sound as it landed on the lid of an old tin of paint. She could see that a small amount of web had remained on the stick and looked like candyfloss that she had eaten at the seaside the previous summer. Just then, a butterfly flew in and brushed its wings on Maggie's leg. Maggie let out a startled cry as she bolted for the door. She had no desire to see the spider anymore.

Outside the shed, Iris and Maggie had planted a little cottage garden containing flox, forget-me-nots and sweet William. Maggie had marvelled that there was a flower with the same name as her father. There was also a patch of wild daisies and buttercups and in the springtime there were miniature daffodils and beautiful primroses. Maggie loved this little garden and smiled at it as she approached the shed door.

She picked up the small bucket and trowel and scooped up some pellets then walked carefully to the chicken pen where her father had placed a small bucket of kitchen scraps. This was Maggie's favourite job and as always the chickens gathered around as she entered. They followed pecking and clucking at her heels as she scattered the feed.

Maggie wasn't scared by the chickens, despite their tendency to peck and they didn't seem to mind when she shoved her hand underneath them, albeit not always gently, as she wriggled her tiny fingers about to retrieve the eggs. She didn't like that the chickens were couped up in pens although they had a lot of garden to wander around in. Her mother had explained that it was to keep them safe from the foxes. Maggie didn't want her chickens to be eaten but she couldn't believe that foxes would eat the chickens as they had such beautiful faces.

"Beautiful faces, whether animals or people, can still do bad things Maggie," Iris had said.

Maggie never forgot this and it would prove to be one of the truest things her mother had ever told her.

Iris watched Maggie through the kitchen window as she washed up William's breakfast things. There was Maggie, a tiny little thing in her pink striped nightie, black wellies and unruly hair, feeding the chickens. It was as innocent and lovely an image as you could get and she felt a rare pang of guilt as she knew this family wasn't what it seemed.

"Maggie," she called. "Time to come and have breakfast, we need to leave soon."

A short time after, Iris and Maggie made their way along the footpath to the barn and workshop. The old-beamed workshop had a slanted, corrugated iron roof and when it rained the sound inside was deafening. A heavy wooden workbench was bolted to the floor where hundreds of new and old saw marks, oil stains, hammer and nail indents had built up over many years by generations long gone. On the far side was a slatted wooden rack suspended from the ceiling by musty old rope where William hung game ready for plucking, skinning and gutting. The smell inside the workshop was a mix of sawdust, oil and animal guts and was unpleasant, particularly on hot summer days.

The barn was the largest outbuilding used for storing their

bicycles and larger items of machinery that William often brought home to mend. It was part of his job to maintain all the Primrose Farm Estate machinery alongside the three other mechanics and farmhands. Maggie enjoyed riding on the tractor with her father. The seat alone was fun as the old spring suspension squeaked each time the tyres dipped into deep ruts causing the driver to sway. Maggie liked to pretend that they were riding a camel across the desert as opposed to a tractor through an apple orchard.

William maintained the hop picking equipment and orchard ladders that varied in length to reach the top of the larger apple trees. Petrol, paraffin and coal were also stored in the barn and with the added dangers of sharp farm machinery, Maggie was forbidden to enter without supervision. William had also fixed on the doors two large bolts secured with a padlock so that entry was out of reach for the farm estate's children. He was very safety conscious and did not want the responsibility of any child coming into harm by being in the barn.

He had also concocted a box seat from an old piece of wood that he fixed to the back of Iris's bicycle and that Maggie had painted yellow. The seat was suspended over the back wheel and attached to the frame. Maggie knew she had to be careful when she shifted to get comfortable because if she moved too much it caused her mother to wobble and then she would get angry at her.

Maggie tried to be good but it seemed her mother often was angry at her and knew she had to try harder to please her mother. On the other hand, it seemed she could do no wrong where her father was concerned. She loved hearing him tell her stories of when her grandpa Harris was the estate's manager. There used to be stables attached to the barn for the estate's horses and when the produce was collected, it was taken to the village train station in large farm carts and wagons and went on to London.

Grandpa Harris had died before Maggie was born and had come from generations of master wheelwrights. They had built and repaired broken cartwheels. William's role had not differed much from his father's day, except that William repaired tractors and trailers instead of horse carts and wheels.

Before William had left for work this morning he had propped Iris's bicycle against the barn. To Maggie's delight she saw a freshly made daisy and buttercup chain suspended from the handlebar gently swaying in the breeze. Her father often assembled her a necklace when he sat outside on an apple log with his morning cup of tea.

"Daisy chain," Maggie giggled.

"Keep still Maggie," Iris said, as she concentrated to navigate the chain over Maggie's head. "You know what happens if you move when I'm putting in on."

Iris placed their packed lunches and drink in the front wire basket attached to the handlebars. She lifted Maggie into the seat and pushed the bicycle down the path and onto Honeysuckle Lane. Once she gained a little speed she mounted the bike and enjoyed the breeze as it lifted the hair from her face.

Maggie dangled her legs either side of the wheel and pulled at the daisy chain. When it broke she held it at one end and let the other end fly in the air. But she didn't hold the chain tight enough and it slipped through her fingers. Instantly, she turned as much as the tiny seat allowed so she could peer backwards to see it fall to the ground. The sudden movement caused Iris to wobble then fight to control the handlebars.

"Maggie, for goodness sake sit still," Iris yelled, "we'll either crash or end up in the blackberry hedge. We're off to Foxden Orchard today, so not too far."

They approached the entrance to Primrose Manor where the Squire lived. On this glorious morning Mr Sutton, the head gardener, was busy trimming the lawn edge near the shingled path.

"Hello, Mr Sutton," shouted Maggie, waving eagerly as they swished passed.

"Morning Maggie, morning Mrs Harris," he said, raising his cap to Iris. "Glorious morning. You ladies take care of yourselves," he called.

"Beautiful garden, isn't it Maggie?" said Iris. "Mr Sutton looks after it very well. How I'd love a garden like this," she added wistfully, more to herself than to Maggie.

"I like all the flowers," said Maggie. Then she burst into her favourite song of the moment: "*Ten green bottles...*" Her father had taught her this to help with her counting.

Iris cringed. Hearing the song morning, noon and night was fast becoming way too much. Iris had urged William to teach Maggie a different song and although he had promised he would, he hadn't yet. She wondered if he did this deliberately to annoy her?

Primrose Manor was easily the prettiest house in the village and whenever they rode or walked by Maggie was captivated by it. In the centre of the picket fence was a large white farm gate secured by black wrought iron hinges that were longer than Maggie's arm. When Mr Sutton wasn't about, William let Maggie step onto the bottom frame and when he opened the gate Maggie would be taken for a short ride as the gate closed. The footpath leading to the house was made of shingle and it crackled and crunched underfoot as if they were walking on brittle autumn leaves. Occasionally, Maggie had seen Mr Sutton raking the shingle. When her father and the Squire talked business, Maggie went with Mrs Sutton, the housekeeper, to the kitchen where she was given warm strawberry jam tarts with a milky cup of tea.

By the time Maggie had sung her way from ten to three green bottles Iris had turned into the small incline leading into Foxden Orchard. Maggie now stopped her singing and, as her mother rode over the uneven orchard in and out of pot holes and deep ruts made by tractors, wagons and hoof imprints Maggie giggled as she was bounced around. This lead to her having a bout of sneezing.

These blessed sneezing fits, thought Iris. *Just like William and his mother.* She wondered if it was hereditary or coincidence? She rode carefully around the deeper indents and stopped at the corrugated shed some hundred yards into the orchard where the workers parked their bicycles, left their lunches, blankets and other possessions. It was the general gathering place for tea breaks at ten and three, and lunch at noon. Iris lifted Maggie down and she was off as soon as her feet touched the soft grass.

"Good morning, Betty," Iris said, as she leaned her bicycle up against the shed wall "Great morning, how are you?"

"Morning Iris, fine thanks. I'm looking forward to having a slice of your rhubarb pie later."

"Not today Bet, I'm afraid." Iris shrugged her shoulders at her best friend. "Not enough flour, it'll have to wait for a while."

"I've some flour ration left, we can make the pie together. I'll make the pastry and you supply the rhubarb. Come over after work."

"Sounds good to me," laughed Iris. The two women linked arms as they walked to the start of their rows. Everyone laughed when Betty laughed. She had a unique chuckle that was highly infectious. They had become good friends ever since Iris married William and moved to Primrose Estate cottages.

When they reached their row they saw the empty apple boxes awaiting them.

"See your William's been busy already," said Betty, "S'pose we'd better make a start then."

They propped up their ladders making sure they were secure in the higher branches.

"Did I tell you the latest thing?" Betty continued. "Eric says he will grow rose bushes between the Anderson shelter and the cesspit after I kept complaining about the smell. Goodness Iris, I tell him every time when we run to the Anderson that it shouldn't've been built so near the damn cesspit, I must have told him a hundred times, and does he listen? Blimey, it pongs." Betty pinched her nose and scrunched up her face causing them both to laugh.

"Are the boys here today?" asked Iris.

"Yes, they're about somewhere, probably up to mischief knowing those two. You need eyes in the back of your head, you do," chuckled Betty. "Eric and I can't keep up but they're good lads with hearts of gold. There's never the need to worry love, they keep an eye out for your Maggie when she's in the orchard and the other little ones too."

"Thanks Bet, yes I've noticed that they are quite protective of Maggie, and she in turn adores Pete and Billy, they are like her big brothers."

"Just one big happy family love." As Betty climbed the tall ladder while holding the apple basket with total control and agility. She had done this for many years. Like Iris, she was in her forties and slightly shorter and rounder in stature. She kept her light brown curly hair under control by wearing a scarf on windy days and under a thin hair net on other days.

The women wore housecoats to protect their clothing when they worked as it was often dirty work navigating in and around the taller branches. Betty had sewn two big pockets down the front of hers to hold all sorts of emergency supplies. The twins were now twelve but over the years she had to contend with many scrapes, cuts, bloody noses, and colds when they were out in the middle of the orchards.

"When you have children, you should never be without an emergency hankie or spare underwear," she would say.

Pete had even asked one day if she had a full roast dinner in there, to which he'd received a playful clip behind the ear for being so cheeky.

"Hey Maggie," came a sudden shout.

Maggie glanced around but couldn't tell where the familiar voice had come from. All she could see were row upon neat row of Bramley apple trees. As delicious as the apples looked, she knew from painful experience that she couldn't eat them uncooked as they gave her a tummy ache and the runs. That hadn't been a good day.

"Maggie, Maggie," the call sounded again.

Maggie jumped up and down with excitement, as she loved to play hide and seek. "Pete and Billy, just you come here." There were two dull thumps behind her in quick succession as the boys jumped down from the thicker lower branches and landed on the luscious green grass leaving two pairs of flattened boot prints.

"What are you doing, Maggie?" asked Pete.

"Where are all the other kids?" asked Billy, as he looked around, "you shouldn't wander off too far on your own."

"They're here somewhere playing hide and seek, but I wanted more buttercups," she explained, "here Billy."

He walked over to her and stuck out his chin as he bent down, used to this procedure.

"It means you love butter," exclaimed Maggie excitedly. "The buttercup makes your chin go all yellowy."

"Yes, we love butter," said Pete, "but we don't get to eat it often with the war on."

"What are you doing?"

"Catapulting," they answered together. "Want to see?"

"Yes please," she clapped.

All three of them walked a short distance further up the apple orchard towards the hop field that was almost ready for harvesting. Pete produced a homemade catapult from his trouser pocket and handed it to Maggie, she thought it was the oddest thing she had ever seen.

"What's it do?"

"Watch," said Billy, as he gestured that she keep her eyes on Pete.

As if by magic Pete produced from his other pocket a very small apple, about the size of a snail shell. Pete took the catapult from Maggie and inserted the apple into its pouch and held it outstretched at eye level. Maggie was totally enthralled, wondering what on earth they could possibly be doing.

"Right Maggie," said Billy "look at that big spider web over there, attached between the gate and the first hop pole, see it?"

"Yes."

"Keep watching."

Just then there was a swift *whoosh* in unison with the twang of elastic as the apple shot right through the centre of the spider's web about twenty feet away. The apple landed a short distance beyond the gate encased in the almost transparent web that gleamed from the early morning dew. Only seconds before the web was intact and securely anchored and now the remains shook from the force; the spider would go without its dinner today.

Maggie stood motionless; she had never seen anything quite like it.

"You okay Maggie?" asked Pete gently, a little concerned.

"I want a turn," she said with excitement as she held out her hands for the catapult. Pete produced another small apple from his pocket and stood behind Maggie to teach her how to fire.

"Not too close to your face or it could hurt," said Billy absently stroking his ear and recalling a time when he'd caught his ear and the elastic had pinged near his eye. "Better to put it to the side, away from your eyes. I'll help you with the first go and then you can do it."

Maggie stood to attention and let Pete guide her hands into position before they fired, aiming at the gate this time. It was a good launch; the apple flew out of the catapult and hit the target splitting on impact. The juice dripped down to the middle section of the gate that would soon be a magnet for all kinds of bugs to feed on.

"Again," she said excitedly.

"Load her up, Billy," said Pete joyfully.

Maggie again stood to attention and unconsciously stuck out her tongue as she concentrated with all her might on hitting the gate. She carefully pulled the elastic backwards and closed her eyes before she released with gusto. To their amazement and amusement, the apple bounced a few inches skywards and then plonked at her feet. All three of them burst out laughing. There was a definite skill involved, as it wasn't as easy as it looked.

For the second attempt they decided to move closer to the gate. Maggie loaded, aimed and fired and the elastic bounded upwards and pinged her fingers much to the amusement of the boys.

"This is heaps fun," said Pete laughing.

"Again," said Maggie, with a more determined look on her face while trying to ignore her stinging fingers. She re-loaded, aimed and fired. The apple left the catapult in a non-urgent manner and landed three feet away. Maggie was impressed at this improvement. Just then, the familiar sound announced the morning break. The echo carried around the orchard as one of the ladies banged on an old metal drum with a small wooden plank.

"Race you," shouted Maggie, dropping the catapult and running towards the shed. Pete retrieved the catapult and tucked it back in his pocket, out of sight of the adults, before running after Maggie. They caught up easily and Billy crouched down for Maggie to climb up for a piggyback.

The workers and children sat together in the orchard in a circle enjoying the glorious late summer's day. The younger children sat on the grass and swished their feet through the long blades whereas the older children and adults sat on apple boxes. Mrs Farley, in particular, believed that if she sat on the grass she wouldn't be able to get up again.

Mothers passed their children beakers of squash and sandwiches and often shared their rations of homemade buns. The adults had flasks of tea and chatted, catching up on local topics and what was happening with the war.

"Do you know what bothers me the most?" said Iris. "It's the fact that the war is all that my poor Maggie knows. She was only three when this started. What kind of a childhood is that? We could be killed at any minute, like when we were out during the air raid recently, my life, and her life, could be over before it has had a chance to start. It's not fair." She bit her lip. It wasn't Maggie's life that she was particularly worried about.

"Ay, know what you're saying love," said old Mr Gibbs, "Maggie'll be alright, you'll see. Kids are pretty resilient, but they haven't the freedom growing up that we knew and took for granted. Yes, I've seen some tragic things in my lifetime with living through both wars, this one'll be over soon, mark my words."

"Maggie's a bright happy child, Iris," said Betty, "We were more or less kids ourselves during the last war. Okay, we were older than my Pete and Billy but we coped unscathed didn't we? It'll be the same for your Maggie, we're tough 'ol birds in the country." She laughed which lifted the conversation.

"You're a real tonic Bet," said Iris, smiling tightly. "You should be Prime Minister."

"I've just about heard it all now," said Mr Gibbs shaking his head, "Goodness help us all. Okay, ladies and gentlemen back to work I believe."

"Are you alright Bet?" asked Mrs Sharp, noticing that Betty looked a little uncomfortable.

Slightly bewildered, she answered, "These trousers are tight but yesterday they were absolutely fine." She ran her fingers around the waistband. When she looked up she noticed the women were staring at her questionably. "Goodness no." Betty flushed, fully understanding the other women's looks. "Nothing like that, it's just these trousers, it's as if the elastic has shrunk."

At the word elastic, Maggie looked up towards Pete and Billy who both gave a swift simultaneous shake of their heads in warning. In that instant all that could be heard was the sudden burst of laughter from Maggie who instantly knew where the catapult elastic had come from. The women looked at Maggie wondering what was so funny? Maggie continued to get the giggles throughout the rest of the day whenever she thought about it.

Chapter Four

Clover's Yard adjoined the Manor and that was where William was working. The tractor he had used to deliver the apple boxes had developed an oil leak and he was underneath it assessing where the leak was coming from.

"What is the damage William, can it be fixed quickly?" asked the Squire as he addressed William's old and worn work boots from under the tractor. "We need this back out in the orchard today to bring back the harvest ready for Parkes & Son's pick-up in the morning."

"Shouldn't be a problem Squire," came William's muffled voice, "I can make it a temporary job today and then take it directly to the workshop tomorrow afternoon after Parkes's truck has left to do a proper repair. It should take around half a day at least."

Smiling at William's satisfactory answer caused the Squire's pencil thin grey moustache to overstretch making a near perfect straight line. He was in his early sixties, tall and skinny as a rake and attired as per a country gentleman with his trade mark flat brown and beige chequered cap.

He had never been shy of getting his hands dirty and had on numerous occasions rolled up his shirt sleeves to help with the maintenance of farm machinery and often drove the tractors around the orchards to collect or distribute apple boxes. Gerald Marsh liked to keep his feet metaphorically placed on the ground in touch with the day-to-day operation of his estate. He effortlessly carried a natural air of authority and breeding of English aristocracy where his attitude of mucking in and helping the workers was a quality that had maintained the respect of his employees and the villagers.

Primrose Farm Estate consisted of six hundred acres divided into a number of orchards harvesting seasonal fruits, vegetables and hops, currently for the war effort. Gerald was a fifth generation Squire and took great pride in the estate that he ran like clockwork.

"Splendid 'ol fellow, that's good news. Now, I'll be in town for the rest of the day at that agricultural meeting I told you about. Let's hope that the blasted idiots on the committee can all agree on our suggestions for better and faster distribution before all our toils are wasted." He nodded slightly to William as he walked back to the Manor.

Over the generations the Manor had been fully restored to its former glory. The thatched roof was particularly worrying in times of war and more so in this part of Kent, known as 'Hell's Corner' due to being en route to London for the German bombers who, on occasions, off loaded their bombs on their return to base. The thatch miraculously survived the First World War so Gerald optimistically saw no reason why it shouldn't survive this war also.

Like many others William admired the immaculate lawns and grounds of the Manor and held Mr Sutton, the head gardener, in high regard. William had the privilege of walking within the grounds whenever he saw the Squire whilst the rest of the workers and villagers only got to see a peek at the glorious grounds twice a year: once at the Summer Fete when the gardens were at their absolute best, and at Christmas time when all the children and Primrose Estate staff were invited for a special party.

A small, mature lake semi-circled the back of the property where the lawns gently sloped down the bank toward the jetty and a solitary rowing boat. Green algae outlined the boat with water lilies growing just above the waterline. It had been a number of years since the Squire had used the boat for fishing. Nowadays, he much preferred to do a spot of fly-fishing from the water's edge as his balance was not as good as it used to be.

In the centre of the lake was a small island just big enough to withstand a family of weeping willows that graciously overhung the side. The tips of the branches danced softly in the water providing protection from the sun for the ducks and swans that nested there.

William brushed himself down and walked across the courtyard that housed the stable block. He picked up eight carrots from the metal bucket and briefly stopped at each stable door where he fed and patted every pedigree horse as he made his way to the tool shed next to the barn. As he gathered all the items he needed to temporarily fix the oil leak his thoughts turned back to the Squire. William knew he had been through tough times starting with the sudden loss of his beloved wife then the turbulent aftermath with his son Adam.

William shook his head. He thought how fortunate he was to have his beloved Iris and Maggie, the apple of his eye. He started the tractor engine and began the slow drive back to Foxden Orchard.

Chapter Five

Iris had taken an armful of rhubarb to Betty's cottage so they could bake the pie together and so Maggie had gone with William to the workshop.

Her father was an excellent storyteller and he often told her of his antics as a boy and the endless mischief he got into with his best friend Bert.

"Daddy, tell me about Bert and Miss Bridges," Maggie pleaded.

"What about them?" he taunted.

"You know, the frogs."

"But you know about the frogs, Maggie."

"Please tell me and do more noises," she said, as she jumped up and down expectantly.

"Alright, come over here then pumpkin."

Maggie ran to her father with outstretched arms and he sat her up on the workbench then continued to plane some wood.

"Well," he began, "Bert and I were late for school, as usual, but this time we were very late as we'd been down to the village pond first. It had been raining and we were soaked by the time we entered the school gate. Playtime was over and all our friends were already inside the classroom.

"We knew the routine, as we'd been late so many times, your grandma Harris used to tell me off for being late but I just couldn't help it. We were only seven and we lost track of time.

Bert and I knew that we had to see Miss Bridges, so she could mark us off as late in the school register, before we could join our friends in class.

"We walked down the corridor and when we arrived outside Miss Bridges' door we knocked but there was no reply, which was quite unusual. I poked Bert in the ribs and he carefully turned the brass handle and opened the door slightly. We both peered in to make sure Miss Bridges was not inside." He gave Maggie a sideways glance and smiled when he saw she was sitting there with legs swinging under the workbench, totally enthralled in the tale.

"Then..."

"What Daddy, what?" Maggie held her breath with trepidation.

"Then we went inside," he whispered.

Maggie caught her breath fearing that her father would be in serious trouble.

"Miss Bridges' office was beautifully furnished with a big polished desk and a huge book case filled with encyclopaedia and on top of the bookcase was a silver trophy. We were not sure what the trophy was for but we were impressed that she had one. A trophy, Maggie is a prize you are given when you win something."

Maggie nodded, clearly impressed.

"Bert opened the drawer to Miss Bridges' desk and from his trouser pocket he popped three frogs into the drawer," William made croaking noises to add to the drama, "*ribbet, ribbet, ribbet,* and then he quickly closed the drawer before they hopped out. Then, we ran back to the door, quickly peeped out in case anyone was outside, then went and sat on the chairs in the corridor to await Miss Bridges' return. I remember the chair I sat on was very old and one of its legs was shorter than the others and I was able to rock back and forth, which made Bert and I laugh out loud.

"Just then, we heard a tapping sound." To support this, William put down the plane and picked up a hammer and tapped it slightly on the workbench. "Close your eyes Maggie, can you see Miss Bridges?"

Maggie did as she was told. *Yes,* she could see Miss Bridges who was a tall elderly lady who always looked angry and seemed to delight in the children being scared of her. Her father had described her on other occasions, so Maggie was able to picture that she had white hair pulled back in a tight bun and wore small spectacles perched at the end of her nose.

"Bert and I stopped laughing and waited for her to turn the corner to her office..."

Maggie, with eyes still closed, could see that Miss Bridges was coming closer…

William continued to tap gently on the workbench, mimicking the footsteps. Then suddenly, he tapped loudly twice, making Maggie jump.

Miss Bridges had arrived.

"'Lateness is not tolerated, do you understand?'" said William, in a high-pitched voice as he mimicked his old Headmistress.

Maggie opened her eyes and giggled at her father, and also to check that he hadn't turned into Miss Bridges.

"Miss Bridges stood there staring at us, she looked like a giant eagle ready to eat us up." William spread his arms and swooped above Maggie making creaking bird noises that made her giggle even more. "She eyed us up and down with a very disapproving look. Mind you Maggie, we did look a sorry sight. Bert and I were dripping wet and our socks and shoes were muddy. We were both worried what our mothers would have to say about that. Bert's shoelaces were undone and because they were wet they left a clear trail on the dusty floor. It looked like a garden worm had zigzagged after him." William wiggled his index finger in front of Maggie then gave her a tickle.

"'Lateness is not tolerated, do you understand?' she repeated, and we both nodded solemnly. 'I want to see both your mothers tomorrow morning, now get back to your class.' Then she left us without saying another word, slamming the door behind her. Nothing about Miss Bridges was ever done quietly.

"We made our way slowly back to class, not because we were ashamed but because we were listening very hard for what we knew was coming. We waited for a while then looked at one another with puzzled looks on our faces. At the end of the corridor we couldn't stall any longer and had no choice but to enter the classroom.

"The whole class, including our teacher, Mr Bennett, fell silent and stared at us wondering what we had gotten up to this time. 'Sorry we are late Mr Bennett,' we said.

"'Goodness look at you two,' said Mr Bennett, 'take your places and open your history books.' We did as we were told and sat down.

"I didn't want to look at Bert because I knew that I would burst out laughing and I knew it was the same for him, so we opened our desk lids and hid behind them, pretending to search for our books while the urge to giggle passed.

"Just then, there was a piercing scream," said William, "Mr Bennett ran from the classroom to get to Miss Bridges and the whole class gathered around us. 'It's you two isn't it?' said Percy. 'Of course it's them, you idiot,' said Henry, 'Mice or frogs?' 'Frogs, big slimy frogs,' I said, still laughing. 'Don't any of you tell, it is a victory for all of us.'

"'We're in for it now,' said Emily, with a very worried look on her pretty little face. 'She'll be worse on us now you'll see.' 'Don't worry, Emms,' said Bert reassuringly, 'Miss Bridges won't know it was us, she doesn't even know we went in her office, I promise. Right, everyone back to your desks, we don't want to draw attention to ourselves. Let's get on with our work for when Mr Bennett returns.'"

"Why was Miss Bridges so mean to the children, Daddy?" asked Maggie, when she had recovered from laughing.

"Miss Bridges was mean to everyone pumpkin, I don't believe even the teachers liked her much either because when Mr Bennett returned a little while later he said that there would be no homework for any of us for the rest of the week and when Bert and I looked at him in disbelief, he just winked at us.

"Now Maggie, you should respect all elders you know that and when you go to school you must respect everyone in your class," said William, in his serious voice. "Okay young lady, time for a wash and off to bed for you before your mother returns and has my guts for garters for keeping you up past your bedtime."

Chapter Six

It was late when the Squire returned from his meeting in town. He closed his car door as quietly as he could and entered through the ornate front doors with the leaded stained glass. On sunny days, the light streamed through creating vivid patterns down the hallway but now the moonlight beamed tones of grey. Mr and Mrs Sutton had long since retired to their annexe in the east wing but even though this was some way away from the hallway, Gerald moved quietly so as not to disturb them.

Although he had eaten earlier in the evening, he suddenly felt quite peckish. He walked down to the kitchen and turned on the gas lamp in the middle of the vast table. He smiled as he read Mrs Sutton's note stating that a fresh salad with cold meats and pickles were awaiting him in the cooler part of the pantry.

"Splendid ol girl, thank you very much," he said aloud. As he lifted the china plate down from the shelf the weighted beads on the ends of the muslin cloth made a clinking sound against the side and a schoolboy smile widened even more when he saw that Mrs Sutton had also made a strawberry trifle as well.

Gerald carried the tray through to the main drawing room and placed it on the oak table. He then went over to the matching cabinet and poured himself a small snifter of whisky; one of life's pleasures and a necessity at the end of a tiring, but productive day.

After his satisfying meal, he poured himself another whisky

and walked down to his study. *The meeting in town hadn't gone too badly*, he thought, *at least there was support from the main fruit and vegetable suppliers in the County, which was half the battle won.* Consensus agreed that even though distribution was adequate, they needed to speed up the process to get the fresh supplies up to Covent Garden. Things were on the up with the newly elected Committee with noticeable results imminent.

Another pressing matter was the start of the hopping season. In two weeks' time, the village would be awash with Londoners for the annual six-week stint. There was still a lot to organise but it was under control. A major meeting would be held on Wednesday with his key staff to finalise details.

Gerald was appreciative of the loyal Londoners' help that was vital to successfully yield the bumper crop on Primrose Estate. Like everyone else, he was also aware of what the Londoners' were going through during this awful war. He had on several occasions travelled up to London on business and the sheer destruction and loss of life was quite distressing. Village life seemed a million miles away from the atrocities in the capital. They had had their fair share of air raids, but it was nothing compared to being in the thick of it all.

His visits to London had invoked vivid memories as he had actively served as a Captain during the First World War. He didn't allow himself to dwell too much on this part of his life as it also conjured up painful memories of his dearly departed wife.

But, equally so, Gerald realised that the Londoners' relished this annual event down to Kent as their temporary escape from the war. They were able to catch up with old Kentish friends and sleep a little more soundly at night, as compared to the brutal noises of war stealing a restful sleep.

Gerald sat comfortably in his antique leather chair enjoying his rare third glass of whisky. He finally gave in to the fact that he was a very troubled man. He believed that his only child would be the imminent downfall of Primrose Farm Estate. If he were honest, Gerald had known for several years that Adam would never willingly follow in his footsteps, although Gerald had tried on numerous occasions over the years to actively involve Adam in the business. He looked up from his whisky glass and sadly gazed at each of the portraits of his ancestors who stared back at him, their oil painted faces seemed to acknowledge the pain he was going through. He had failed them, failed in his responsibilities to his tenants and their families, and most of all, he had failed his son.

Due to unforeseen complications, his dear wife Mary had passed away during child birth and for many years Gerald could not bear to be in the same room as his son, blaming him entirely for her death. Since day one Adam was cared for by a succession of nannies ensuring that he wouldn't become too attached to one person. Mr and Mrs Sutton could do nothing but watch on helplessly as the Squire would pay the nanny an extra month's pay and immediately hire another to take her place. Adam often woke in the morning to find a new nanny had replaced the one before without being told of a reason or even a goodbye. Thinking it was for the best, Gerald packed Adam off to boarding school when he was just ten years old.

Kent was rich with excellent boarding schools, achieving outstanding academic reputations, but Gerald opted to send his son to Priory Square down the West Country in Dorset. Adam had now completed five years out of eight and over those five years he had returned to Kent only three times. The atmosphere between father and son during those visits was distant, as they were strangers to each other. It wasn't long before Adam began making excuses not to return home during the holidays, opting to stay with friends and sometimes staying on at boarding school to avoid going back to Kent altogether.

Gerald knew that he was solely to blame for not having a relationship with his son as he had been so tied up in his own bereavement. He now wanted to make amends but had been bewildered on what to do next. There had been too much lost time. He decided that when Adam came home for the Christmas holidays in a few months' time he would try his utmost to salvage what was left of their relationship.

Chapter Seven

As the working day ended the following day, Iris gathered up their things in Foxden Orchard. She packed away their lunchboxes, beakers, blanket and a couple of Maggie's toys into the basket on the front of the bicycle. "We've got to go to the Post Office first to buy a stamp before we go home, hold on, here we go."

The ride out of the orchard was as bumpy as the ride in as Iris snaked her way around potholes with Betty following behind. The twins quickly caught up gathering pace and sped past the ladies to rush on home.

"Pete, put the kettle on love," shouted Betty, as the boys flew past.

"Righto Mum," he said, waving in the air then disappearing around the corner, closely pursued by Billy.

"See you tomorrow, Bet," said Iris, as the two women peddled out of the orchard in opposite directions.

After a couple of minutes Iris and Maggie pulled up outside the village Post Office and Store. Iris lifted Maggie out of the seat and propped the bicycle against the wall. The familiar 'ding' of the brass bell over the door chimed as they entered.

"Good afternoon ladies," said Bill Dwyer, the Postmaster.

"Good afternoon, Mr Dwyer," said Iris.

"Hello, Mr Dwyer," said Maggie.

"What can I do for you today, Mrs Harris?"

"Just a penny stamp please." Iris placed a penny on the counter. "I'm writing to my aunt who lives up north, she hasn't been too well lately I'm afraid."

"I'm mighty sorry to hear that Mrs Harris, I hope she recovers soon. Now young Maggie, what have you been up to lately?"

"I've been playing hide and seek in the orchard."

"That sounds like fun," said Mr Dwyer, as he continued to serve Iris.

Maggie wandered over to the counter top. It was at eye-level to her and she had to stand on tiptoe to see more. Maggie liked Mr Dwyer. He was much older than her father and had a kindly face; he wore small round spectacles and was always dressed in a smart suit. She was fascinated by his baldhead. It was very shiny and she often wondered if he polished it with beeswax like her mother polished the sideboard and cabinet. Just then, she spotted something.

"What's that?" she asked, pointing to an envelope on the counter top, her eyes dazzled with interest.

"Maggie, that's rude, you mustn't do that," said Iris. "So sorry, Mr Dwyer."

"Not at all, Mrs Harris, not at all." He turned the envelope around and pushed it towards Maggie.

"Maggie, please be careful," whispered Iris, wondering what had captured her so.

Bill Dwyer walked around to the other side of the counter and slowly crouched down to Maggie's level. One of his knees cracked as he did so.

"What's this?" she asked.

"It's a koala stamp Maggie," said Mr Dwyer

"Koala," repeated Maggie slowly, "what's that?"

"A koala is an animal that mostly lives in trees and carries its babies on its back. It lives in a country called Australia. That's where this stamp came from."

"Where's Australia?" asked Maggie, excitedly.

"It is far far away. Thousands and thousands of miles away and it is very hot there too. This letter has travelled a long way to get here. I have a cousin who lives in Australia and from time to time he sends me letters and I write back. But this letter is from Jack, my cousin's son who is about five years older than you are."

"Is that near Maidstone?" asked Maggie, relating to the only far-away place that she knew.

"Goodness gracious no, Maggie," he said smiling gently. "It's much further than that. You see, Maidstone is about eight miles away from here and Australia is thousands of Maidstone's away." Bill Dwyer could see that Maggie was truly captivated by the stamp. When she finally handed the envelope back to him, he reached for a pair of scissors and cut around the koala stamp. He popped it with Iris's stamp into a small bag and handed it to Maggie.

Both Maggie and Iris were taken aback when he did this.

"Mr Dwyer, that's very kind of you, but not necessary," said Iris.

"Mrs Harris, it is my absolute pleasure. I have many stamps from Australia and I would be delighted if Maggie would take care of this one for me," he said smiling. "Would you do that Maggie?"

"Thank you, Mr Dwyer," she said breathlessly, "I will look after it, I promise."

"I know you will," he smiled. He opened the door and waved them goodbye.

Maggie was unusually quiet as they cycled home. Iris was enjoying the peace and the afternoon breeze when suddenly,

Maggie spoke.

"I like Australia and I will go there one day to see a koala."

"Will you now, Maggie?" Iris laughed. "That's just grand and you can send us a letter with a koala on it too," she said sarcastically.

As soon as they arrived home, Maggie raced off in search of her father who was working on the tractor in his workshop to get it ready for the next day.

"Daddy, look what I got from Mr Dwyer," she said. "It is a stamp from Australia, which is longer away than Maidstone."

"I should say it is, Maggie," said William, as he stopped what he was doing and wiped his oily hands on his overalls and examined the stamp she was holding. "Yes, very nice it is."

"It's a koala. Have you been to Australia, Daddy?"

"Goodness no Maggie, it's a long way from here."

"I am going there one day to see koalas," she said matter-of-factly as she walked back towards the house.

Chapter Eight

Early September was the start of the hop season and as always, the busiest time of year for the village. The steam train pulled up with a deafening hiss at Marden village station and the platform became awash with running children, stacked luggage and noisy chatter.

The few men who were not of fighting age or had been medically discharged, disembarked with all kinds of battered suitcases, bags and possessions tied up with belts and odd pieces of string. The women tried to round up the excited children as they held babes in arms, and toddlers, frightened by the pandemonium, clung to their legs. Locals turned out with handcarts ready to help the hop-pickers to their accommodation that would become their home for the next six weeks.

Horses and ponies waited patiently in a row outside the station harnessed to trailers ready to be loaded. Mr Sutton was there as well, ready to assist but also standing strategically near the horses, eagle-eyed with a bucket, never missing a chance to acquire good quality manure for the Manor's precious roses.

The Squire, William and a few other key members of Primrose Estate were positioned down the platform, each carrying a clipboard with family names to indicate which hop-pickers hut to report to. The estate workers assisted with settling in the newcomers but the majority of them were seasonal regulars to the village and knew where to report. Like generations before, the hop-pickers converged upon the village at the invitation of the Squire who carried on the tradition of subsidising their train fare for the round trip.

Hopping season wasn't all rosy for Kent as a whole. It was common knowledge that some villages had troublesome and uninvited guests turn up. But, in recent years extra policemen were stationed in the villages for deterrents where word soon got around. Mostly, the villagers looked forward to catching up with old friends.

Although this was work, comprising of hard, dirty manual labour, it was a holiday too, and the London mothers were grateful that their children would have six weeks of clean air and were able to run around freely and safely without getting into too much trouble.

On average, a family could expect to earn enough to ensure that their children had warm clothing and boots to see them through the winter months with perhaps a few luxury extras along the way if they budgeted right. The majority of the men who were dockworkers, sometimes came down at weekends to help out and also to have a few pints at the two village pubs.

It was all quite exciting and a little scary as Maggie had never seen so many people in one place before. She worried she would lose her mother in the crowd. She was also quite puzzled when she saw several people carrying what she thought were curtains.

"Why do they carry curtains?" Maggie asked her father just before they left for the orchards.

"They are to black out the light from inside the hut, so no light shines through. You know how we block out the light in the evening? It's the same for the huts. Why do we do this Maggie, can you remember?"

"So the planes don't see any light and drop a bomb on us, that's why we cover the windows."

"Yes, that's good Maggie."

"So why are all these people here, what are they going to do? Some were carrying pots and pans too!"

"Well, the hoppers cook their own dinner down at the huts so they need the pots and pans for this. They are here to pick the hop vines because there are too many hops for the estate workers to harvest. We need all the help we can get during this busy time and also help with clearing some of the trenches in the orchards in case there are air raids, because it doesn't take long for the earth to fill them in again. We have to make sure they are safe.

"I'll take you down there this year Maggie and you can see for yourself all the work that is done there."

"On your bicycle?" she asked gleefully.

"Yes, on my bicycle!" he laughed, knowing full well that Maggie loved to ride on the back as he zoomed down the lane much faster than Iris.

Late in the afternoon, Maggie accompanied her parents to Foxden Orchard. A stocky man with a grey beard and wearing a flat cap and braces over his shirt came over to them. He had an air of dependability about him as he puffed on his pipe.

"Albert, good to see you again," said William, extending his hand to greet the man.

"William, likewise," said Albert, as the friendly handshake continued.

"Mrs Harris, you're looking well," said Albert, tilting his cap to Iris. "And who is this little lady?" He bent down towards Maggie.

"I'm very well Mr Dunn, thank you," said Iris. "Maggie, this is

Mr Dunn. He has been coming to Kent ever since he was a boy and now he brings his family."

"Pleased to meet you young lady, you were just knee high to a grasshopper last year and too young to remember us I would imagine, but you had fun playing with all the children from London. I'm sure you'll catch up with them in the next few days, there's my Tommy and Vivien for a start."

"Settled in alright, Albert?" asked William. "Anything more you all need for tonight?"

"We'll be snug as a bug in a rug, William. The strange thing will be the silence would you believe, but we'll all be out like a light in no time at all, it's been a long day. It will make a very pleasant change sleeping out under the stars and not in a packed out underground station. Well, I know you've your rounds to do, so I bid you goodnight and see you at six in the morning."

"Goodnight Albert, I'll catch up with all the family tomorrow."

The next month went by quickly, with the village adjusting to the hustle and bustle of the newcomers. The villagers had been horrified to hear the dreadful stories about the Blitz and the devastation that was happening only forty miles away. Sadly, there was always someone who knew of someone who had been killed either in the bombings or loved ones who had been killed serving in action.

Adults and children renewed friendships and everyone participated in the harvest of the hop vines. The weather continued to be excellent enhancing the crops with bushels aplenty and except for a few night air raids, as time went on, the war was almost forgotten.

Maggie and her parents became firm friends with the Dunn

family and Maggie soon realised that Mr Dunn, like her father, was a master storyteller. Albert Dunn was a retired dockworker and he told stories of faraway places and people who travelled on impressive vessels. One day, Maggie heard him speaking about ships that came from Australia and the next day she excitedly showed him her Australian stamp. He was mighty impressed.

During a morning break, when adults and children alike were sitting having a drink and bite to eat, Albert decided to tell a story about one of the ships that docked.

"It was late in the afternoon and people were coming and going offloading their cargo…" he began. "Just then..." he stopped and looked around, engaging everyone's undivided attention, "there was a strange noise." He lowered his tone, as if to tell a secret. All hush surrounded the group who waited until he spoke again. "There was a thump, thump, thump noise," he said, banging his fist on an upturned apple log. "Everyone around me on dockside stood still and we all looked at each other as puzzled as you could ever be. We hadn't heard anything like it in our lives and we listened and listened some more. Suddenly, it became louder and louder and an echo carried the noise that seemed to surround us completely. There was nowhere for us to go and this noise was becoming more scary." Albert stopped speaking and slowly lit his pipe, fully aware that his audience were hooked and awaiting his next word.

"Mr Dunn, what happened?" demanded Maggie, eyes wide with anticipation. He looked around the group and saw people nodding their heads, agreeing with her. He stood up and placed his pipe on the apple log, and without saying another word he walked slowly around the outside of the circle. All eyes were on him. In a split second, he swept Maggie up into his arms as she let out a playful scream. "And out came this big kangaroo," he cried, "who bounced around the ship." He bounced up and down like a kangaroo holding Maggie who was now giggling loudly. The rest of the group began to laugh as well and the young children applauded.

"Your stories get wilder all the time, Alby," said Mrs Dunn laughing. "I don't know where you get them from, husband of mine, I really don't, just when I think I've heard them all, you come up with this."

"Just a piece of fun me 'ol treacle, no harm done," he said, placing Maggie back on the ground. "Right me china's, back to work for the oldies and you young 'uns can clear the tea things away."

Chapter Nine

At the end of the hopping season, the Londoners returned home. For the first few weeks the village seemed empty but then, over time, everyone reverted to their usual routine and with the exception of a few air-raid warnings, life in the village settled down to business as usual.

It was time for Maggie to start school and despite knowing all of the village children she was quite nervous about her first day. William and Iris took some time off from work to accompany her. She insisted on carrying her own lunch, her reading book and her gas mask.

"I do want to go to school but I also want to stay and help in the orchard," she explained, as they walked towards the village.

"You will be fine, young Maggie," said William "you are growing up fast and it will be good to learn new things and you can still play with your friends at play time."

"I suppose," said Maggie. "But what if I don't like it?" She looked at her father in alarm. "Will I have to go back tomorrow?"

"Of course, you will like it," said Iris briskly. "You need to get good learning to get on in the world. Off you go."

"Look," said William. "There's Sally Vinter over there. How about you go and talk to her because she's new to the village, it will be harder for her. Go and make friends and everything will be alright. You can tell us all about your day later."

"Alright, Dad," said Maggie, as she hugged her parents and trotted off in Sally's direction.

As Iris and William were walking back towards home William said, "Not sure where those five years went, are you?"

"No, they went by very quickly," said Iris, secretly she thought that the five years hadn't gone quick enough. But now that Maggie was at school, she would have a whole six hours a day that were Maggie-free.

"She'll be fine," said William, mistaking Iris's quiet mood for concern about their daughter. "She makes new friends easily enough and she'll have the class teacher eating out of her hand in no time," he said laughing, "she has a way about her, she will be fine whatever she does in life.

"Iris, if you don't mind, I'll leave you here as I'll pop into Foxden Orchard to check on a few things before I head back to the workshop. See you later, love." He pecked Iris on the cheek as he ventured off towards Foxden.

Iris joyfully made her way back home in readiness for peace and quiet and having the house to herself. She had no intention of going back to work today. She had only been home around twenty minutes when something caught her eye by the kitchen window. She looked closely towards the vegetable patch and noticed that every now and then, the tall potato plants seemed to shudder. There was no breeze so she wasn't sure what was causing them to move like that. Perhaps there was a stray cat about or… Iris quickly looked towards the chicken coop wondering if the chickens had escaped. She could see that the gate was still latched. She wiped her hands dry on her apron and ventured out towards the vegetable patch, clutching a shovel, just in case. As she got closer to the potato plants she could hear loud sniffing sounds.

Just as Iris reached out to part the leaves, Maggie sprung up like a jack-in-a-box and stormed towards the house.

"Don't like it," she sniffed. "Don't want to go to no bloody school."

"Maggie!" exclaimed Iris. "No bad language young lady, where on earth did you hear that from?"

"Pete and Billy said it once. I know it's wrong but I don't want to go to bloody school." Maggie turned, hand on hips, facing her mother. "I want to stay home with you. I can help here. You said I was good at home."

"You have to go to school or the village bobby will be upset with us, don't you see? And as for Pete and Billy, well they shouldn't use bad language in front of you. I will speak to Betty about that. Now, come inside, we'll clean you up and I will take you back."

Maggie reluctantly complied. She didn't want to be in trouble with the bobby and she didn't want her parents to be in trouble either. She had enjoyed talking to Sally before school but when the time came to walk inside the school hall she had bolted for home.

Iris walked Maggie back to school and discreetly spoke to her teacher. There was only one desk available and that was in the front row right under the teacher's nose. *How lucky was that?* Iris hurried back home, annoyed but eager to enjoy what time she had left on her own.

Maggie and Sally bonded straight away through the most bizarre turn of events. While the teacher was writing his name on the blackboard, Maggie had tilted her chair backwards and leaned on Sally's desk behind for support.

"What are you doing?" whispered Sally. "Get off my desk."

"Can I borrow a pencil?"

"No, get off my desk or I'll bash you with my ruler."

"Go on then, I dare you."

Sally hit Maggie over the head but this caused her old brittle wooden ruler to smash in three pieces. Sally's face reddened in shock and those who saw what had happened, burst into laughter. Maggie joined in.

"Sally Vinter and Margaret Harris," said Mr Turk quite sternly as he turned around from the blackboard, "come here please." He put down the chalk and a hush descended over the classroom. "Quite a first day, wouldn't you say?"

All eyes were on the girls who looked a picture of guilt as they stood shoulder to shoulder and looked at their teacher. He was relatively short and Sally thought he was very big around the tummy. Her father said it was rude to call people fat but all of a sudden she had the urge to giggle because when she looked down slightly she saw that his tummy was covered in fine white dust from when he had turned around and his tummy had rubbed off some of the chalk from the blackboard.

"You will please go and stand in separate corners of the classroom with your backs to the class in silence for the next ten minutes, is that understood?"

"Yes, Mr Turk," they both muttered.

"Maggie," said Maggie. "My name is Maggie, not Margaret."

"Very well, Maggie it is. Now off you go." He pointed to the far corners. The girls walked away, not really understanding how long ten minutes would be.

Their friendship was strangely set up for life from that day onwards.

When William arrived home that afternoon Iris told him of the morning's events. They decided to make no reference to it because Maggie seemed much happier now. Maggie told them both over supper that she and Sally had decided to sit together in class.

"We're also going to share my ruler because Sally broke hers," she said, smiling innocently. She shrugged. "School doesn't seem so bad. I might go tomorrow."

Chapter Ten

The mornings and evenings started to become darker and colder as the summer gradually turned to autumn.

"Good morning, Mrs Sutton," said Pete and Billy together as Mrs Sutton stood at the Manor's kitchen door wiping her soapy hands on an extremely white tea towel.

She eyed the boys closely with their red rosy cheeks and beaming smiles. "Morning boys," she said, "what can I do for you today?"

"Well, it's rather what we can do for you, Mrs Sutton," said Pete enthusiastically.

"And what may that be?" she asked, noticing a small puddle forming behind the boys on the doorstep. She crossed her arms and eyed the twins suspiciously.

"Hey presto," exclaimed Billy, as they brought their arms round from their backs and held out two decent sized rainbow trout strung up on fishing line.

"Well," marvelled Mrs Sutton, "Rainbow trout, the Squire's favourite. Where did you get these from boys?" she asked, placing her hands on her hips.

"From Purchets stream the other side of the village, Mrs Sutton," said Billy. "Aren't they grand? And they are yours for only two shillings each."

"Are they now?" she laughed. "Two shillings? I'll pay you one shilling each or not at all you cheeky boys."

The boys looked at one another and shrugged in agreement.

"Not bad for a morning's work," said Pete to Billy as they ran along Honeysuckle Lane towards home.

"That's a good profit too," said Billy. "I knew she'd knock us down but I thought it would be lower than a shilling a piece."

"Not a word to Mum or she'll go mad," said Pete. "Let's get that other fish."

"Hello Mum," they said together as they entered the kitchen. "Look what we've brought for tea." They held up another large rainbow trout.

"Goodness, that's a beauty," said Betty, "We'll have this tonight with some vegetables. Where did you get it from?"

"Purchets," said Pete.

"Purchets?" repeated Betty, as she looked from one son to the other. "That's good work boys, really good." Betty stood thinking for a while then repeated again, "Purchets?"

"Yes Mum," said Billy.

Out the corner of her eye, Betty saw Billy slightly nudge Pete. "Oh my goodness," exclaimed Betty, raising her hands in the air. "You got them out of the Squire's lake didn't you?"

"Mum, really," protested Pete, a hurt look on his face.

Betty stood with her hands on her hips just staring at her boys, her eyebrows raised. There was no need for any words on an occasion such as this as Betty's eyebrows did the talking for her.

"Okay Mum, yes from the Squire's lake. It's full of them and no one saw us and we saw no harm in it," said Pete. "It's only one fish."

"Bye Mum, gotta go," said Billy, as both boys flew out of the kitchen door. If only she knew the whole story!

Chapter Eleven

Mrs Sutton had been meticulously planning for months to make Christmas 1941 a special time at Primrose Farm Estate. This year would mark her fortieth year of organising the festivities for the Squire and all the staff and she still delighted in making little changes each year.

She was a stickler for detail and perfection and it was all those details that made the event so memorable. At sixty-five she still thrived on running the Manor like clockwork. She was small in stature and dwarfed by the Squire whom admired and respected both Mr and Mrs Sutton. He was grateful for their hard work and above all, their companionship.

She had mastered the art of calligraphy as a young girl and in October she spent two weeks carefully writing invitations to all the families of Primrose Estate. By the beginning of November she had delivered each one of these. Of course, official invitations were unnecessary, as every family knew they were invited, but Mrs Sutton liked things done properly. More often than not, the invitation would take pride of place on mantle pieces awaiting Christmas Eve.

The Squire allowed Mrs Sutton to call upon three members of staff to help with the heavier manual preparations. This particular year she called upon Mr Edgars, Mr Milton and Mr Connor to help gather, chop and store plenty of firewood to keep the large hearths burning for a warm and inviting welcome for everyone. She also required them to collect sufficient holly from the hedgerows for decorating the Manor in traditional yuletide fashion and asked them to collect any mistletoe they could find so she could tie them in bunches and hang under doorways.

Above all, they were to chop down the Christmas tree that she had personally selected from one of her many afternoon walks around the estate's woodland and to safely deliver it to the Manor. To ensure the correct spruce was delivered she had attached an old tartan scarf of hers around one of the lower branches.

There were a few good contenders to choose from this year, but the one Mrs Sutton had selected was just under ten feet tall and satisfyingly broad and full at the base. The spruce was in excellent condition and the deep forestry aroma would fill the Great Hall with no difficulty at all.

"Hey Pete," as Billy nudged his brother, "Look at that over there," he said indicating the spruce with the scarf attached as they cut through the woodland. In fact, they frequently used the Manor's grounds as their personal thoroughfare, being mindful of Mr Sutton's whereabouts.

"Looks like the chosen tree for this year's party," said Pete as they ran towards it. "This must be Mrs Sutton's scarf," as he held it up and draped one end over his shoulder.

"Very fetching, lad," laughed his brother, "let's tie it to another tree as a joke."

"Yes, let's." As Pete started to untie the knot he felt that it was frozen stiff in the middle from being out all night.

"No, hold on," exclaimed Billy as he suddenly covered his brother's hand with his own. "I'm wrong, we'll leave it. It's funny now, but…"

"But we want to see the best tree decorated, just like everyone else," finished Billy.

"Yes, we do. Come on, race you."

The twins sprinted for home.

For Mrs Sutton, the only worry about the Christmas holidays was that Master Adam was home from boarding school. The atmosphere instantly changed for the worst when he arrived. He hardly ventured out of his room, sleeping day and night, and when he was awake his mood was so dark, that she was quite frightened to be around him. She remembered Adam as a polite but very reserved little boy and was genuinely saddened to see what he had become.

"Pardon me, Squire," said Mrs Sutton, after she had knocked and entered the study.

"Come in, Mrs Sutton." The Squire instantly put down his fountain pen and swivelled his leather desk chair around to face his housekeeper. "What can I do for you?" He ushered her over to the fireside chairs. "Mrs Sutton, is everything alright?" he asked, with a little concern as he could see that she looked quite worried and pale.

"This is rather delicate, Squire. I feel duty bound, so I'll just come straight out with it," she said. She sat with her back bolt upright and looked the Squire in the eye. He knew that she wouldn't come to him without good reason and let her proceed without interruption.

"It's to do with Master Adam."

The Squire flinched slightly, knowing already that his son was causing a problem.

"Yesterday when I took up his lunch tray, I found him in a drunken stupor lying in a vomit covered bed. Made me feel very queasy as I opened all the windows to get some fresh air in. He stirred a little and was quite abusive. Don't ask me to repeat what was said because I won't. I tried to get him out of bed so I could at least change his sheets.

"He's only fifteen Squire, he shouldn't be behaving like this. It isn't right and I am sorry but I refuse to take up any more food trays. If he is hungry, he can come to the dining room like everyone else.

"There. I've said my bit, won't say any more about it. Just wanted you to know how I feel."

"Thank you for bringing this to my attention, Mrs Sutton. I had no idea it had gotten this bad and for that I apologise profusely for my son's unacceptable behaviour towards you. Rest assured, I will have strong words to say to him." The Squire stood and placed a gentle hand on Mrs Sutton's shoulder for reassurance as she left the room.

The Squire was furious as his loud footsteps could be heard on the polished floor as he marched down the hallway going from room to room collecting whisky bottles as he went. When his arms were full he suddenly felt extremely foolish and naïve, realising how much alcohol he had in the house. The bottles clinked against one another as he carefully made his way to the kitchen and tipped the contents down the sink.

The liquid sloshed and gurgled and the fumes made him momentarily intoxicated as he emptied each bottle. He then walked outside to clear his head and was pleased that a positive decision had finally been made, albeit a little late, but a decision none the less. He would tackle Adam when he had sobered up and the house was less busy.

Much later that evening, Adam sauntered down to the dining

room to see if any food was on offer. When he found it all in darkness he went in search of Mrs Sutton.

Where is that little busy body? She should be in the kitchen to prepare me my dinner, I'm famished, he thought.

"Kitchen's closed," said the Squire who was sitting at the far end of the kitchen table cloaked in darkness.

Adam ignored him and made his way to the pantry. *If I have to, I'll make my own food,* he thought.

"Nothing to eat until we come to an understanding on how you conduct yourself while you are under this roof," said the Squire in an authoritative manner. "Sit down and explain yourself, son."

Adam was still drunk, but not too drunk to pick up the irony of what his father had just said.

"Son?" he questioned. "All of a sudden, I am your son?"

The Squire decided to let that one go and admitted to himself that it was a poor choice of words. "Sit down I say," he bellowed, as he watched Adam pull out a chair. "You owe Mrs Sutton an apology," he began. When he saw the boy smirk he felt like leaning over and grabbing him by the scruff of the neck. "You will do as I say and will sincerely apologise first thing tomorrow. Is that clear?" he said as he locked eyes with Adam who initially returned his stare but then looked away, defeated.

"Good," said the Squire. "Secondly, the house is clear of whisky, and so there is no room for misinterpretation, if you are caught drunk again or in possession of alcohol, I will cease your boarding school fees and you will be forced to come back here to live and attend the village school."

The instant look of horror on Adam's face confirmed to the Squire that he had played an ace card. Leaving the boarding school was the last thing in the world that Adam wanted to do.

He had no choice but to abide by his father's rules. After a moment, Adam realised it wouldn't be too bad. He had had the hindsight to stockpile a secret stash of alcohol that no one could ever find. He just had to be a little more careful and condense his daily intake.

Chapter Twelve

When William left Primrose Cottage before sunrise on the twenty-third of December to make his rounds he discovered that Jack Frost had been extremely busy overnight. Shutting the back door as quietly as he could he stepped gingerly onto the white glistening path. His footsteps crunched loudly and left imprints as he walked slowly towards the barn to get his bicycle.

Management of the estate was a year round job and over the Christmas period he was responsible for making sure that the gates and workshops were locked and that all the animals were safe with enough feed, water and straw.

The fresh icy air stung his nostrils with every breath in and white puffs escaped from his mouth as he breathed out. He glanced upwards towards the bedroom windows and wished that he was still snug and warm tucked up in bed. Dawn had not quite broken and the lane was still cast in bright moonlight. William took in the beauty of the picturesque winter scene courtesy of old frostie as he peddled along admiring the freshly painted iciness over the roofs, hedgerows and trees.

Proof that anyone was out and about this frosty morning was the snake-like trail left by his bicycle tyres and a slight squeak indicating that the pedals needed oiling. White vapour puffs billowed behind him like a miniature steam train as he cycled down Honeysuckle Lane. He would only be working for a few hours today as pre-arranged with the Squire as he planned on getting back before seven to look after Maggie because Iris was helping Mrs Sutton at the Manor today for the party preparations.

On that same cold early morning, Mr Winchett, the village butcher, delivered to the Manor's kitchen two of the estate's pigs that he had expertly prepared and primed into proportionate cuts ready for cooking. As a thank you, Mrs Sutton cooked Mr Winchett a hearty breakfast including all the cups of tea that he could manage.

When Iris and Betty arrived at the Manor's kitchen a short time later they began preparing and cooking six fattened turkeys, twelve of the Manor's plumpest chickens, ten ducks and the two pigs. The traditional twelve-seater kitchen table was heaped with cooking and cooling trays, cake tins, mixing bowls alongside cake and pie ingredients and three rolling pins that were floured and ready to use. The prepared meats were positioned on the table in batches waiting to be cooked and Mrs Sutton had set up an orderly assembly line to maximise the oven space to its best advantage. The kitchen was also equipped with two large and extremely heavy coal and wood-burning range cookers especially designed for this amount of cooking.

Back in the Manor's heyday, the many functions on the social calendar catered for every season. The old Squire of the early 1800s employed a head cook, two kitchen assistants, a butler, housekeeper and several maids in which to run the Manor efficiently. Nowadays, particularly during the war, Christmas was the only time of year that Mrs Sutton had use for both range cookers and she relished every moment.

The meat preparation and all the cooking would take fourteen hours and be completed in four batches while the savoury dishes and sweet puddings would be completed in two batches using both ranges. It was a long but an enjoyable rewarding day. As the morning continued, the delightful waft travelled beyond the kitchen and by early afternoon the whole house was filled with a wonderful mouth-watering aroma to make any tummy rumble.

The aroma was so enticing that you could easily imagine that the ancient suit of armour positioned outside the library being tempted down from its plinth to queue up at the kitchen door and hold out a plate in anticipation of slices of hot turkey, pork, chicken and duck.

"Goodness me," said Betty, as she entered the kitchen. "You can smell the cooking down the hallway all the way to the Great Hall, it's the most beautiful smell ever."

"Are smells beautiful?" asked Iris, as she looked up from washing up. "Never thought of smells as being beautiful before."

"This one definitely is." Betty turned her nose to the air in an exaggerated way.

"You are funny Bet. How's the holly decoration going?"

"It looks just grand love," said Betty, as she placed her index finger to her lips. "Those holly leaves are something to be reckoned with though, lost count how many times they got me, the little blighters."

"Ah, ladies, time for a break I think," said Mrs Sutton. "Come, take a seat and a well-earned rest." She placed a freshly made pot of tea and three china cups, saucers and tea plates on the table. Even though the temperature outside hadn't lifted much beyond five degrees all day, the kitchen was as hot as the ovens, even with the door and windows open.

Betty washed her hands then sat and buttered two thick slices of warm bread each. To have butter on a weekday was truly a treat she thought, as the knife made gentle clanking sounds against the side of the glass butter dish. Iris brought over a plate containing succulent turkey slices that were still oozing juices and Mrs Sutton poured the tea.

"Cheers," said Mrs Sutton, as she held up her teacup.

"Cheers," said Iris and Betty together.

"Now for the best bit," said Mrs Sutton gleefully, "Tuck in ladies and enjoy."

The kitchen was silent with the exception of the range cookers activity where hissing fat and popping noises from the burning apple logs could be heard. The women all had rosy cheeks and shiny noses from the heat of the kitchen as they devoured and savoured the fruits of their labours on this bitterly cold day.

"My goodness, that was good," said Mrs Sutton as she dabbed her napkin over her mouth.

"Sure was," said Betty with eyes beaming.

"I'll say," smiled Iris in agreement, feeling a rare sense of contentment.

Just then, a loud, long and liquidy belch echoed through the room. They all turned to look at the kitchen doorway. Out of the corner of her eye, Iris saw Mrs Sutton's expression change as the blood seemed to drain from her face. Iris stood and put her hand on the older woman's shoulder in support as Adam literally stumbled into the kitchen.

"Ah, ladies, ladies," he slurred. "What a wonderful sight you are, and what a lovely aroma emanates from the kitchen."

But not from you, thought Betty, as she wrinkled her napkin under her nose to block out his repugnant odour.

"Where's my father?" he demanded, as he tried to focus his glassy eyes on Mrs Sutton.

"He's in town picking up a few things for the party," she said dutifully, looking away to avoid his cold stare. Even though he had apologised profusely for his ungentlemanly behaviour the other day, she didn't believe he meant a word of it.

"Ah, is he now?" Adam walked over to the pantry supporting himself by the table and worktop on his way.

Where did he get the liquor from? thought Mrs Sutton. She knew the Squire had got rid of all the whisky. Adam returned from the pantry empty handed, obviously not finding whatever he was searching for.

"Will we see you at the party, Adam?" asked Iris with interest. Adam was only fifteen but he was the Squire's son and one day he was going to inherit all this land and money. She envied him, he had an easy life ahead. He could do anything.

"Bloody hell no woman, are you mad?" Adam saw Mrs Sutton flinch at his language. "Sorry, Mrs Sutton," he said. "No, I'll not be here, thank Christ. I'm going to a friend's for a few weeks, leaving tonight. Stay here? With all that joviality? Fraternising with the lower classes? Hell, no." And with that, he was gone, although his stench lingered.

Betty was stunned. She couldn't believe that anyone, especially a child, could be that rude. "He's only fifteen," she whispered, "Completely out of control. If my Pete or Billy spoke like that I'd whip their behinds." She shook her head in disbelief.

"We'll have another cup of tea with a warm mince pie then we'll crack on," said Mrs Sutton, suddenly perking up as she poured the tea. She was embarrassed by Adam's offensive statement but extremely relieved to hear that he would not be around for Christmas or New Year. That was the best Christmas present ever and she also said a private prayer that it would be perfect if he just buggered off at least until next Easter holidays.

After their mince pies and another cup of tea it was time to get back to work.

"How about you ladies swap jobs this afternoon to give yourselves a break?" suggested Mrs Sutton. "I'll start to decorate the tree."

"Good idea," said Betty. "Beware of that holly Iris, it bites."

"Mrs Collins, you are meant to arrange it, not fight with it." Mrs Sutton laughed. "Come on ladies, work to be done, schedule to keep." She marched off towards the Great Hall suspending a tea towel high in the air in the direction of travel like a headmistress leading a school group.

The Manor was not the only hive of activity that morning. All the ladies of the estate were busy baking cakes, scones, cheese fingers, sausage rolls and all kinds of party food ready to take to the Manor. Food ration coupons and points had been cleverly spent and where possible, non-perishables stored up little-by-little ready for the Christmas period.

Chapter Thirteen

Christmas Eve and the day of the Primrose Farm Estate Christmas party had finally arrived much to Maggie's delight. She traipsed into the kitchen wearing a huge grin. She had been looking forward to this party ever since Mrs Sutton's invitation had dropped through their letterbox a month ago. "Can we go now?" she asked.

"Yes, we're all ready and with a brisk walk we'll be there before four o'clock," said Iris.

"Righto girls, let's be on our way." William ushered Maggie and Iris out the door while he buttoned up his coat. Being a cloudy day, it was nearly dark already as they walked down Honeysuckle Lane meeting up with other families on the way. The ladies carried their food contributions wrapped in wicker baskets covered with tea towels to keep out the winter's chill. The children followed closely behind and every now and then wafts of freshly cooked mince pies, sausage rolls and butterfly cakes streamed through the air.

"Betty love?" said Eric as he stepped up beside his wife, "Let me help and carry the basket for you, looks quite heavy."

"I don't think so," chided Betty, playfully slapping his knuckles as they hovered over the basket, "I've spent hours on this lot and I don't want them accidently tipped over, or, to be more frank, for you to slip your hand underneath the tea towel to sample before we get there Mr Collins. I know what you are about." Betty laughed as she saw the shocked look on his face.

"Goodness love, I am truly hurt by that remark," he said, breaking into a laugh also. "You know me all too well 'ol girl, that'll I say. I'll have to wait until we get there then. Mind you, the one I sampled before we left the house was truly scrumptious," he said, rubbing his stomach in appreciation.

"You are impossible Eric, now come on, or we'll be late."

There was constant chatter and excitement in the air as adults and children alike turned from Honeysuckle Lane into the Manor's long driveway. Their footsteps crunching on the pathway leading to the front door sounded like a herd of cows munching on packs of biscuits.

"I bet Mrs Sutton has laid on a good spread," said Pete.

"Oh yes, from what Mum said the Squire has pulled out all the stops. Do you remember last year?" asked Billy.

"That was the best ever, I love this time of year," said Pete.

"I don't remember much at all," said a sad-looking Maggie as she walked alongside the boys.

"You were a little poorly last year and slept through most of the party," said Billy.

"You'll remember it this time round, I promise," said Pete.

Completely satisfied with this, Maggie picked up a smile as one-by-one they were greeted at the door by the Squire and Mr and Mrs Sutton. They placed their coats on the hooks in the hallway and as they filed through the adults took a glass of sherry and the children were given homemade blackcurrant jelly drinks.

There were gasps of pure delight as everyone felt the sheer warmth and marvelled at the festive scene before them. It wasn't called the Great Hall for nothing as it could easily accommodate the seventy people attending today. Everyone agreed that Mrs Sutton, Iris and Betty had done a grand job with the decorations.

Apart from the beams, oil paintings and tapestries, the main feature of the Great Hall was the magnificent Kentish Ragstone fireplace with its slate hearth. It was part of the original building and was twice Maggie's height and at least three times her in width. The fire had been ablaze for several hours, courtesy of Mr Sutton. It roared vivid reds, yellows and raging oranges and purples in full glory and completely heated the room.

Garlands of fresh holly were placed across the deep mahogany mantle and carefully balanced along the top of the antique mirror suspended on the wall above. Each garland boasted deep red holly berries that seemed to have been buffed to their finest.

Mr Sutton had placed a generous pile of apple logs to one side of the fireplace and about a foot away from the grate stood a freestanding ornate metal fireguard that fully enclosed the fire. He saw fit to supervise the fire, as he feared that the little ones would venture too close. Also one or two of the apple logs had been spitting and occasionally small pieces of burning log would shoot out onto the hearth. On closer inspection these pieces seemed to pulsate and were quite mesmerising to watch. When this happened Mr Sutton would swing the hinged guard back slightly and used the fireside tongs to pick up the burning wood and replace it safely inside the grate.

Mrs Sutton had made rows of paper chains that were now hung from the beamed ceiling. But by far, the finest of all the decorations was the magnificent Christmas tree that stood proudly in the far corner.

Maggie stood completely still; her eyes transfixed on the Christmas tree. She had never seen anything more beautiful in her life. It was like she had stepped into a magical storybook owned by a beautiful princess.

"Come with us Maggie," said Pete, rescuing Maggie's drink that was tilting at a precarious angle. He grabbed her hand and whisked her away to look more closely at the Christmas tree. "Isn't it grand?"

"It's beautiful," she whispered as she looked up at the tree craning her head right back so she could see the elegant fairy suspended at the very top. "Look at all the colours," she said, as her mother came up beside her.

"Yes, it's very pretty," said Iris, "See how Mrs Sutton has decorated the tree? The decorations are very old and some are as delicate as egg shells and are painted by hand. Come with me Maggie, let's go and look at all of the food that has been prepared then you can join the other children."

Maggie and Iris went over to the long table where the ladies of the estate were proudly arranging their dish to its best advantage. Although this was a joyous occasion where everyone participated, there was still some serious competition amongst the ladies.

"My, my Mrs Harris," said Mr Wells, "Your sausage rolls look as good as always."

"Thank you Mr Wells," Iris said, noticing that he had four on his plate.

"Ladies and gentlemen, may I have your attention please?" requested the Squire as he banged a small brass gong sending a soothing echo around the room. "Thank you," he said, as a hushed silence fell. "First of all I would like to say a very big thank you to Mr and Mrs Sutton who have put so much effort and work into this year's Christmas party at the Manor."

The room roared with cheers, whistles and applause as all eyes settled on the couple. Mrs Sutton's cheeks blushed in embarrassment.

"This marks the fortieth year in which Mrs Sutton has organised this great event. So, everyone please raise your glass. Well done and thank you, Mrs Sutton."

"Mrs Sutton," repeated everyone in the room raising their glasses in the air.

"Special thanks also to Mrs Harris and Mrs Collins for assisting in the meat cooking and with the decorations. Also sincere thanks to all helpers who have spent so much time in making this occasion so special, because without your help, this would not have been possible. And lastly, but by no means least, a special thank you to all the ladies of the estate for your splendid contributions. They are truly delightful."

More rapturous applause followed.

"I would like to say with heartfelt gratitude a big thank you to all Primrose Farm Estate workers and families for your continued hard work over the past year. And my goodness how quickly this year has flown by. They say that as you get older, time goes quicker."

"You're not wrong there, Squire," said a voice in the crowd, followed by more cheers and laughter.

"Yes, thank you for that," smiled the Squire, holding up his hands for silence. "Now, before the festivities begin I would like you to again raise your glasses to the King and for an end to this awful war and hope our boys and girls return home to us safely. God Save the King."

"God Save the King," everyone announced, raising their glasses.

"I wish you all a very Merry Christmas and a happy, safe and healthy 1942. Now, go and enjoy yourselves." The Squire raised his glass to all in the room.

When the cheers died down, the ladies went over to the food

table and removed the remaining tea towels from their trays, plates and dishes alongside the medley of meat dishes ready for the party to begin. The adults formed groups and started conversations while the children ran around savouring the fun of the early evening.

With the party going so well, Mrs Sutton was joyous. Everything had come together nicely and the families seemed to be having a wonderful time. She did feel a little guilty and selfish however in thinking that it was good to forget the war, albeit briefly.

"A glass of sherry, Mrs Sutton?" asked Iris as she held out a dainty glass.

"No, thank you, Mrs Harris. I'll wait until later on. Don't want to appear squiffy now do I?"

"You have worked so hard, Mrs Sutton. One small sherry won't harm. Come on, it's Christmas," said Iris still holding out the glass.

"Well, yes I have, thank you, why not?" smiled Mrs Sutton, as she accepted the small sweet sherry. "I'll drink this then perhaps you could help me bring all the pickles, chutneys and preserves through? The jars are already laid out on the kitchen table, they just need bringing through."

"I'd love to help but I need to check on Maggie, perhaps I could ask Mrs Collins to help?" said Iris sweetly. *I'll be damned if I am expected to keep working,* she thought. She watched Mrs Sutton closely as she sipped her sherry.

"Mrs Sutton, forgive me if I am wrong, but I can't help noticing that there's a way of, how can I put it? A way of 'intrigue' about you at the moment."

Mrs Sutton burst out laughing and winked.

Iris was shocked. This was totally out of character for Mrs Sutton, something was definitely going on. "What are you up to, if you pardon my being forthright?"

"Oh my dear. As you know I love to do something a little different each year. But, I believe this year will surpass all. Not even the Squire knows. It is just too delicious for words." She took another sip of sherry. "And please don't ask me because all will be revealed very shortly," she said, tilting her head back to finish off the sherry. "Now, pickles, Mrs Harris. Pickles."

The hall was buzzing with different conversations and Mrs Sutton selected a few ladies to help distribute another round of food. As the ladies moved around, offering the trays of food they were privy to snippets of conversations on all sorts of topics. Mrs Sutton had purposefully selected those ladies who she believed were nosy parkers. This was a ruse by her to keep them occupied so they wouldn't notice what she had planned. Over a ten-minute period some of the men discreetly left the room: one here, a couple there, until about twenty men in total had left.

At just the right time, Mrs Sutton banged the small brass gong and waited as the chatter died down. "May I have your attention please," she asked. "Thank you. Now, if you would all be kind enough to put on your coats and follow me outside to the rear of the Manor. All will be revealed for this year's treat."

"Where's Daddy?" asked Maggie, as she spun around trying to locate her father.

"Now, don't worry anyone," said Mrs Sutton, before Iris could reply. "There are some folk who have gone on ahead. Please follow me and could the last one out close the door, as we don't want to lose all this heat. Off we go. Quick, quick."

There was excited chatter as everyone filed down the hallway to retrieve their coats. Mrs Sutton led them through the main front door and around the side of the Manor to the back of the house.

To maintain order over the group Mrs Sutton banged the gong again. "Now, if everyone can gather in a tight semi-circle and please be silent," she said, as she pressed her index finger to her lips and arranged everyone accordingly. "I believe we may have a treat in store."

Maggie was confused. Why were they now outside in the cold night? She had been lovely and warm inside and wanted to stay with the Christmas tree.

"Do you know what's happening love?" whispered Betty, as she stood beside Iris wrapping her arms around Maggie's shoulders.

"No idea, Bet and I can't see William, what about Eric?"

"He's not here either, or the boys," said Betty, as she looked around. "I hope this is worth it. It's too cold to be out here when there is a glorious fire going to waste inside."

There had been no overnight air raids upon the village during the past week and Mrs Sutton had prayed it would continue. She had decided to take a risk and discussed it at length with all her co-conspirators who had agreed that it was worth it. It was just as well that the Home Guard had not been invited this evening as they may not have agreed.

"Look," exclaimed Maggie, as she pointed excitedly towards the lake. All eyes followed Maggie's direction as a sheer hush descended on the captivated audience. When everyone's eyes adjusted to the darkness they could see a distant flickering flame that appeared to be gliding and dancing towards them through the air. Accompanying the light was soft music.

"That sounds like my Eric's accordion," whispered Betty.

The flame and music gradually became clearer as a rowboat softly glided towards the water's edge. The lantern silhouetted Eric and reflections danced over the concentric circles that moved toward the jetty like inky silk waves as the sound of *Hark the Herald Angels Sing* embraced the night.

In synchronisation, more flickering lights gradually appeared from the surrounding woodland like tiny dancing stars. The male voiced choir walked slowly towards the lawn, their dulcet baritones blending with the accordion. Each held homemade lanterns that were glass jam jars hanging from wooden poles as their formation mirror-imaged the audience thus completing a huge circle on the Manor's lawn. As the rowboat arrived at the jetty, Pete, who had been rowing, and Billy, who had been holding the lantern, helped their father from the little boat. Eric, miraculously, didn't miss a note as he stepped out of the boat. He and the boys made their way to the circle of people.

When the carol finished the audience erupted in an enthusiastic applause through their gloved and mittened hands. Eric played a few notes of the next carol to which the choir once again burst into song, the harmony was perfect. They finished off with *Silent Night* and everyone joined in. The music carried into the night chased by plumes of white puffs of air from the singers.

This perfect moment would live on in everyone's memory and be talked about for many years to come. It was one precious memory that Maggie would always remember as being truly magical.

Mrs Sutton, once again sounded the gong for attention. "Thank you to The Manor Male Voice Choir," she said proudly. "Now, lights out gentlemen and if everyone could file back into the house where there is hot mulled wine for the grown-ups and warmed blackcurrant jelly drinks for the children."

There was much talk as everyone made their way back inside to the welcome warmth of the fire.

"Not so fast you two," whispered Mrs Sutton as she caught Pete and Billy by the arm. They easily towered above her but she held them firmly back from the crowd. "I've been meaning to catch up with you both for a while."

The boys looked at one another with puzzled looks.

"Now. Rainbow trout? Ring any bells?" she asked, looking from one to the other.

Caught off guard, the boys looked at her blankly.

"Mrs Sutton?" said Pete, hoping his brother could come up with something.

"Purchets," she said. "After you'd left those fish I realised that something was not quite right. Then when I was talking to Mr Dwyer in the Post Office the other week, it suddenly dawned on me that there hadn't been any rainbow trout in Purchets stream for a number of years. So 'gentlemen', I put it to you that you fished in the Squire's own lake then had the audacity to sell the fish back to his estate for profit. What do you say to that?"

Pete and Billy knew they had been caught out. Billy just shrugged and Pete opened his mouth as if to speak and then closed it again.

"Now, gentlemen," Mrs Sutton said, "Our future arrangement will be as follows,listen carefully: I give you permission to fish in the lake during the trout season ONLY and for that the estate will pay you one shilling per week for two fish per week and you can also take one fish home to your mother. It's your choice, take it or leave it. Or, if you prefer we can discuss this directly with the Squire?"

Pete and Billy looked at one another and then with a mutual nod, both said, "Done."

"Good. Now that's all arranged, perhaps you'll accompany me

back inside the house. It's too cold out here to stop and chat."

At the end of the party, everyone applauded the Squire for his hospitality and bade him and Mr and Mrs Sutton a Merry Christmas as they filed out of the Manor. The clouds had cleared and the moonlight was sufficient to guide the party goers down Honeysuckle Lane.

"I didn't suspect a thing," said Iris, feeling unusually cheerful. She linked arms with William in a rare show of affection. "When did you all meet for practice?"

"We only managed three meetings in all, didn't we Eric? It was a miracle it came off so well."

"Yes, just the three meetings. That Mrs Sutton is a force to be reckoned with isn't she?" Eric put his arm around Betty and the twins nodded their agreement knowing they would be extra mindful of Mrs Sutton in future.

Just then from the back of the group someone started to sing *Silent Night* and soon everyone had joined in. The carols continued until the last family had reached home. The tone fading in voice as each family arrived at their cottage and waved goodnight to their friends and colleagues as the snow started to fall in time for Christmas Day.

"Out like a light," said William, as he walked back into the kitchen from taking Maggie to bed. "I was about to start one of my stories but she was already asleep." He smiled at the memory of his daughter's sleeping face, knowing that she had had a truly glorious day.

"She had a very busy day," said Iris. "Now, William, if you can bring the tree in we'll start decorating, it won't take us long."

An hour later, William and Iris stepped back and admired

their handiwork. The medium sized spruce looked truly grand in all its decorated glory standing in an old coalscuttle in the corner of the parlour supported by logs to stop it from toppling over. Iris had salvaged and stored the flour that was ruined from the spillage back during the summer's air raid and had mixed it with a little water to make a glue-like substance. Over the past couple of evenings when Maggie had been in bed she had made tiny paper-chains to hang around the tree.

She quite enjoyed being creative and thought if only she had had lovely Christmas memories like Maggie was having as a child. Life might have been very different indeed.

"Maggie loved the party today and she'll remember this Christmas I'm sure. She has grown up so much this last year and will remember things better from now on. I know she was poorly last Christmas, but with everything else we went through last year perhaps it was for the best that she doesn't remember it.

"I know we said we'd never mention last year, but seeing how happy she was today, she deserves so much better. Childhood is precious."

"Well, for some children it is," Iris spat back. "And. We. Agreed. Never to talk about last year. Remember? You forgave me at the time. I thought we had moved on. I am trying very hard here. Do not dig this up now. Please William."

"Yes, I'm sorry love. I only meant to say that life is so much better now."

"I'm turning in," Iris said curtly. "It's been a long day."

Chapter Fourteen

"We have a tree," yelled Maggie. "We have a tree. I need the lav, need to go, need to go," she sang as she ran out the kitchen door.

Iris and William couldn't help laughing as they watched their daughter sprinting down the garden path scuffling her wellies with her nightie, dressing gown and hair billowing.

"Think it's about time Maggie had her potty back under the bed," said William. "Time to try again and hope she doesn't kick it over or spill it coming down the stairs."

"Yes, I agree," said Iris, "it's getting too cold out there of a morning."

"That's better," exclaimed Maggie, as she ran back into the kitchen and plonked her freezing hands into the warm washing up water.

"What do you think?" asked Iris, as they filed into the parlour.

"It's beautiful, our own tree and just in time for Christmas." Maggie wrapped her arms around her parents.

"We're glad you like it, Maggie" said William. "I fed the chickens when I came in from work this morning so you don't have to do them. After breakfast we'll open your presents."

When Iris and William gave the huge stocking to Maggie she was amazed. Iris had made it from a hessian sack and decorated it with red stitching and a material bow. Maggie tipped it upside down and out rolled an apple, an orange and, as she dug down deep, she retrieved a pair of knitted mittens and a hat to match. Nestled in at the toe of the stocking was a small wooden box about the size of a new potato. William had whittled the box over many weeks out of old English oak. It had ornate carvings with a small, hinged lid. Maggie carefully opened the lid and found it was lined with red velvet and within the box were two sixpences sitting on top of another Australian stamp, courtesy of Mr Dwyer.

"This is the best Christmas ever," she said, her eyes shining in awe.

After Christmas dinner, William put on the wireless to listen to the King's Christmas speech acutely aware that Iris had been sneaking rather one too many sherries. Late in the afternoon there was a knock at the back door followed by a slightly out-of-tune rendition of *Jingle Bells.*

Maggie opened the door to reveal Betty, Eric, Pete and Billy standing together with beaming faces as they all chanted: "Happy Christmas."

They all ploughed into the kitchen and took off their coats, hats and gloves. Pete and Billy brought out an old pack of playing cards and began teaching Maggie how to play Snap. Eric handed William some beer bottles while Iris fetched clean glasses from the cupboard and gave the children warm home-made blackcurrant jelly drinks. She then poured Betty and herself a large glass of sherry. Betty placed a tray of freshly made chicken sandwiches and sausage rolls on the table for supper.

Everyone was having fun on this Christmas night, as the adults reminisced in the parlour over the past year and the children played cards at the kitchen table.

"Are you alright, love?" Betty whispered gently to Iris as they sat on the settee. She thought that Iris was a little squiffy when they arrived and had watched as her friend had downed at least three more glasses since their arrival.

"Fine love, here have another." Iris attempted to top up Betty's glass.

"Not for me thanks love," said Betty as she covered her glass with the palm of her hand, "I'll call it a night, why don't I put the kettle on? I'll make us a cuppa."

"Perhaps I don't want a cuppa, Betty. Then what?" challenged Iris, as William and Eric picked up on the abrupt tone. "Come on, it's Christmas for Chrissake."

"NOT in front of the children," William said quickly before Maggie or the twins heard. He turned to Eric. "Perhaps you'd better go, sorry. I should've done something earlier, this has been brewing all day I'm afraid."

Betty quickly moved into the kitchen and passed her sons their coats.

"But, we're in the middle of a game," protested Pete.

Iris's voice could be heard from the parlour and the twins caught the look in their mother's eye. Instantly they realised what she was doing as she was also holding Maggie's coat.

"Hey Maggie," said Billy, "How about coming home with us this evening so your father can look after your mother? It's been a busy day. Come on, the fire is stoked and we'll finish the game at our house."

Maggie looked at Betty, who was holding up her coat.

"Okay, Maggie?"

She nodded in agreement and held her arms out. Her father had closed the parlour door.

Iris was in a rage and she wasn't holding back. "YES, I had an affair," she flung her arms in the air, "we all know that, the whole bloody village probably knows that. BUT, YOU FORGAVE ME," she hissed at William who stood stock still. "TELL ME WILLIAM, tell me, what do I have to do for you not to bring it up? Of all the days of the year, you have to pick bloody Christmas Day."

"I did forgive you, I still forgive you and we have moved on..."

"WE HAVEN'T MOVED ON AT ALL!"

"Yes, we have. I am sorry I mentioned it last night. I didn't mean it like that. We should have talked it over then instead of it festering like it has."

"FESTERING? Is that what it was? Have YOU been festering all year, William?"

"Look, we'll talk about this in the morning when we're a little brighter..."

"A little brighter? You're pathetic," Iris spat back. "Why don't you just come out and say that I'm too bloody drunk? Be a man, William. Stop being so damn polite all the time, IT MAKES ME SICK. YOU MAKE ME SICK."

William knew very well what his wife was provoking. He stood calm, which only infuriated Iris more.

"Don't just stand there like a wet blanket," she taunted.

"Rant all you like Iris," he said quietly. "I'm not your father. I won't strike you. You married the wrong man for that."

"That we agree on," she said as she pushed past him to head up to bed.

Chapter Fifteen

Since Christmas night, Iris and William had worked hard for Maggie's sake to settle the unpleasantness of their row. Iris knew she had to make amends all round to salvage her place at Primrose Cottage.

She made Betty a rabbit pie and stood on the Collins' doorstep apologetically. When Betty opened the door and greeted Iris with a warm hug, Iris felt relieved.

Maggie was quickly turning into a bright and knowing child and in the coming months after school she became her mother's shadow. Iris tolerated this. She knew she should be grateful for all she had but sometimes she just wanted to scream. It seemed that every time she turned, Maggie was right there in front of her. At the end of the working day Iris just wanted her own time and breathing space but Maggie wouldn't let her be. She wanted to help with the baking, all of the household chores, with the sewing and knitting. She was an eager pupil and picked up new skills quickly.

"I reckon," said Iris to William as they sat by the range cooker having a cup of tea at the end of the day, "That soon enough Maggie will be more than capable of running a household."

"Yes," he said. "You've taught her well and she knows the names of all the tools in the workshop as well. We could both retire tomorrow and Maggie could run the place," he joked. "She's a good 'un alright and we are truly blessed to have her." William didn't notice Iris cringe at this remark.

Maggie and Sally's friendship continued growing until they were quite inseparable. At first, Iris hated the idea of Sally coming over to the house all the time after school as it meant that she had to spend extra time feeding two children instead of only one and the fact that there was an extra person around. But Iris soon changed her tune when she realised that with Sally there, Maggie had someone else to be with and that meant Iris had more free time. She realised it was in her interest to encourage the friendship.

However, one day Maggie asked at the dinner table if Sally could stay for the up-coming weekend. Iris was about to decline, she couldn't think of anything worse than having two children around for the weekend, when William answered and said it was a splendid idea. Maggie whooped with joy and William beamed with excitement for his daughter.

"We should have talked this through together," said Iris, when Maggie had gone to bed that evening.

"What's the problem love? They will have a good time."

"It would've been nice to have given my opinion. It's as if I don't have any say," she said, as she dried up the dinner things, rubbing the saucepan ferociously.

"You don't want Sally to stay over?"

"It's not that," Iris said quietly, forcing herself to remain calm. How could she say that she never wanted anyone to come over to stay? That the whole world could take a running jump with William and Maggie at the front of the line? She felt trapped but knew she could never reveal her true feelings.

"All I meant was that we should discuss these decisions away from Maggie first. Look at it from my side of things. You will be at work for the majority of the time and I will be here all of the time. I should have had a say without being made to look like I am the bad person who doesn't want Sally to stay. It's a lot of responsibility looking after someone else's child. What if there was an accident or something? Or they go wandering off and we can't find them? We need to think of these things."

"Righto love, I see where you are coming from. Next time we'll say we will talk about things first and then get back to her. But it will be fine, you'll see."

Iris was seething. All through the week her tension continued to mount up and when Friday afternoon arrived she was dreading the end of school.

"Iris?" called Betty, as she knocked on the kitchen door. "Are you home love? Iris?" She peered into the kitchen window looking for Iris and even looked at the outbuildings and lavatory but still couldn't locate her. *That's strange,* she thought, *Iris said to come round for a cuppa before the children came home.*

Just then, Iris seemed to stagger slightly through the parlour door into the kitchen. Betty rushed into the kitchen to help her.

"Iris? What's wrong? You look terrible, if you don't mind me saying." She assisted Iris back to the parlour and sat her down on the settee. "You're very pale, are you sick? Let me get you some water."

"It came on all of a sudden Bet, I have this blinding headache and feel queasy, must have been something I ate. I need to get Maggie and Sally from school. Sally is staying the weekend."

"You can't go in this state. I will get Maggie and explain to Sally that you are unwell and to make it another time. Do you want me to fetch the doctor?"

"No, that's not necessary. I will be alright. Thanks for getting Maggie, you are a good friend."

"That's what friends are for love. Now you go on up to bed and lie down, I'll bring round something to eat for you all later and I will leave a note for William. Off you go and get better, do you need a hand?"

"Thanks Bet, I will be okay. Thank you." Iris turned and walked gingerly towards the stairs and unbeknown to Betty, smirked in victory. *That was easier than I thought* as she hoped she had done enough to have gotten out of a very long weekend with two brats and also there was no supper to cook. She didn't feel guilty at all to lie to her friend; it came so easily to her. Betty was a natural born mother and a good cook so there was no harm done, and besides, she wanted to finish reading her book, so this was perfect timing.

About an hour later Iris quickly put away her book as she heard Betty enter the house and gently call out, asking if she was all right. Iris feigned sleep and stirred groggily when Betty entered the bedroom.

"How are you feeling love?" Betty sat down beside Iris and looked at her with concern.

"Just a bit groggy but I will be okay. Is Maggie here?"

"All good, love. I walked the girls back to The Oak and the Vinter's were really good about it. They could see how disappointed the girls were so they offered to have Maggie for the weekend so you could rest up. I've put a casserole on the kitchen table for William when he gets in and there is some for you as well, if you are up to it."

"Thank you Betty, that is so lovely of you but I just want to sleep at the moment."

"I will leave you be. William will be home shortly and I will pop in and see you tomorrow, take care love."

"Bye Bet, thank you." Iris couldn't believe that she would have a whole relaxing weekend on her own. *It is just perfect,* she thought. But she knew that she shouldn't play too much on it, as William would insist on the doctor and he might even call someone else in to work his shift at the Manor at the weekend. Iris knew she had to play this just so.

After William read Betty's note he checked on Iris who was genuinely asleep this time. He left quietly and stopped by Eric and Betty's to thank Betty for the meal.

At seven that evening William stood outside The Oak Pub wondering how noisy and boisterous it would become around closing time. He did not know Edward or Gwen Vinter personally but, from what he did know of them, they were decent people. He did not blame Betty for allowing Maggie to stay at the pub because she was caught in the middle of things but something didn't feel quite right.

Pubs were no places for children and Maggie was only six years old. But then again, William reasoned with himself, their daughter Sally was the same age and she seemed a fine little girl. William had to put his mind at rest, so he walked inside, approached the bar and extended his hand.

"Mr Vinter," he said.

"Mr Harris, nice to see you, what'll you have? And it's Edward."

"William. It's nice to finally meet you as well. Look, sorry, this is a bit awkward, I didn't come for a drink..."

"You just wanted to check on Maggie because you don't think a pub is a suitable place for a child to be in. Is that correct?" asked

Edward.

"That about does it," William said, relieved that the point was out in the open.

"Those were my exact concerns before we took on this place. But rest assured, Gwen has got the accommodation upstairs just so and you wouldn't even know it was connected to a pub, apart from the noise sometimes. Sally knows that she isn't allowed in the bar at all when it is open and we said the same to Maggie when she first came over. Not sure if you have ever been upstairs at all but there is a separate secure entrance and no one can get upstairs from the bar area, so everyone is completely safe. That was the first thing I made sure of when we came down for a viewing prior to buying."

"That's good to know Edward. I appreciate you saying all this. No hard feelings?"

"None whatsoever. I would have done the same in your shoes. Sure I can't tempt you?" he said, gesturing to the beer pump.

"Perhaps another time, I must really get back to Iris."

"Another time it is then and hope Mrs Harris recovers soon."

"Thank you, and could we keep this to ourselves?"

"Mum's the word William. Goodnight."

Iris wasn't the only one who had a good weekend. Maggie and Sally had such fun together. Sally, her parents and older sister had moved from London the year before. Sally and Maggie spent hours talking about Sally's early life in London and Maggie heard all the antics of living above a pub. London was a very noisy, busy and frightening place to be during wartime so Sally's parents had decided to move.

They had sold their furniture business to buy The Oak Pub in the village. Even though they had never run such an establishment before they were hard workers. And Edward Vinter could certainly handle himself behind the bar where his main concern was detracting overzealous advances towards his eldest daughter, Pamela, more than anything else.

On the flip side, Pamela hated the countryside. She was bored and wanted to return to London. She wanted to go out late with her friends and to get into secretarial work, as she could not see a future for herself in the village. The pace was too slow for her. She understood her parents reasoning for the move, but she yearned for the life she loved in the city, however dangerous.

After some serious and sometimes overheated discussions with her parents, Pamela reluctantly agreed to give it a year to see how things progressed. Her father said that if she still felt the same after that time then they would consider letting her go and live with her aunt in London.

Pamela adored Sally and was initially worried about her settling in to her new life. Although, since she had made friends with Maggie, Pamela could see the special bond between the girls and loved them both equally.

Chapter Sixteen

"Are you alright love?" asked Betty as she walked back from the village store to the orchard with Iris during their lunch break.

"Fine. Why do you ask?"

"It's just that the twins overheard you telling Maggie off yesterday in the orchard and said that she was rather upset…"

"Isn't that the point of telling off?" said Iris a little sarcastically, "Maggie is fine, you know how she is."

Betty bit her lip wondering if she should say more. "They said what you were saying was cruel, …"

"What is this Betty? The third degree? Can't I reprimand my own child without being questioned?"

"I'm not saying that..."

"Then what are you saying? What did the twins 'think' they overheard?"

"That you wished that Maggie hadn't been born. Did you say that Iris?" Betty stopped and looked at her friend.

"Look, it was something and nothing, the boys have their wires crossed that's all, that's what happens when you hear only some of the conversation. They misheard Betty. Why would I say that to Maggie? Answer me that, why?"

"It wouldn't enter my head," said Betty.

"But it would enter mine?" Iris let that hang as an awkward silence descended. "Do you ever tell the boys off?"

"A lot, you know that," said Betty.

"Well then. Why can you tell off your children, but I am questioned when I do the same?" Iris was agitated and annoyed with herself for letting the boys overhear. She should have waited until they were home to reprimand Maggie. She would be more careful next time.

"I was just asking, Iris. Nothing more. I'm sorry." Betty was annoyed too. She should have got more details from the twins. From Iris' reaction, Betty was now questioning what her sons had told her.

"It's alright Betty, I don't want to fall out over this misunderstanding. Let's get back to the orchard, have a gossip and grab a quick cuppa before we start work."

"Talking of gossip," said Betty, thankful that the conversation had moved on, "I over-heard Mrs Wilks and Mrs Bates say that they saw you last Tuesday…"

Iris' heart began beating rapidly. Had she been caught in her afternoon liaison with Harvey? Damn, how could she be so stupid? It was bad enough that William had caught them in their bed the previous year. She didn't want to go through that again as it had taken months to get William back on side.

"Iris? Are you okay?"

"Sorry, you were saying?"

"I had to laugh, but 'apparently' last Tuesday, you were seen in town coming out of the movie theatre with a man and they said that you were kissing him and the man was not William!"

"Is that so?" Iris was thinking rapidly for an excuse.

"Yes, I know it's strange. They said that you were dressed to the nines, hair, makeup, the whole works."

"It wasn't me, love." Iris reassured. "How on earth could it have been? How could I be in town on Tuesday when I was at work? How exciting though, if you think about it, it seems that I have a glamorous double!" She thought that she had downplayed enough to deter suspicion. "To be honest, I'd much rather be at the movie theatre as opposed to working, wouldn't you?"

Betty was confused. She knew full well that Iris had excused herself yet again from work on Tuesday morning saying that she had one of her headaches and Betty had taken Maggie to school.

This made Betty recall all the other times Iris had made excuses to leave work early and in her heart of hearts she knew that Iris was still having an affair with Harvey. Eric had told her about William catching them in bed together. Eric had told Betty in confidence so there was no way Betty could tell Iris she was aware of this without landing her husband in trouble.

Betty decided not to say anything else, after all it was none of her business, but it did anger her to think that Iris may be continuing the affair while lying to William.

Chapter Seventeen

"Quiet please," said Mr Turk. "Get out your English books and turn to a new page. Today we are going to learn a new rhyme."

The class quietened down and all that could be heard was the sound of the desk lids being raised and lowered.

"You can see that I have written the rhyme on the board. It is called *Monday's Child* and the rhyme is for learning the days of the week. Please copy it into your books now."

Monday's child is fair of face,
Tuesday's child is full of grace,
Wednesday's child is full of woe,
Thursday's child has far to go,
Friday's child is loving and giving,
Saturday's child works hard for a living,
And the child that is born on the Sabbath day
Is bonny and blithe, and good and gay.

"I also have a calendar here," Mr Turk continued as the children were copying the rhyme, "so you can tell which day of the week you were born on if you do not know it. Who wants to go first?"

Maggie shot up her hand.

"Yes, Maggie, when is your birthday?"

"Sixteenth of July, 1936," she said as she waited with baited breath while Mr Turk looked it up.

"Ah, here we go," he said. "You were born on a Thursday and according to the rhyme you have far to go."

"Sir," called out Gregory, "she only lives down the lane, not far at all." The whole class roared with laughter.

"Yes, very funny Gregory, finish up writing. Look everyone, to save time I have already prepared a list of your dates, that I will pass around. Please look up your name, copy your date down and then pass it onto your neighbour."

"You're a Thursday with far to go," said Sally as the girls walked back to The Oak that afternoon after school, "and I'm Tuesday and graceful."

"You're always graceful, Sally," said Maggie to her best friend.

"Oh, that's kind Maggie. When you go to Australia, then you will have travelled far! Isn't that amazing?"

Chapter Eighteen

Maggie looked at the church noticeboard with delight. The date of the village Summer Fete was going to be held on Saturday, 17 July 1943, the day after her seventh birthday. The Fete was to be held within the grounds of Primrose Manor, courtesy of the Squire. Maggie couldn't wait to tell Sally at school the next day, because Sally had not yet seen all the Manor's grounds. The previous Summer Fete had, for some reason, taken place on the village green.

Maggie had sneaked Sally within the grounds of the Manor on a few occasions on the pretence of visiting her father in the workshop. She knew that the Squire and Mr Sutton wouldn't mind. But eagle-eyed Mrs Sutton would have carted them off back home if she'd seen them. The Summer Fete would be the perfect opportunity to explore the grounds together.

The summer days leading up to the Fete were lovely and hot, and the forecast for the Fete was much the same. The girls wore cotton summer dresses, ankle socks and their best shoes. Mrs Vinter gave them both a new ribbon for their hair and Sally said that they could pretend the whole Fete was being held solely for Maggie's birthday and that they were the guests of honour. Maggie liked that idea and looked forward to the day eagerly.

When the day of the Fete arrived, the whole scene looked like a jolly watercolour painting. Decorated stalls were set up on the front lawn selling all kinds of produce and yummy delights. There were prepared jams, chutneys, pickles and preserves. People could buy fresh produce from inventive displays ranging from vegetables to seasonal fruits, eggs and home made cheeses.

There was a refreshment marquee that was very popular too. The Women's Institute, or the WI as everyone called them, paraded up and down like protective mother hens wearing their best floral pinny's while serving appreciative customers cups of tea with either a slice of cake, fresh strawberries and cream or raspberries and cream. This was also a good place to take refuge from the sun and ladies could be seen fanning themselves to get a little welcome breeze.

The marquee was primarily used for the cricket season and still smelled a little musty inside despite being out to air for a week as per Mrs Sutton's instruction. She had strategically placed several seasonal bouquets around the area and no one dared comment on the smell within Mrs Sutton's earshot.

Pete and Billy were gently guiding two ponies that were giving the children short rides around the grounds. The ponies had ribbons plaited in their tails and through the reins. The twins charged a penny for a ride and all proceeds from the afternoon's Fete were to be shared as deemed by the village and church committees between the village fund for the war effort, and some for all kinds of good causes for the village.

When one set of rides had ended, Pete motioned to Billy to follow him with the ponies behind the tea marquee. When they were out of sight, Pete quickly retrieved a paper bag that he had hidden beside the tent earlier.

"What are you doing?" asked Billy.

Out of the bag, Pete produced a small straw bonnet with a silk sunflower on the side.

"That's Mum's," exclaimed Billy. "I remember, she bought it at the jumble sale a while back."

"Yes it is, but before that it belonged to..."

"No!"

"Oh yes, dear brother. Now, I am going to tie it on good 'ol George here. If this goes according to plan, there will be a bonus magic show because once this is seen there'll not only be ponies, but you-know-who'll have kittens!"

Both boys roared with laughter.

"If we're rumbled within a couple of minutes, I'll do the washing up for the next week," said Billy, as he recovered from laughing. "But if it goes beyond that, then you can do it. Deal?"

"Deal!"

The boys sauntered back toward the queue of children leading plod-along Frank followed by George who was still chomping on a carrot and sporting a brand new hat. They had hardly gotten beyond the marquee when Mrs Sutton descended quicker than gravity.

"What is this?" she exclaimed. "What on earth are you doing?" She pointed at George.

"Hello, Mrs Sutton," they said, trying their best to keep straight faces.

"Don't you 'hello Mrs Sutton' me. What have you got to say for yourselves?"

"Mrs Sutton, if you want a ride then you will have to queue up like everyone else," said Pete. Billy's jaw dropped, he could barely believe what his brother had just said.

"Yes, yes, very amusing. But surely," Mrs Sutton said haughtily, "everyone knows that you do NOT plait a ribbon through a pony's tail." And with that she turned around and walked away.

Ha! she thought. *That got you! It's a good hat but not mine any more.* She smiled to herself. She had a bit of a soft spot for those mischievous boys, although she'd never admit it.

Around four in the afternoon the Fete was coming to an end and the Squire gave out presentation cups for the afternoon's competition winners. He thanked everyone for contributing towards the worthy causes.

"And lastly," he said, "let's wish a belated happy birthday to Maggie Harris. *Happy Birthday to you …*"

Everyone joined in singing happy birthday and Maggie beamed with pride. This had been her best birthday ever.

Chapter Nineteen

A few weeks after the Fete, William noticed that Maggie had been behaving quite oddly.

"Are you all right pumpkin?" he asked.

"Well, Pete and Billy..."

"I might've known it would have something to do with them two, what have they done now?"

"They said that the ghost of an old wicked Headmaster roams the school corridors," Maggie blurted out, "and that he takes away the small children so they never see their parents again and that if you hear his footsteps he is coming for you." She looked up at William, fear all over her face.

"Is that what they said?" William sat Maggie on his lap. "Pumpkin, answer me this: if you are told something by your parents or Pete and Billy, who would you believe?"

"You of course, Pete and Billy play tricks on me sometimes."

"Well, Maggie, I do believe that you have just solved your own problem."

Maggie was thoughtful for a moment and then she beamed. "They are rascals aren't they?"

"That's one word for them."

During the next few weeks the air-aids became more erratic and the village committee held weekly meetings, keeping up to date with new procedures for evacuations, blackouts and emergency treatment posts.

Families sat by the wireless for current news on the war. Church services were filled with prayers dedicated to their fellow countrymen on the frontline, friends in London and for the safety of the King. The WI gathered once a week in the village hall, where they unpicked stacks of well-worn old jumpers, cardigans, socks and other woollen items and knitted balaclavas to be sent to the frontline for the forthcoming winter. These gatherings were also a time of socialising and exchanging news and village gossip.

Pete and Billy were walking home from meeting friends in the village one evening and as per usual they took the shortcut through Foxden Orchard.

"Shhhhh. Did you hear that?" whispered Pete, as he suddenly stood stock-still.

"Yeah, where did it come from?" Billy whispered back.

"Dunno, strange sound though. Can you place it?"

"Nah, new to me."

Guided by the moonlight, they crept quietly through the trees. As the breeze picked up, the apple branches and leaves swept ghostly shadows across the path ahead.

"Look, there's the hop-pickers hut," said Billy.

At that moment there was a loud bang and an awful sound that they had never heard before. They froze in their tracks standing shoulder to shoulder in utter fear for their lives.

"Animal or human?" mumbled Billy nervously.

"Dunno, let's get out of here quick."

Just as they turned by the hut they saw the path in front of them awash in a soft light and before their eyes a giant shadow appeared. As they looked up they saw a grotesque thing, masked from top to toe in black, that stood nearly as tall as the hut itself. It wasn't human and it yielded the biggest sickle the boys had ever seen. The sinister blade caught the moonlight and cast what appeared to be blood spraying off the end in an arc as it swayed to and fro. Then they heard a spine-chilling growl.

"Run!" shouted Billy.

They ran, stumbling and slipping over dew-covered apples that had dropped from the trees. When they finally arrived at the gap in the hedgerow they tried simultaneously to get through. The hedge wasn't used to coping with two escapees at the same time and its thorns tore at their outer arms as they pushed through together. Adrenalin had kicked in and they felt no pain for the time being, but it did not look pretty.

"Ma'll go mad when she sees all this," panted Billy as he bent down and picked some long grass and wiped his arm.

They ran down the lower field and eventually came to the wooded fence at the back of their long garden.

"What the bloody hell was that thing?" asked Pete.

"I dunno," said Billy, trying to catch his breath. "Thought the bugger was gonna get us though. Thought we were done for."

"Blimey, I need the lav." Pete ran for the small outhouse already adjusting his trousers.

Meanwhile, back at the orchard Eric helped William climb down from the hop-pickers stilts and both men laughed so much they ached.

"Did you see that?" exclaimed William as he gathered up the blackout curtains that they had used to dress 'the monster'. "I've never seen them run so fast."

"Cor blimey, my stomach hurts, haven't laughed like that in ages. Serves them right, they will think twice before playing tricks on young Maggie again."

"Come on Eric, let's get back quick as we can. I want to see those two when they get home."

"Righto, we'll talk about this for years to come no doubt."

"My my, you two look a little flustered, what happened?" asked Betty, as she looked up from ironing as the boys wandered into the kitchen.

"Nothing Mum," said Pete catching his breath. "Hello Mrs Harris, nice to see you."

"Hello boys, had a good evening?"

"Not bad," said Billy, "thought we'd have a race back and caught our arms in that hedge a way back."

"Nothing too serious," said Betty as she put down the iron and quickly examined their arms. "My, you do look very flushed and you're as jittery as I don't know what. What have you been up to this time?"

"Goodness, a full house," said Eric as he and William opened the kitchen door. "Hello boys, looks like you've seen a ghost. Or worse, doesn't it William?"

"Certainly does Eric, certainly does. Where do you want this sickle?" asked William as he gently and carefully swung round the sickle in front of the boys and winked at both of them before placing it in the corner.

"Cor, Dad," blurted Billy "you scared us into next week."

At that point the adults burst into laughter and the boys just stared at them in disbelief.

"Lesson learned lads, I believe," said William. "If you scare my Maggie again with tales of ghostly Headmasters or any scary story I'll have your guts for garters understand?" He stood between them and placed his hands on top of their heads.

"Understood Mr Harris, sorry Mrs Harris, sorry to you all," said Billy.

"Yeah me too," said Pete.

"The boys will be 'round in the morning William, to apologise to Maggie," said Betty. "And they will help with all the chores for the next two Saturdays."

The boys looked at one another in great disappointment but nodded their heads accepting their punishment.

Chapter Twenty

When the time came for Adam Marsh, the Squire's son, to graduate from boarding school in April 1944 he wrote to his father making it perfectly clear that he didn't want him to attend the ceremony and to ignore the official invitation sent by the school. The Squire pondered the dilemma over the following weeks and decided to ignore Adam's wishes and attend anyway. He was discreet and sat at the back of the packed hall among the proud parents and families. What surprised the Squire most of all, was the fact that his son had clearly worked hard over the years to accomplish his outstanding results. He felt a touch of pride for what his son had achieved.

However, through the ceremony, Adam had spotted his father, and while the Squire felt pride – Adam felt the day that was to be HIS special day, not his father's, had been irreversibly marred. Later that evening, Adam drank heavily and started an unprovoked fight. Adam had known John Dalby ever since they had started Priory Square together when they were ten years old. They were peers, but it wasn't a friendship. Adam hadn't bonded particularly well with anyone, preferring to keep to himself.

All the pent up frustration and anger that he had felt all his life exploded in this one instance of sheer madness. John had to be hospitalised with four broken ribs, a broken nose, fractured jaw and a concussion. The altercation cost Adam dearly as well.

He was arrested for grievous bodily harm and his submission to stay on as a History Master for the new intake, a submission that was precious to him, was immediately revoked. The Headmaster informed him that he had half a day to pack before he was escorted off the grounds in disgrace.

Adam stood outside the school boundary in his best suit with two brown leather suitcases at his feet. He felt totally bewildered and had no idea of where he could go next. He was just eighteen years old and now exiled from the only home he had really known. He had been at Priory Square for eight years and in that time he had achieved outstanding academic qualifications but now, all his hard work was blemished with a letter of deep disappointment from the Headmaster alongside a criminal record.

Adam felt a surge of self-pity. He had been shunned yet again, just like he had been by all those nannies. They had left him without a care or a goodbye and he had never been able to fathom out just what he did so wrong to be treated that way. He was now left out in the cold again, and this time, it was his father's fault.

Adam vowed to make his father pay.

The Squire received the first letter within days of Adam leaving Priory Square. It stated that he was responsible for Adam getting into trouble that had led to his dismissal therefore, he should pay Adam the total annual salary that he would have earned had he not been dismissed.

Adam thought he was pushing his luck with the huge demand but felt desperate enough to try it out. He thought he could always argue that the money would be used for him to live until he found himself another position.

He was extremely surprised when his father agreed to the

demand without any hesitation. The Squire did this to appease his own guilt. He knew Adam's troubled behaviour was a result of his poor upbringing. If his mother had been alive he would have been a very different young man. Adam received a year's salary without having to do a solitary day's work.

Chapter Twenty-One

The news of D-Day on June 6 1944, spread like wildfire through the village as reports that American and Allied troops had invaded Normandy. This was the largest invasion by land, sea and air in history. Celebrations were in place as everyone rejoiced with the prospect that the war may finally be coming to an end. The mood in the village lifted considerably and thoughts were spared for the hop-pickers in London as to what they were going through. There would certainly be ample news to share when the hop season was due to start in September. The villagers were glued to the wireless for daily updates and eager for the war to end and getting back to normal after all these years.

Twenty-seven days after D-Day, the village was changed forever with its own personal disaster.

Maggie's eighth birthday was fast approaching. Her parents had asked what she wanted to do for it and she had replied that a birthday tea with some of her friends after school would be grand. She had gone to bed thinking of party games and telling Sally about it in the morning.

Later that evening, Eric and Betty burst in through the kitchen door.

"Iris!" called Betty. They were breathless and the look of alarm on their faces made Iris drop the newspaper on the kitchen floor as she stood up from the old grandfather chair. She instinctively knew that something fatal had happened.

"Dear God," she whispered, "William?"

"A flying bomb's been shot down by anti-aircraft fire," said Eric, as calmly as he could. "It landed in Spindler's Lane. It's a God awful mess."

"William was down that way tonight," Iris said in alarm. "He said he'd be back before I knew it." She looked at Betty as if imploring her to confirm that William was safe.

"I know, he told me earlier as we passed in the lane," said Eric, his voice thick with emotion. "He'll be all right love, you'll see. We have our bikes out front, we're on our way there now."

"No," said Iris. "I'm coming with you. Betty can you stay with Maggie? She's asleep, we were planning her birthday tea, she's out like a light."

Betty gave her a brief hug.

"We'll bring him back won't we?" asked Iris. "He only popped down there quickly to take old Mrs Mews some fresh eggs, said he'd be back for a cuppa in no time. You know how he is? Oh Betty, I couldn't bear the thought..." Iris was genuinely trembling.

Betty squeezed her arm. "Why don't you let Eric go…"

"No," Iris said suddenly. "Cycling will take longer, we'll run the shortcut through the orchards, you up to it?"

"Righto," said Eric, pleased that Iris was thinking rationally. "You be alright love?" he looked to his wife and kissed her on the cheek. He could see the anguish on her face and knew she was worried.

Betty nodded, fearing words would bring tears.

Iris drew on all of her strength as she and Eric sprinted like young athletes through the hedgerows, over ditches and dodging trees using the moon as nature's torchlight. The only sounds were their deep breathing and the swishing of the long bladed grass underfoot.

Soon they detected distant sounds that were unfamiliar to them. This wasn't London, this was a country village for goodness sake. These eerie sounds had no right to be here. Throat choking smoke hung in the air that grew stronger the further they ran into it.

As they burst through the last orchard and ran out onto what used to be quaint Spindler's Lane, nothing could have prepared them for the devastation they found. Intense heat stung their faces and the hairs on their arms felt as if each one had been singed. Sickly smoke billowed around them burning their throats and stinging their eyes. It felt as if they were in some kind of a cruel nightmare, but the nightmare was real. An immense fire raged in a pit before them as if a monstrous dragon had awoken.

Iris doubled over to catch her breath and retch, her chest heaved as she fought for fresh air amongst the thick smoke and coughed uncontrollably like everyone else around her. She reached into her housecoat pocket for a handkerchief to cover her mouth and nose all the while her eyes darted around trying to pick out William from the crowd. Her eyes streamed in protest from the smoke and she had to constantly blink to make out the faces. Why couldn't she see him? Where was her husband? At one point, all she could see before her were swirling waves of thick black smoke and roaring flames that gleamed in the sweat that ran from peoples foreheads.

When she couldn't see William amongst the bustling crowd she looked in vain at the spot where the four cottages had proudly stood. She looked at old Mrs Mews' cottage and saw with dread that the roof had caved in and the windows blown out. "Dear God in heaven," she whispered, as she carefully and slowly made her way to the cottage, dodging people, fires and endless debris.

It seemed the whole village was rapidly turning out. People were milling about in chaos and confusion. The six members of the Home Guard tried to clear the crowds back from the deep crater that stood before them and away from the danger of fires and toppled cottages. The two village bobbies were completely surrounded by frantic people all shouting questions and asking for help, as if wearing a uniform meant they had all the answers.

Women were crying in fear and shock and small children clung to their mother's housecoats scared out of their wits. Eric could see the young Jessop's lad dressed in his small blue-stripped pyjamas, his shoulders were heaving up and down like he had an exaggerated bout of hiccups. Tears streamed down his angelic face but most of all it was the three-year-old's eyes that drew Eric to him. They were wide open in fear and the fire's reflection in those deep brown eyes would forever stay with Eric, haunting his nightmares for years to come.

It seemed unbelievable to imagine that only that very afternoon four chocolate box cottages had been standing in glorious sunshine. There were flowers around the doors and windows, children playing in the gardens and the cottages were full of life. Wafts of inviting country baking had escaped open kitchen doors and windows and sent mouth-watering aromas out on the mid-afternoon.

Now, it was as if an angry giant had stepped down from the clouds and crushed the cottages in a single stomp. Chimneystacks had tumbled, looking totally out of place amongst a bed of yellow roses, now painted with coats of dirty ash and soot.

People were drawn to the crater's edge as if hypnotised by a side-show peddler promising to show glimpses into some forbidden treasure. But there was no sideshow, no illusion, just the destruction of a peaceful village lane.

As she approached where old Mrs Mews' cottage had been,

Iris spotted William. He was consoling a woman with a child that was typical of his kind nature. Iris's heart leapt from her chest, she praised God and ran as best as she could with her arms outstretched towards him. She tried calling him but her throat burned as if she had gargled a piece of coal coated in razor blades. As she neared she realised it wasn't William at all, but Mr Jenkins. They had the same coat and at the realisation she felt the strength sap from her legs. Hope totally diminished as she once again peered at Mrs Mews' destroyed cottage.

Eric stood still and scanned the crowd. A piercing scream jolted everyone into action. A hysterical woman had spotted a bloodied arm protruding from under some bricks and began clawing at the rubble with all her might. Two men quickly rushed in and took over, forcing the woman back. The men unearthed a young woman from the village.

Everyone stood completely still as the tearful anguish of a young man broke their hearts as he knelt, cradling the lifeless body of his wife. They all knew this woman, had watched her grow up, had seen her in church every Sunday, had seen her at village fetes, worked with her in the orchards and just last year, seen her married at the village church.

The Squire arrived with a screech of tyres. He jumped from his car leaving the engine running and the door open. He knew all of these people and felt their pain and anguish, but at this moment, organisation was needed. Tears, condolences, compassion and rage, would come later. Lives came first and they had to act quickly.

Every village had a drill for bombings and at this time nothing was happening as it should. It was hardly surprising, but he needed to take control and restore some order. He climbed onto a brick garden wall about two feet high and still in relatively sturdy condition. Once stabilised he took a gleaming brass whistle from his tweed jacket pocket and then let a continual steady loud breath out. The urgent high-pitched sound pierced the scene getting the attention that was needed.

"Attention please," he bellowed, "Attention everyone please."

People turned around to see the Squire on the wall.

With a few coughs in between he spoke. "Everyone, gather around. First things first, we need to make this area as safe as we can before we assess the damage and start rescue. All the women from the WI, you know your groups from the village action plan. Please proceed as practiced by escorting all the women and children to the village hall out of immediate danger.

"Please also prepare suitable areas for a makeshift hospital if it is required and make provisions for hot beverages and food for the helpers. The town hospital is aware of what has happened and doctors and nurses are at this time on their way here, as are the town and neighbouring fire brigades and police. Mr and Mrs Dwyer from the village store are opening up for provisions and making arrangements for delivery to the village hall as I speak. Mr and Mrs Sutton are also bringing down provisions and medical supplies from the Manor helped by Mr Dawson and they should be here shortly.

"All members of the Home Guard and Constabulary come forward. The remaining men please split yourselves into equal lines behind them. You are divisions one to eight, remember your division as it will be extremely helpful to organise this properly." The men quickly filed equally behind the eight men, mostly grateful that someone was taking control. There were the odd few still milling around in a daze with a look of bewilderment, dread and emptiness. The Squire appreciated that these people were probably looking for missing loved ones.

In startling alarm, he saw Iris, and the deep torment etched on her face. *Was William missing?* The Squire quickly put that thought to the back of his mind to concentrate on organising the divisions.

"Listen please, a reminder of your divisions and duties." The Squire brandished a clipboard in the air. "Harry you are division one, Albert division two, Henry division three, Charles division four, Matthew division five, Stephen division six, James division seven and Simon division eight. As we haven't a pump in the village, division one quickly get to Foxden Orchard. You'll find stacks of buckets that are kept in the hop-pickers barn, it's bolted so one of you kick down the door and bring the buckets back here. In the meantime, division two and three make easy access to Bill's Pond by getting rid of a portion of the hedgerow while you are waiting for division one to return. Then division one join division two and three to form a chain to put out the fires until the brigade arrives.

"Division four and five, access the danger points in the immediate vicinity and secure as much of the area as you are able to. Then slowly move outwards to the five cottages on either side of the road in the immediate area. Be vigilant of weakened chimneystacks, roofs, supporting walls and declare if you think they are safe to return to or not, though I have my doubts. I'll have a team of builders up here in the morning for a thorough check. Division six to eight, locate and perform rescues where you can safely. I will send over the doctors and nurses when they arrive. Everyone remember your division leaders and report back to me as a central point of information. Now go."

The Squire jumped down and located Iris at old Mrs Mews'

cottage and saw that Eric too was approaching. "Mrs Harris?" he said, as softly as he could but loud enough to be heard above the commotion as he placed a hand on her shoulder.

"He's missing sir," she said in barely a whisper. "My William is missing, he was here with Mrs Mews this evening, no one has seen them." Iris broke away to continue her search with Eric following behind.

The Squire bowed his head, thinking at that brief moment, of his dear departed wife. *But at this stage,* he reminded himself, *Iris still has hope, she has to hope and pray with all her might that William is safe and that all the missing villagers are soon to be found safe and well.*

Over the next few hours, the emergency services and personnel, together with the eight divisions the Squire had assembled, began to take control of the chaos. Casualties with minor wounds were well cared for at the village hall. The more seriously injured were driven back to the town hospital. Eight fatalities had been recovered with three more people unaccounted for, William being one of them.

Back at Primrose Cottage, Maggie was blissfully sound asleep and in the kitchen below, Betty was beside herself with worry. She kept busy by washing up a few pots and pans and even washed the kitchen floor. She finally put the kettle on the range cooker and sat, silently praying for William's safe return. Mostly, she prayed for Maggie, at nearly eight years old she was much too young to lose her father.

"Goodness me, stop it," she said aloud. "William is alive and well and any minute they will burst through the door and we'll all have a cuppa and talk late into the night." The oak grandad chair creaked slightly as she leaned over the side to pick up Iris's floral knitting bag and placed it onto her lap and reached inside to see what her friend had been making. From the pattern Betty could see that Iris had been knitting a light pink cardigan for Maggie. She admired the front panel, which had interwoven cable stitch with the three needles still attached. There were also three little white crochet daisies that Iris would sew onto the front and it all looked beautiful. Perhaps it was a birthday present? Betty had always admired Iris's knitting skills.

Iris who was assisting clearing debris when she felt a gentle but firm touch on her shoulder. She knew that the news she had been dreading had come. She turned to face not Eric, but the Squire, and saw that his pale blue eyes were watered.

"God in heaven no," she said, shaking her head in disbelief. "Not my William, no."

"I am so sorry," he said compassionately.

"I must go to him, where is he?"

"Think it best not, Iris," said Eric as he stood beside her. "The doctor said we'd better tell you, better coming from friends, you know. He said it was quick, William wouldn't have felt a thing. I am so sorry."

Iris looked up at Eric's face and could see the hurt and pain as tears flowed down his cheeks. He clung to her in a heart-felt embrace.

"He was only fifty-four Eric. Fifty-four. We had years left, how can this be true? "You've seen him haven't you?" she gently pushed him away and searched his face for some kind of acknowledgement. "You're sure it's him? You've seen it's William?" she urged.

"That I have." Eric suddenly found an inner strength, he had to pull himself together for her sake. He clutched Iris's upper arms and looked her in the eyes. "Please Iris, I plead of you, it is better you not see him. Remember William as he was. He would want that I am sure."

"How? Tell me how it happened?"

"He was found with Mrs Mews, they were buried beneath the rubble. They've taken them to the village hall. We need to be strong. You need to be strong Iris, for your sake and for your Maggie."

"MAGGIE," blurted Iris. "Oh my God, Maggie. How can I do this? How can I tell her?" Iris broke into heart-breaking sobs as Eric embraced her while the Squire slowly backed away knowing that Iris was in safe hands.

In the days that followed, the whole village pulled together united in their grief, bewilderment and the sheer determination to not let the enemy win. People looked out for one another, families opened up their homes to their neighbours, giving them accommodation, food, comfort and support where they could.

Maggie was inconsolable. Even Sally was temporarily shunned away. Maggie stayed by herself in her room where she cuddled her father's favourite jumper that still had his scent along with a touch of sawdust. Betty had taken Maggie some food and drink up to her room as her mother didn't seem to want Maggie near her.

Maggie was lying on top of her bed crying into her pillow when she heard her grandma's familiar voice downstairs. She sat up and dabbed her eyes wanting to go to her when she suddenly heard raised voices.

"We don't want you here, GO AWAY," shouted Iris at her mother-in-law.

"I've come to see my granddaughter," said Dora Harris as she entered the kitchen carrying a wicker basket filled with a freshly homemade pie and placed the basket on the kitchen table.

"She's asleep and doesn't want to see you. We thank you for the pie, now please go."

"I have a right to see my granddaughter," Dora said as she locked eyes with Iris. She could see that the woman looked genuinely bereaved and so in a more softened tone, she added, "Iris, how are you bearing up?"

"As if you care how I am bearing up. Things haven't changed between us, you are still unwelcome here."

"He was my son, I am grieving too," Dora pleaded.

"HE WAS MY HUSBAND," Iris retorted.

"WHEN IT SUITED!" Dora had had enough.

"Here we go again, this old chestnut." Iris flung her arms in the air then pointed at the woman angrily, "get out and don't come back you old witch."

Maggie was still crying and through her tears she heard every angry word as she clutched her father's jumper. She sat on the edge of her bed wishing they would stop arguing.

Dora regretted her last statement. She had come for Maggie and Iris always fired her up. The bad blood between the two women had to be put aside for Maggie's sake.

"Look, Iris. Let's start again. We'll all get through this together, be united for William's sake. I'll put the kettle on..."

"Nothing has changed. We don't want you here. And," Iris spoke with relish, "hear this so there is no mistake. You are not welcome at the funeral."

It took a few moments for that to sink in for both Dora and Maggie listening in.

"You are banning a mother from her own son's funeral?" Dora shook her head in disbelief. "You cannot do that."

"Yes I can. Stay away or you will never see your precious

granddaughter ever again. Do you hear me?"

Maggie couldn't listen to another word. She ran down the stairs and into her grandma's arms.

"Grandma!" exclaimed Maggie.

"Maggie, dear child." The two embraced.

This was all Maggie wanted. To be warm and safe in someone's arms. Her mother had kept pushing her away over the past few days and not wanted to have anything to do with her.

"Very touching," said Iris as she prised Maggie away. "Go back to your room." She gave Maggie a push towards the parlour. "Grandma cannot stay, it's just us Maggie."

"You can't do that," protested Dora. "William wouldn't want it this way. Why are you doing this? Can't you see that the child is upset? She has just lost her father."

"OUT, NOW!" Iris then pushed the woman out of the house and slammed the door in her face.

Chapter Twenty-Two

One week later, the funerals of eleven village members were held in the packed village Church. The whole village turned out for the solemn occasion to mark their mutual respect for loved ones, friends and neighbours.

The Squire had arranged for a brass plaque to be erected in the Church vestibule as a sign of respect and dedication to the brave souls who had so tragically lost their lives on that day, July 3 1944. In an immense show of reverence, people travelled from the local town and surrounding villages and also a few of the regular hop-pickers travelled down from London to pay their respects. The Squire opened up a few of the hop-pickers huts for their short stay, indebted for their thoughtfulness. Some of the men even stayed a little longer to help with the clean-up of Spindler's Lane.

In what had been the saddest week of Maggie's life she somehow found the strength and courage to attend the service. She sat quietly beside her mother in the second pew alongside other mourners listening to the Vicar's speech and the condolences of friends.

She tried to hold her mother's hand as she looked back and forth between the horrible box that held her precious father and the statue of Jesus on the cross. She did not understand why her parents, school and Sunday school had all said that Jesus looked after people. He hadn't looked after her father.

At that moment she felt extremely guilty and bowed her head

in shame. Her rich brown curls hid her face, as she didn't want people to see her. She hadn't any more tears left. She thought that if people saw that she wasn't crying they would think she didn't love or miss her father and how so very wrong they all would be.

Maggie idolised her father. She yearned to see him again and to be lifted upon his big strong shoulders. She wanted to hear his wonderful stories and to be whisked around the garden in the bumpy wheelbarrow as she held on the sides for dear life while laughing non-stop as he took the corners at precarious angles.

And not so very long ago, they had both sat here in this very spot, holding hands during the Sunday service. He had tickled Maggie's palm and she had wriggled to break free and even laughed in the middle of the sermon, only to get a stern look from her mother.

Her father's hands. They were big hands. Hands that were rough to touch, hands that bore cuts and the odd black fingernail when he misjudged the nailhead to hammer his finger instead. How Maggie had squirmed when he peeled back a gunky damaged nail to reveal a new one growing underneath.

Upon hearing a brief but distinct cough in the crowd, Maggie lifted her head and was uplifted when her eyes met her grandma's. A clever ploy by her grandma to let her know she was there. They gave each other a brief smile. Iris grabbed Maggie's hand and tightened the grip as she cursed under her breath at her mother-in-law's defiance.

Iris was grateful for everyone's kindness in the weeks and months that followed. Betty brought regular meals, as did Mrs Sutton and the ladies of the WI. The Squire said that Iris could take her time in returning to work, as it was important that she spend quality time with Maggie.

Slowly, Iris and Maggie coped by taking each day as it came. Maggie's eighth birthday came and went without even an acknowledgment from anyone, including herself. A subtle transition was happening, so subtle that Maggie was not even aware that the roles were reversing as she slowly started to take care of her mother. Maggie possessed the same will and determination as her father. She was more than capable of running a household, both her parents had told her that and she was now needed to do so.

Betty popped around each morning to check if everything was all right and she began to observe the transition herself. Iris was withdrawing and although Betty tried hard to reach out to her friend, Iris seemed trapped in a world of her own. She had some good days but mostly they were not. Iris would go to work but then would leave early and Betty would cover for her. Maggie seemed focused on keeping busy and did most of the household chores without question after school.

Mrs Sutton regularly gave Iris some homemade stew to take home. Iris said there was no need but Mrs Sutton insisted, saying that she had baked too much. Iris took it in good grace, knowing Mrs Sutton was just trying to help as best she could, she had never 'baked too much' in the past.

Eric started to work from William's workshop at the Manor and at Primrose Cottage as per the Squire's request, temporarily taking on the manager role. When things needed to be repaired at the cottage workshop he would do this in the evenings with help from other estate staff. Betty would go with him and keep Iris company after dinner when Maggie was asleep.

Maggie coped pretty well at school. Her friends rallied round and Pete and Billy looked out for her and would walk her home when Iris was working. Sally and her parents also looked out for

Maggie and had her stay regularly to give Iris and Maggie a much-earned break from each other. Simon Dwyer, the Postmaster's son, also took it upon himself to look out for Maggie. He had liked her since they were small and he would often come through to the shop whenever he knew Maggie and her mother were in the post office.

"Maggie, how are you?" smiled Mr Dwyer, genuinely pleased to see her again since her father's funeral.

"Hello Mr Dwyer, hello Simon," Maggie said, as Simon appeared in the doorway. "I am well, thank you. Just two things today, I need to buy some flour and I also wanted to tell you that I borrowed a book from the school library about Australia."

"That's good Maggie," said Mr Dwyer, "perhaps next time you come in you can show me, I would like to see it."

"Yes, I will," she beamed.

"I'm pleased you've popped in, I have something for you," he said beckoning for her to approach the counter. It didn't seem that long ago that she could barely see over the high counter, now she was a good head taller and the counter didn't seem that big anymore. He smiled warmly as he opened a drawer beside him and placed an envelope on the counter. With his long index finger he pushed it slowly towards her.

Maggie's eyes widened in excitement as her own name appeared on the envelope:

Miss M Harris
c/o Marden Village Post Office
Kent
England

A letter addressed to her! She had never received a letter before. Then she noticed the Australian stamp.

"What is this Mr Dwyer?" she asked in confusion.

"A letter for you Maggie that has come all the way from Australia. It has travelled thousands of miles to get here. My cousin, Mr McKinnley, who I have told you about when I gave you the stamp, has written to you. He said he would in his last letter because I mentioned that I talk to you about him and his family. So he thought he would tell you more about his sheep station out there."

"Thank you so much Mr Dwyer, this is just the best thing ever, ever, ever," said Maggie in excitement as she turned the envelope over and over in her hand in sheer wonder. Mr Dwyer couldn't have been more pleased. The timing was perfect. It was good to see Maggie smile again after so much sorrow. The letter itself had arrived a few days ago and Mr Dwyer had sought out Iris to give her the letter. If truth be told, Mr Dwyer didn't think that Iris was all that interested but that was understandable considering. She did say that it would probably mean more if he gave Maggie the letter himself, as he had been the bearer of Maggie's excitement with the first stamp.

Maggie rushed home to tell her mother the good news. Her mother was lying down so she took her a cup of tea and was buzzing to tell her the news.

"You're looking pleased with yourself today," said Iris, guessing why her daughter was looking as she was. She hadn't looked happy for so long, it was almost warming to see.

"Look," exclaimed Maggie as she waved the envelope in front of her mother's face.

"Don't tell me your teacher is saying 'well done for getting to school on time'?" Iris teased.

"Oh Mum, very funny."

"You came first in hopscotch?"

"No."

"The King of England says 'Hello Maggie, how are you'?"

"No."

"I give up, what is it?"

"I have a letter that has come all the way from Australia. It's addressed to me. Can you believe that? It is from Mr Dwyer's cousin and he tells me of his sheep station in the outback of Australia. Also his son, Jack and daughter Sylvia say hello as well."

"Well, that's mighty kind Maggie, perhaps you'll read it to me after dinner."

"Yes I will and I am still going to Australia one day Mum, you'll see," said Maggie as she turned to leave. Just before she reached the bedroom doorway she stopped and turned back to her mother. "We will go together," she said. Then she was gone.

Iris had no intention of going anywhere. This was where she belonged and as hard as it would be for Maggie to leave her behind she would not stand in her way. In fact, it would be the opposite, as she intended to encourage Maggie to leave.

Even though she relied on her every day, Iris thought that if Maggie left, she would at last be on her own. She had genuinely mourned her husband but she was adjusting quite well now and couldn't help but think, one down, one to go.

Chapter Twenty-Three

The loss of William Harris affected the Squire badly. He considered William to be a personal friend and confidant, as well as the estate's manager. He was grateful that Eric Collins had temporarily agreed to step into his shoes to keep things ticking over and the rest of the estate's employees had banded together in support.

As hard as it was, the Squire was concerned regarding the business side of things. At some point, Iris and Maggie Harris would need to vacate Primrose Cottage for the arrival of a new manager and family to move in. He knew things were tough and was also aware, courtesy of Mrs Sutton, that Mrs Harris was not coping at all well.

"Good morning Squire," said Eric as the Squire approached the workshop at the Manor.

"Eric, good morning. How are things?" He gestured around the workshop.

"Pretty good, things are ticking over nicely."

"Splendid, splendid. Look, the reason I am here is to ask if you would..."

"Ah, I was wondering when that was coming," replied Eric as he put down the spanner on the workbench and walked over to the Squire. "With all due respect Sir, to yourself and to William, I couldn't take over as Manager of Primrose Farm Estate. It wouldn't feel right stepping into his shoes like that."

"I do understand Eric, but I firmly believe you would be excellent in the role…"

"Sorry Squire, but the answer will always be no," he said with the utmost sincerity.

"Understand 'ol man, had to ask, you know that."

"Yes, I do. It's a big compliment so thank you. But, I will gladly continue to fill in in the meantime."

"More than acceptable. Do you know that in a way it warms my heart because I know that none of the farm hands will wish the position either. It just shows the respect William had from his fellow workers. I will advertise the position shortly."

They shook hands.

"Thank you Squire, we miss the 'ol fellow. You know, I half expect him to come wandering in at any time…"

"Yes, me too. Good day," sighed the Squire as he walked back across the courtyard.

Like the other bereaved families, Iris and Maggie had had their share of ups and downs in the months that followed the tragedy. Maggie's release was going to school where everything appeared as normal, but sometimes she dreaded going home. Her mother had become moody and withdrawn and Maggie yearned for things to get back to how they were, knowing that was impossible. Betty would pop around frequently to try and cheer her mother up but was unsuccessful most of the time. It seemed that the only time Iris had any enthusiasm was when she encouraged Maggie to spend the weekend at Sally's place. She even suggested Maggie go and visit her grandma more, although Iris would not have her in the cottage.

Early one morning, the sound of sawing stirred Maggie from her sleep with the familiar tone and rhythm as the blades sliced through timber. She had grown up with the comforting sound and in her mind she could even smell the rich fresh aroma of freshly sawn timber. For a second, Maggie assumed it was her father out in the workshop and she smiled, until fully awake, she realised no, it couldn't be him. It was just Mr Collins starting work early. That had been a cruel start to the day.

Finally, on May 8 1945, the war ended in Europe and the whole country celebrated the great news. Maggie and Betty were thrilled because this seemed to lift Iris out of a dark place since the ten months after William's passing and for a while it seemed as if this could be the start of better times.

The village rejoiced with a succession of street parties and the Squire opened up the Manor. Mrs Sutton put on a good spread as always. Both pubs were open for longer hours and had outdoor stalls serving home-made blackcurrant squash for the children. The WI decorated the church and village hall and people celebrated like it was New Year's Eve. Eric and his trusted accordion merged with the barbershop singers where they paraded up and down the village green receiving requests along the way. The vicar announced that there would be a special evening service to give thanks and prayers in remembrance for all the fallen souls.

Three months later, the Squire visited Primrose Cottage. Iris knew he would be popping around for a visit as Mrs Sutton had cycled by earlier that afternoon enquiring if she and Maggie would be home.

"Good afternoon ladies," said the Squire, tilting his cap as he walked into the kitchen.

"Good afternoon Squire," they said together.

He carried a wicker basket packed by Mrs Sutton and placed it onto the table. He then carefully unravelled a chequered tea towel revealing freshly baked scones that were still warm from the oven, some blackcurrant preserve and a small jar of clotted cream. Iris fussed around the kitchen putting on the kettle and Maggie set the table wondering why the Squire was bringing them such delicious scones.

"I'll come straight to the point, Mrs Harris," he said gently, suddenly aware that he towered over them he sat down to make himself more equal in stature. "I appreciate how difficult things have been this past year or so..."

"Thank you Squire, but it's time for us to move on isn't it?" said Iris.

"Well, er, yes. I am sorry to say this Mrs Harris, but the estate has to move forward and I need to appoint a manager to oversee the running of the business."

"We understand, don't we Maggie?"

Maggie nodded sombrely. She was just nine years old and would be leaving the only home she had ever known.

"And we are grateful that you have let us stay on here all this time. When do we need to move?"

"Mrs Harris. Iris. As you know I respected William very much. He was a good man and an excellent manager, as was his father before him and I also considered William a dear friend. With all good intentions and not meaning to offend, I have taken the liberty of making some enquiries and plans of my own. As well as the estate, I own a small cottage on the outskirts of the village. It is currently vacant and is in good repair. I will not see you out on the streets, but would consider it a favour to me if you and

Maggie were to move in."

"That is very kind of you to think of us Squire. But, forgive me, Primrose Cottage is tied in. I am indebted to you that you had lowered the rent on the cottage after the loss of William's earnings. But, without seeming ungrateful, I would not be able to afford full rent on the new cottage."

"I appreciate your concerns," he said, "I apologise. I should have said that I will draw up a contract stating that the cottage would also be tied-in on your earnings. You will continue to work for Primrose Estate as before, and all financial arrangements will be the same as they currently are. The only change will be moving to the new cottage. If you agree, I will allow four weeks for you to arrange the move and to paint the cottage as you see fit. You may ask Mr and Mrs Collins to assist if you wish, on company time. If you think this all sounds amicable I will give you a few days to think about it."

"Yes, it sounds very amicable. Thank you Squire. It is a very generous offer and we gladly accept."

"Splendid. I will have the papers drawn up by the end of the week. Now, young Maggie, where is this tea?"

Sally stood by the school gate. "Good morning Maggie," she called. "Not long till you move to the cottage, how are things going?"

"Hi Sally, Mr and Mrs Collins have been helping with moving things and nearly everything has gone now but it is quite sad leaving it all behind." Maggie looked down and added softly, "It feels like we are abandoning my dad."

"Your dad is wherever you are," said Sally reaching out for her friend's hand. "I heard someone say that once someone dies they carry on in your heart, so it doesn't matter where you live, does it?"

"I like that Sally, thanks." Maggie hugged her friend. "I feel better about it now. Hopefully, it will be a new start for us. At least we are in the same village and everyone has been very nice about it all. It'll take longer to get to school but I will get used to it. Pete and Billy have kindly said they will walk me home after school, although I think Mrs Collins had something to do with it. I just wish grandma was allowed to come over or I could visit her more. Mum hates her, it's so horrible Sally because I feel that I am caught in the middle."

"You poor thing. That's horrid. My mum said you are welcome to come over to stay anytime Maggie, you know that. Perhaps we could invite your grandma for tea, then you could see her?"

"Thanks Sally that's a lovely idea. Your mum is great whereas mine seems grumpy all the time."

"She'll come around. Come on or we'll be late and Mr Turk will have a fit. Oh, I almost forgot, Simon Dwyer keeps asking about you."

"Why?

"Asking if you need any help with the move."

"I have been trying to avoid him lately. He seems to be everywhere I go so I have been trying to dodge him."

"You are funny."

Chapter Twenty-Four

Two years flew by and Maggie and Iris had settled in to the small cottage despite it being so much smaller than what they had been used to. Being on the outskirts, they had more of a walk to the village shops, school and orchards, which wasn't so bad when they took their bicycles.

One afternoon as Maggie came out of school she spotted her grandma across the road. Before she excitedly ran over she quickly caught up with Pete and Billy who were now eighteen and working in the orchards. They still stopped by at least once a week at the school gate to accompany Maggie back home and catch up with all the news.

"You know we're fine with you seeing your grandma, Maggie," said Pete.

"But your ma will go mad if she knows," said Billy.

"Yes, I know, I won't tell if you won't. Come on boys, you know how much I love my grandma, this is the first time I've seen her in ages. Please… just this once, and I will see you next week I promise."

"Okay, Maggie, mum's the word," said Billy.

"Literally," said Pete as they walked away laughing and waved over to grandma.

"Grandma!" Maggie said as they embraced. "So lovely to see you, it seems ages since I last saw you. How are you"?

"Very well Maggie and even the better for seeing you. Goodness you are growing up fast, cannot believe you are eleven already. How are you honeybee?"

"I am okay but I've been worried. I haven't seen you for so long."

"I was a bit under the weather but I am fine now. I fancied a bicycle ride to get some fresh air and thought I would surprise you after school."

"A lovely surprise. Do you know that the strangest thing happened the other week? Even after all this time Pete, Billy and I were talking so much as they walked me home that it was as if I still lived down Honeysuckle Lane. I started to walk down Primrose Cottage path. When I realised, I sprinted back down the path and bumped straight into Mrs Collins. She had seen me from her lounge window and clipped Pete and Billy behind the ear and told them to walk me back home. We all laughed about that."

"The boys mean well. How is your mother?"

"She seems okay. She doesn't talk much these days. It's as if I am not there half the time. And lately, she hasn't even been home when I come in from school."

Dora raised her eyebrows questionably as Maggie continued, "She says she's been out to do some shopping but she doesn't bring anything home with her and when she is at home she sleeps a lot."

They continued strolling along out of the village.

"Do you sit together and talk at mealtimes?"

"We don't talk much at any time and we rarely eat together."

"But when do you eat?"

"I make sandwiches for lunch in the morning before I go to school and if there is no bread, I pick some apples on my way home or Pete and Billy give me some of their food and at the weekends I go over to Sally's. I wish I could stay with you sometimes grandma, but mother won't allow it. Why can't things go back to how they were? I don't understand. I still miss Dad so much." Maggie's eyes filled with tears.

"Oh child. This won't do at all." Dora shook her head. *This is appalling,* she thought. "I'm coming home with you now, I need to talk to your mother."

"I don't think that is a good idea, grandma." Maggie stopped and turned to face her. "She may be sleeping. Perhaps another day."

"Maggie." Now Dora was perplexed. "What is going on?"

Maggie's shoulders slumped and her whole face seemed to crumble. "Oh grandma, it's very scary," she began, as she fought back tears, "for a while she has been disappearing for a few days at a time and doesn't tell me where she is. Mostly, there is no food in the house and last week I actually stole someone's lunch from school. I still feel very bad about that. I pray for weekends to come around faster so I can go to Sally's. Her parents and sister are all very kind to me and the chicken stew Sally's mum cooks is too delicious for words. I make that much fuss that she gives me plenty to take home and I make it last for a couple of days. I feel so ashamed that I can't tell anyone. Not even Sally. The only things in the cupboards are a few bottles of alcohol, but I don't touch those. Dad would never have been like this. He would be horrified I am sure."

When Maggie looked up she saw that her grandma had tears running down her cheeks. "Oh, I'm sorry grandma, I didn't mean to make you cry. Please don't tell anyone."

"Maggie, child." Dora hugged her tightly. She was enraged that she had not known what was going on with her granddaughter. William would never forgive her for not intervening. It was all because of Iris. The way Dora felt right now, she could easily knock Iris off her lazy arse and into next week. And even though she had never sworn in her entire life 'arse' was the right word. *Arse. Arse. ARSE! There, be damned to high heaven,* she thought.

Maggie leaned the bicycle against the fence and they walked in silence up the garden path. The front door was unlatched so they went straight in. The room smelt stale and musty from a combination of alcohol and cigarette smoke.

The living room was completely cluttered with rubbish and it was obvious that Iris was in a drunken stupor. Dora resisted the urge to throw a bucket of water over her and shake some sense and responsibility into her. The way she felt, a bucket of water would be too kind. Perhaps a bucket of bricks…

"Right Maggie," she said calmly "go and pack some things to tide you over, you are coming to stay with me."

While Maggie went up to her room, Dora picked up the few bottles of gin that she could see and tipped what was left down the sink. She did a quick sweep of the kitchen and tipped away the contents of a couple more bottles and cursed the day her son had met this woman. She knew that William had not had an easy time in the marriage although he had worked his socks off to give his family a good home. Iris was nothing but a parasite that had latched onto her son.

William and Iris had married within a few months of meeting, much to Dora and Lionel's concern that it was too soon. All they could do was support their son and trust that he knew what he was doing. It was a bit of a squeeze, with both couples living in Primrose Cottage with Iris and Dora having to adjust to a whole new routine.

Lionel was the estate manager and William worked under him

for many years so nothing really changed for them. With another woman in the house, Dora was the one who was most affected. She had originally thought that it would be easier with two women sharing the chores but within just one week, Dora discovered that Iris was lazy and manipulative. The men would leave the cottage at six and Iris would still be in bed until around ten o'clock. She would get up, spend ages getting ready and saunter around the place arranging the cushions or just sitting reading magazines.

Even though Dora worked full time in the orchards there were a number of occasions when she had to pop back home during the day. Usually she dropped in for a cup of tea on her way to another orchard only to find Iris still asleep.

Dora knew of Iris' unstable upbringing and initially felt sorry for her but no matter how much she tried to get close, Iris had pushed her away.

"I have a weak, useless excuse for a mother already. I don't need another one," she had said.

One evening as they were all having dinner Dora asked Iris if she wouldn't mind baking an apple pie for their dinner the following day. Iris had reluctantly agreed as there was an audience and she couldn't get out of it without causing a scene. *That will get her doing something,* thought Dora.

The next evening Iris produced a lovely apple pie and the men agreed it looked and tasted delicious. Dora was enraged as Iris had plenty of time on her hands to bake an apple pie; all the ingredients were literally on her doorstep with apple trees in the garden. But, instead of baking a pie, she had bought one from the village shop. Dora was furious. Wasting money when she could have baked!

"Lovely pie, Iris," said Dora. "How much does Mr Dwyer charge for pies nowadays?" Iris shot up and slammed her palms on the table before storming off. Dora felt guilty that she had caused William trouble.

Dora had tried to make amends, but it was not reciprocated. From that day onwards the atmosphere between the women was tense. Iris began plotting to get her revenge. A couple of days later she made sure that she was alone in the house with her mother-in-law.

"Cup of tea, Dora?"

"Thanks Iris, that sounds just the ticket," said Dora, surprised at Iris's offer. "Seems like I am forever darning socks, I say to Lionel that the vegetable patch is full of spuds without them appearing in his socks as well." She laughed at her own joke as Iris looked at her blankly.

"It's time you and Lionel retired and moved out," Iris said as she poured the tea.

"Pardon?" Dora wasn't quite sure she had heard correctly.

"You heard. Move back into your old family home on the hill. Wouldn't take much to do it up. I went up there recently to have a look around."

"Oh did you now!" Dora took off her glasses and stared at Iris. "And why would you do that?"

"I didn't take too kindly to you showing me up like that in front of everyone over that apple pie."

"All this because of an apple pie? That's absurd."

"Like I said. Retire. Give the newlyweds a chance to be on our own for once. Impossible with you both always here, it's enough to dampen any marriage. Plus your son will be the new manager of the estate. It's about time Lionel retired, give him a well earned rest before he dies. Persuade your husband to move out or I will make trouble between you and your son. And you don't want that do you?

"Jam tart to accompany your tea?" Iris politely offered a plate of pastries, "they are bought as I couldn't be bothered to bake."

"You disgust me," said Dora calmly. "I have tried with you and every time you push me away. Why are you so difficult? And whatever did my son see in you?"

"You really want to know?" Iris smirked and sat back slowly to enhance her ample bosom.

"Like I said, you disgust me you two-bit trollop." Dora left the table and heard Iris burst into laughter.

Shortly afterwards, Lionel passed away after a brief illness. At the wake held in Primrose Cottage parlour, Iris said to Dora, "You probably won't believe me but I am genuinely sorry about Lionel…"

"You are not capable of being genuine about anything," Dora retaliated.

Iris leaned in slightly so only Dora could hear her. "You will make your excuses to William and you will move out within a fortnight or life will get very difficult. If you tell him about this I will deny everything. Make no mistake, he will believe everything I tell him." And with that, Iris walked away from her mother-in-law leaving her debating whether she should take the risk to speak to her son or not.

When Dora moved out, William tried to convince her to stay, saying that it was too soon for her to move away. She was welcome to live at Primrose Cottage to the end of her days, he had said, but the look of horror and menace on Iris's face had said otherwise. Dora realised she had lost her husband and also her son. She was tired and just wanted peace and quiet, so she moved out hoping this would appease Iris. However, even after this, Iris remained cold towards her mother-in-law and made snide remarks whenever William was out of ear shot.

And now, as Dora waited for Maggie to pack her things she looked at her pathetic, comatose daughter-in-law sprawled on the sofa. She bent and whispered, "What goes around, comes around." When Maggie came downstairs with her bag she took her hand and they walked out the door and headed for home.

Chapter Twenty-Five

Over the seven years that Maggie lived with her grandma, they had many picnics in the garden and fancy teas inside in the drawing room. Endless music played through the house courtesy of the wireless, Dora's records or Maggie and Sally playing the piano. Sally often came to stay for weekends.

Dora loved having Sally over. When the weather was fine, Dora set up a picnic tea for the girls on the table outside and loved to hear their chatter and laughter.

"Hello Sally," she said, "you two go through and I'll bring out the goodies, I insist before you protest, off you go and catch up on all the vast amounts of important news since you last saw each other – yesterday wasn't it?" Laughing, she walked through to the kitchen.

"Your grandma is funny," Sally said, "I love this garden Maggie, it's so wonderful and cosy and peaceful and welcoming." She accepted a glass of squash and sat in the wicker chair. "I could just snooze the afternoon away here," she said as she stretched her arms and legs out and took in the tranquillity of the garden.

"Please snooze away, that means more goodies for me," laughed Maggie as she sat in the chair beside her friend. Her grandma returned with a host of delicious sandwiches and pastries. Maggie loved these days.

Dora loved these days too and enjoyed the girls' company. After she had eaten with them, she excused herself and sat under the shade of the old chestnut tree and continued her knitting.

The girls took a moment to be quiet and savour the serenity of the afternoon. The only sounds were the buzzing of a persistent fly who had discovered the pastries and the pleasant tapping of knitting needles.

These were happy years for Maggie and her grandma.

Chapter Twenty-Six

February 6 1952, the village was devastated to hear that King George VI had died. A special church service was held the following Sunday in the King's honour and afterwards the congregation lined the village green as the brass band marched passed in respect. In the afternoon, the older folk gathered for a remembrance tea in the village hall to reminisce and to raise a cuppa to their beloved King.

Maggie was now sixteen and still dreaded visiting her mother.

"Do we really have to go?" pleaded Maggie, "You know this is the only down side to living with you grandma."

"Flattery will get you nowhere child." Dora joked back.

"Why do we keep trying? She doesn't want us there. She never wanted me."

It broke Dora's heart to hear Maggie say this, but they both knew deep down that this was true.

"She's your mother, Maggie. You only get one."

"Well, I'm her daughter and she only got one. Doesn't mean anything to her."

They made their way to the cottage in silence. Most times, Iris wouldn't let them in beyond the front door. These past few years she had not only alienated her daughter and best friend but most of the villagers. She had become unsociable and rude whenever she ventured out and was fast becoming the village nuisance.

Despite their turbulent history, Dora took over Iris's rent and paid the Squire every week out of her own pocket. Dora was adamant that this arrangement was to be strictly between them. As far as Maggie knew, her mother still paid the rent. As for Iris, she did not give the rent one iota of consideration and was oblivious to the lifeline bestowed upon her from the most unexpected source.

Eric and Betty had tried to maintain the friendship but everything was thrown back at them. Pete and Billy told them that it wasn't worth it and they should move on. They all loved Maggie and saw her often in the village and sometimes went to her grandma's for tea. They were sad for what Maggie had gone through but they were pleased she was so happy living with her grandma.

One afternoon, Betty was studying her shopping list in Mr Dwyer's Post Office store, when Iris wandered in.

"Iris love, how are you?" Betty was genuinely pleased to see her old friend but quickly noticed how unkempt and dirty Iris looked.

"Fine," Iris responded tartly as she pushed passed.

"Would you like to come over for a cuppa and catch up sometime?" Betty asked.

"Not really." Iris picked up a packet of sugar and walked back to the counter to pay.

"Iris. That's rude."

"Betty," Iris turned to face her. "I don't really care. What are you going to say? That we used to be friends? Told each other everything *la la la de da?*" She placed the sugar on the counter and walked back to Betty. "Look, *love.* Let me spell it out for you because I know you country folk are a little slow. In a nutshell, I only ever came to the village to get out of home. I married William because he was there. I never wanted a child; I tolerated it, but thankfully no more, as she is living with the witch.

"Now, all of you do-gooders mind your own business and I will mind mine. And as for you?" Iris stepped back slightly and looked Betty up and down. "Well, talking to you at work was just something to do to make the day go quicker. I never liked you or your runt family anyway. Leave me alone. Is that clear enough?"

Betty couldn't believe what she had just heard. Tears started to well up as she calmly followed Iris to the counter. Betty noticed that Mr Dwyer was approaching the shop from the back storeroom and as evenly as she could gather herself, she called out asking him if he'd mind fetching some more humbugs as she'd noticed the jar was empty on the shelf. Mr Dwyer apologised and turned back to the storeroom.

"Iris?" called Betty.

Iris turned to face her.

With as much force as she could muster, Betty slapped Iris hard across the face. The impact caused Iris to stagger backwards and Betty's hand stung so much it went numb.

"You are a cold-hearted bitch," snapped Betty, "you are a drunk and a mess. I curse the day William met you. He was a decent man and Maggie is worth a hundred of you. Clean yourself up, you stink." She pushed passed her and walked out of the shop.

Not long after, one early evening when Maggie was at the Oak Pub with Sally, they heard a woman shouting outside and went to the top window to peer out. Maggie was mortified as her mother was cursing in the street demanding to be served a drink.

The girls ran down the stairs and around to the street and saw that the pub door was open and that Iris was being jeered at by the men inside. Sally and Mr Vinter felt sorry for Maggie to see her mother in this way as she staggered up and down demanding to be served.

"We'll get her inside up to the flat," said Mrs Vinter kindly as she followed the girls.

"No. Thank you, Mrs Vinter," said Maggie not wanting her mother to spoil anything. Maggie was highly embarrassed and watched as the men she knew insulted and laughed at her mother despicably.

Mr Vinter saw the anguish on Maggie's face and admonished the men and ushered them inside then closed the door.

"What'yer doing? Get off me," shouted Iris, as the girls tried to steer her away from the pub towards home. "I just want a drink."

"You've had enough," said Maggie as she supported her mother on one side and Sally the other.

Walking Iris home as she ranted was the longest fifteen minutes of Maggie's life. Sally felt so much for her friend and, even though she was the more placid of the two girls, she became more and more angry as they neared the cottage.

They plonked Iris onto the couch and while Maggie went to the kitchen to fetch a glass of water, Iris started up again.

"Stupid girl, she's like a noose around my neck..."

Hearing that felt like a line had finally been crossed and Sally snapped. She pushed Iris back down onto the couch.

"You weak, selfish woman, you have tried everything to bring Maggie down to your bitter level. It will never work. Leave her alone. She is far better off without you.

"Come on Maggie," said Sally as she steered her friend toward the door. "Nothing more to do here, let her sleep it off."

Chapter Twenty-Seven

The village had been in planning mode for weeks to make the Queen's Coronation on June 2 1953 a special occasion. Maggie and Sally were nearly seventeen and were looking forward to the dance being held in the village hall the following evening.

The atmosphere was almost like Christmas Eve, but in the summertime. Villagers were out before the Coronation making sure their cottages were ready for the big day. There were red, white and blue buntings displayed on every cottage and commemorative tea towels and Union Jacks were suspended from upstairs windows.

Maggie and Sally observed the work in progress from the lounge window of the pub. Being more or less centralised to the village, the pub had an excellent vantage point. They could see the men walking towards the green carrying chairs, then tables, from both the village and church halls in readiness for the street party and brass band.

Orchard workers climbed their tallest ladders to attach buntings from the top of the great oak tree in the middle of the village green. The other ends were then draped across the green and secured to the top of each shops' guttering giving the effect that the tree and village green were underneath a large canopy.

The girls were back in the kitchen preparing their last batch of cheesy sticks. Sally was cutting up the cheese and Maggie was putting the mixture on the baking tray ready for the oven. Just then, the whole block of cheese slipped from Sally's hand, fell and rolled on the floor. The girls looked at one another in horror then burst out laughing.

"That's really not funny," said Sally.

"No it isn't," agreed Maggie. Then they laughed some more.

"This is the last of the cheese," said Sally, as she retrieved the block from the floor. "Goodness, it's covered in bits, look."

"Wash, or cut it off?"

"Can you wash cheese? Won't it go soggy?"

"Don't know. Let's cut it off then."

Sally started to cut the cheese but it slipped from her grasp again and rolled on the floor. Both girls fell into rapturous laughter.

"Ah, no," said Sally, as she again retrieved it from the floor.

"You're hopeless," laughed Maggie, clutching at her sides.

Just then Gwen popped her head round the door. "Doesn't sound like much work going on in here," she said.

Sally quickly plonked the block of cheese into the bowl with the other ingredients before her mother could see that she'd dropped it.

"What did you do that for?" asked Maggie after Gwen had left.

"Goodness, I don't know. I panicked."

"Now there are bits and stuff all over it."

"We'll cook it and say nothing and for goodness sake don't eat any tomorrow," said Sally, "hopefully no one will notice."

"You think?" said Maggie with a doubtful look.

Later that evening just before they all settled for bed, Edward Vinter walked into the lounge munching on a cheesy stick. Both girls looked at him in horror.

"These are nice, a bit grittier than usual, but nice. Night girls."

As he left the room he heard a sudden burst of laughter. *Those two laugh at absolutely anything,* he thought.

The jam-packed schedule started at eight the next morning with a church service followed by a morning tea that was held on the village green. Around lunchtime, the Vinter's had organised a pram race with the other public house. The race consisted of two teams of six to represent each pub. The men dressed up as nannies (some looked quite scary), and their wives were dressed as babies and seated in prams. The 'nannies' had to push the 'babies' around the village green circuit. When they arrived at each pub, the nannies had to drink a half pint of ale before moving on. The winner was the one who completed three circuits in the quickest time. One nanny, Mr Parks, was disqualified after taking a corner so abruptly, that he nearly capsized Mrs Parks into the pond.

There was also a fancy dress competition where it appeared that the vast majority of entrants came dressed as the Queen, complete with a crown. The three judges awarded the winner to a little boy who came dressed as a chimney sweep and everyone agreed it was the diplomatic option.

At three o'clock the children excitedly took their seats along the long line of party tables and tucked into a very delicious Royal tea. There were paste sandwiches, tomato sandwiches and orange squash followed by wobbly jelly and blancmange plus lots of other goodies donated by different households. The children wore red, white and blue hand-made paper hats and were given paper streamers that they could throw. The party whistles deafened out the brass band as they serenaded the older folk under the shade of the oak tree.

The adults were milling around the children and helped the younger ones by topping up drink beakers. Some leaned over to pinch a sandwich or two from the tables. Gwen Vinter was very surprised that the cheesy sticks were not going down as she expected as there were a couple of trays with half eaten ones. She would have tried one herself but she didn't like cheese much.

Maggie and Sally were among the helpers making sure that the children were having a good time. The girls had decorated their dresses with red, white and blue sashes made out of crepe paper. Later on, they sat on a bench by the village green and made crepe paper posies for the little girls to carry.

That evening, the village dance was the big hit as all had expected. The Squire had lent his record player as it had a decent speaker and when people arrived they brought their favourite records to be played. Most were hits from the forties and everyone was happy to dance the evening away to the hits of the era.

Maggie and Sally started dancing together but from time to time they were interrupted with requests to dance from admiring young men. Simon Dwyer breezed Maggie around the floor and she was extremely surprised at how good a dancer he was. He explained that his parents had always been keen dancers and he used to watch them dance in their living room.

The girls took a break and stood to the side of the hall while Simon went to get them all a drink.

"What a lovely day," beamed Sally.

"It has been a beautiful day," agreed Maggie, who took their drinks on Simon's return. Just then Sally was whisked off to dance by Trevor, an estate mechanic and Simon led Maggie outside where it was a little quieter and cooler. He asked if she would like to go dancing in town the following weekend. Maggie felt embarrassingly trapped yet again. She had turned him down a few times with a number of excuses. She liked Simon, but there was no spark there for her. Yes, they had gone on a couple of dates in the past but at the end of the evening when he kissed her, it didn't feel right at all.

To alleviate this, she had tried fixing Simon up with Sally when they had gone into town to the movie house a few times. The sad thing was that Sally really liked Simon and even though they had had a good time she had felt a little awkward knowing that he liked Maggie more. It just wasn't fair.

Now, as they stood outside the village hall Maggie declined yet again saying that her grandma hadn't been too well lately, which was the truth, and that she would be staying in with her.

"Maggie, I like you, you know that. I understand about your grandma, but I am sure she would want you to be happy and to be going out and having fun."

"Yes Simon, she would and she really insisted that I come out today to celebrate the Coronation even though she was too unwell to come herself. I felt a little guilty, but I came on one condition that I would stay with her in future. My grandma is the world to me."

"I know and respect that. Perhaps I can come over and visit you?"

"Grandma would like that, but Simon..." *this has to be it,* she thought, *I have got to say something otherwise I will be going around in circles forever.* She took a deep breath. "Simon, I am sorry, but this evening proves that I cannot be your girlfriend. Your dance moves far excel mine and I am likely to get you arrested for bad taste..."

Simon knew what Maggie was saying. He had known what she had been saying for a long while in fact, and he finally admitted to himself that he was too stubborn or unwilling to accept. It was time to move on. He burst out laughing, and she laughed with him, grateful he had understood what she had tried to tell him.

"Maggie Harris, you are a lovely person, inside and out and I am very glad to have you as my friend." He emphasised the word 'friend' and kissed her gently on the cheek. He would always be fond of her.

When they parted, they looked each other in the eye and smiled, realising they were starting a new chapter in their friendship.

Chapter Twenty-Eight

The village was still buzzing long after the Coronation celebrations had ended and soon it was hop season once again. Maggie continued to enjoy her long running correspondence with the occupants of McKinnley Station and it was always a welcome joy when she received a new letter. Jack McKinnley sounded like a nice man and he often wrote of the antics of the station, telling of sheep shearing stories and about the kelpie dogs and horses. He wrote more than his sister Sylvia who hadn't really written at all since Maggie was a small child. Mr and Mrs McKinnley frequently mentioned that she would be welcome to stay anytime and had even offered her a job. Mr McKinnley believed that they could make use of her farming skills and mechanical knowledge.

Maggie often daydreamed about living in Australia. She wondered what it would be like if she were to take the offer seriously. Out of curiosity, she began to write up a plan. Was there anything holding her back? Well, her grandma and Sally for a start. She would miss them dreadfully. As for her mother... if Maggie were truly honest, she knew she wouldn't miss her at all. The real thing holding her back was money, she hardly had a bean to her name so she would have to start saving seriously.

She had spent a lot of time talking to Mr Dwyer and Simon about Australia and had built up quite a picture in mind of

McKinnley Station and its occupants.This helped a lot whenever she received letters because she could almost picture everyone there. Mr Dwyer's cousin, Ben McKinnley ran the station with his wife Judith. Ben's parents had immigrated when he and Mr Dwyer were children and Judith was born in South Australia to second generation Australians. Ben and Judith had two children, Jack and Sylvia who were five and three years older than Maggie respectively.

She had learned that McKinnley Station was around one thousand square miles, but it was quite small in comparison with the bigger stations. They farmed an average of five thousand Merino sheep and some of the biggest problems they encountered were lack of rainfall, wild dogs and the harsh climate.

Out of necessity, if she were to seriously consider moving to the other side of the world she would have to brush up on her horse riding skills, as well as keeping her hand in with the mechanical side of things. As a child she used to tinker a lot in her father's workshop and under his supervision she had used all of the tools and assisted him when he was under the tractors. She decided that she would look into getting some more experience in this field.

Chapter Twenty-Nine

In the nine troubled years following his graduation, the Squire's son, Adam, had not returned to Primrose Farm Estate. His pride would not allow him to give his father the satisfaction of knowing he had failed or to live what he considered a dull and boring life of a country Squire, surrounded by endless simpletons. The only communication between them was when Adam wrote to his father demanding money.

The Squire, on the other hand, did not like to think too much about how much money he had sent his son since his disbandment. He regretted having given in so easily to Adam initially. For an astute businessman, he had made some personal costly decisions.

Adam had built up a string of bad business deals and mounting gambling debts so when the Squire received yet another demanding letter the previous month, he refused to pay. Common sense prevailed, forcing a penniless and homeless Adam to return to the fold aged twenty-seven.

The two men couldn't have been more different in manner or appearance. The Squire was tall and wiry and Adam shorter and stocky. Adam was an excellent academic at boarding school but since his expulsion he had been too idle to use his intellect. He looked down his nose at the middle and lower classes, and the huge chip on his shoulder governed that the world owed him the biggest favour.

"Jesus Christ!" Adam exclaimed in frustration as he burst into his father's study and sat down heavily on the fireside chair, "how the hell do you put up with it here? It's so bloody boring."

"Morning Adam," said his father trying not to show his displeasure. He didn't approve of blaspheming, but in the circumstances he let it go. "Would you like some tea?"

"No, I would not like some tea. That would mean I would have to see that busy body and she grates on my nerves, twittering all over the place." He reached over to pick up the newspaper and turned the pages loudly in front of him, shielding himself from his father.

"That's enough of that, I will not hear a bad word against Mrs Sutton, she is the backbone of the Manor and don't you forget it," admonished the Squire, "what are your plans today?"

"Making as much bloody noise as I can," he said sarcastically, "how the hell do you stand it? I cannot think because it is too bloody quiet. I'll have you know that I could stand at the other end of the building and fart and you'd be able to hear it plain and clear."

"There's no room for that inappropriate schoolboy talk here."

Adam noisily billowed out the paper in response then a few seconds later he snapped it closed, stood up and threw the paper on the chair and paced the room.

"If you want something to do, help me with the accounts today…"

"Give me strength," Adam said impatiently, as he walked back out the door.

Chapter Thirty

The 1953 hop season yielded a bumper crop and the Squire reported an impressive number of bushels. The rain had kept at bay, making life a lot easier. As the last Saturday of the hop season arrived, the men folk currently residing at Oak Barn Orchard and Foxden Orchard were ushered off to the village pubs. This gave the women the opportunity to pack their belongings without the men getting under their feet.

In a jovial mood, the men headed to the village where both pubs were packed to the rafters on their last evening before they all returned back to their London lives. Old friends shook hands and wished each other well and the villagers turned out to wish their friends a safe journey home. The noise was deafening inside The Oak Pub and Edward Vinter was enjoying the busy evening. As landlord, he was offered many drinks as he tended bar and collected glasses and he thought that if he'd accepted every one Gwen would have had a fit.

The night was humid and all the men crammed inside. Even with the doors and windows open, it was still impossibly hot. The air was thick with the combination of pipe smoke, roll-ups and the smell of fresh and stale beer, as the men tasted the fruits of their labour. But the most dominant odour of all was of hard working manual perspiration. The men were shouting to make themselves heard and everyone was in high spirits. There were frequent shouts of 'open the door' when anyone left or entered the pub and accidentally closed the door behind them.

"All the best, city person," joked Charlie, a Primrose Estate employee, as he patted Joe on the shoulder, "at least going back to the smoke you won't come across any of the critters that we have down here."

"You still laughing about that?" smiled Joe, "I tell you for the thousandth time, that insect was as big as my house."

"Goodness, it grows ten-fold each time you tell it," said Charlie as he finished his pint.

"Bloody big thing it was. And camouflaged, it could've done some real damage... What's so funny?" laughed Joe.

"Joe, 'ol man. You need to spend a little more time in the country, you city people are so funny."

"I'm not taking any chances, Charlie. Next year I am keeping my boots firmly on at ALL times."

"Joe. It was a grasshopper."

"Exactly!"

"One for the road?"

"Line them up 'ol man." as the two friends weaved their way to the bar.

Edward Vinter couldn't help but laugh at hearing this as he collected some dirty glasses from the tables. He understood both sides to the story as he had moved from London himself. The bugs took a little getting used to in the country but now they didn't bother him at all. He remembered one particular occasion a few years back when a hop-picker had asked Edward with some concern if the red spot on his arm caused him any grief? Edward had tried to keep a straight face as he informed the hop-picker that it was just a ladybird.

With a handful of glasses Edward made his way back to the bar.

"Say, George, how many bushels this year?" said one old cockney as he held up a pint glass giving a toothless smile to his friend. "The way you're slowing up mate, I'll be surprised if you didn't break the duck."

"I'll tell you, Harold," said his equally aged friend "If I'd packed as many bushels as you've teeth then I've doubled my load, you 'ol wind-up merchant. Another beer, mate?"

"Hey squidger," someone shouted across the room "How's yer bum for spots?"

"Oi, Smithy," laughed Tommy, 'Squidger' Dunn. "Me bum's fine, how's tricks?"

"Good mate," said Smithy, as he started to zigzag across the room to his friend "Remember me to the family."

As Smithy raised his glass a man staggered passed and knocked his arm, causing Smithy to spill the majority of his drink over his shirt.

"Oi mate, watch where you're going," shouted Smithy, brushing his shirt with his hand, "that beer cost me thruppence."

"That's about all you're worth anyway," slurred the drunk, as he turned back and squared up to Smithy.

"What'd yer say?" shouted Smithy, as he looked into the eyes of a madman.

Tommy and a few others saw what was about to happen and quickly gathered around Smithy looking at the man they had seen before but couldn't place.

"Alright lads," said Mr Vinter who also observed and rang the 'last orders' bell to get attention. "No trouble in here," he barked with authority. "Take it outside." He pushed his way through to the men.

At the sound of the bell, protests began that it wasn't yet closing time. When they realised that there was some trouble brewing a hush immediately descended over the room.

"What's yer problem?" asked Smithy as he eyed the stranger.

"You're my problem. *Boy,*" hissed the man, who looked Smithy up and down with a look of disgust on his face.

Instantly, without his eyes leaving those of the stranger, Smithy stepped to one side and brought the top of his beer glass down hard on the side of a table. The remains of beer and shards of glass crashed to the ragstone floor, then he lunged the splintered remains of the beer glass towards the drunk's face.

Tommy reacted in a split second and captured the offending weapon, a few others stepped in to separate the men.

"You're drunk," snarled Smithy, as he broke free and shoved the madman backwards to land with a thump onto a wooden bench.

"And you're all worthless pieces of shit," ranted the madman. "Bugger off back to that sewer you call home. A band of cowards the lot of you." He regained his unsteady feet.

"Who the hell do you think you are?" said Smithy. "Come on, outside and we'll see who's a coward."

"They'll be no such thing," said Mr Vinter. "This is the Squire's son. I'll take him upstairs where he can sleep it off." As he made his way to Adam to steer him away.

"I don't need your help, you stupid man, get your hands off of me," slurred Adam, "All of you leave me alone. I want a beer and I demand you give me a beer now," he said, as he walked towards the bar.

"I'm not serving you Adam, you've had enough already. Go on home son."

"I said I want a beer. I order you to serve me and I'm not your son." As he thumped his fist on the bar top.

"Let's escort the gentleman outside," said Tommy, as a few men approached Adam. The crowded pub suddenly divided, giving a clear pathway to the street. Tommy had a flashback to when he was a small boy in the East End of London and when he briefly attended Sunday school. He remembered the story of Moses and how he commanded the parting of the Red Sea. It was like that now.

"Bloody cowards," Adam bellowed as his arms were restrained behind his back and he was marched out the door. "What's this? Five on one, very big of you," he said, struggling to free his arms. "I want a beer," he shouted, "I came here for a beer and I demand you criminal moth-eaten peasants let me go."

"Hey Tommy," said Smithy, "our friend here demands a beer, what'd ya think lads? Come on Tommy, give him a beer."

Tommy calmly walked up to Adam and slowly poured a full pint of Kent's finest over Adam's head, causing him to struggle even more through sheer rage.

"It's not a beer you want," snarled Tommy, as he and Adam stood nose to nose. "It's manners son. No one speaks to my friends like you just did, toff or no bloody toff." And as quick as lightening Tommy thrust his fist into Adam's stomach causing him to double over and retch in pain.

"Our friend here deserves a lesson in manners boys and I know just the tree for the job," said Tommy. He and Smithy dragged Adam through the village and marched him to the back of Foxden Orchard. Once there, they tied him to the biggest apple tree they could find.

"You can't just leave me here you imbecilic idiots," protested Adam as spittle flew from his lips. He was powerless though, bound to the tree with his hair, face and shirt sodden with beer.

"My father will sack the whole lot of you, you bunch of gutless thieves, you're the dregs of society, all of you. Cowardly bastards."

"No son, no," said Tommy calmly, as he gently patted Adam on the side of his face. "Your father will not be sacking us. He is a decent man and I don't know what he did to deserve a runt like you. No, it is you who is the dregs mate.You cross my path again, I'll hurt you real good, do you hear me?"

"Pretty little sister you have," said Adam, changing tactics and licked his lips suggestively.Tommy's eyes fired with rage and Adam knew instantly that the sister was the key to hurting Tommy.

Vivien was four years younger than Tommy and at just sixteen she was already a stunner with long auburn hair and a film star figure to match. She gathered the attention of many boys and men wherever she went. But, despite her beauty,Vivien was a shy girl who didn't feel confident around the company of men and she often wondered what all the fuss was about.

Tommy was smart enough not to play into Adam's hands and forced himself to unclench his fists. His upbringing had been tough, like many in the East End, where he had found solace in boxing. He was building up to become fly-weight champion of his region. Mr Doherty, his trainer, had instilled discipline in him and had taught him not to rise and react to personal remarks, however bad they were.

"Nice try 'ol son," said Tommy as he tried to cover his initial anger. "We'll bid you nitey nite now and someone will set you free perhaps in the morning when we've all gone back to the smoke."

As Tommy and Smithy walked away they could hear Adam as he ranted, "Next year mate, you'll keep 'til next year. And that pretty sister of yours, I'll show her what a real man can do. She'll be mine, do you hear that? She'll be mine for the taking willing or not. DO YOU HEAR ME PEASANT?"

"Leave it Tommo," said Smithy grabbing his friend's arm firmly sensing Tommy's anger was rising. "We'll fix him next year, let him stew. Vivien will be okay, she's a good girl."

Tommy smiled at his friend and knew he was right. Boxing had taught him discipline and patience. He knew he could wait and he knew that the squire's son would be worth it.

Hell, he was looking forward to it already.

Chapter Thirty-One

Grandma's health slowly deteriorated, and she passed away peacefully in May the following year. After the funeral, Maggie accepted the Vinter's invitation to live with them at The Oak Pub. Pamela, Sally's older sister had long moved out so Gwen was delighted when Maggie agreed to stay. No one else quite loved her chicken stew like Maggie did.

Maggie grieved her grandma in a different way to her father. It was the shock of her father's death that she would never be able to shake. She had gone to bed and her father was alive and when she woke in the morning he wasn't. With her beloved grandma, Maggie had known she was dying and was able to prepare herself for it. Dora had been in ill health and elderly and as much as Maggie missed her, she hadn't wanted her grandma to live on suffering.

Sally and her parents were as good as kin and they rallied round as families do. They talked about grandma and of the good times and as much as Maggie hurt, she knew that she would get through this sad period. As a small final defiance, her grandma had instructed that the wake be held in the pub. Maggie had laughed out loud when she heard this, as her grandma had never really gelled with the WI brigade. She knew that her grandma would be smiling at the vision of the WI ladies' disapproval. The wake was well attended and smiles, laughter and reminiscing were on the menu, as per her grandma's request.

Maggie was stunned to learn that her grandma had left her everything, as this was something they had never talked about. Dora had been a shrewd woman as it had always been her way to tie up loose ends. Iris was the only exception to this rule that had frustrated her. Dora hadn't wanted Maggie to be burdened by her passing so she had given precise instructions to her solicitor as to how she wanted things handled.

Even though the Squire was getting on in years he was still an integral part of the village. Since William's death he had felt a connection and loyalty to Maggie and in looking out for her best interests. He willingly helped Maggie put her grandma's property on the market. Also, unbeknown to anyone, he waived Iris's rent on the cottage so that Maggie wouldn't have to worry about her mother's security. Dora Harris's house was sold not long after and the proceeds went towards securing Maggie's future.

She was still determined to travel to Australia but now it would be sooner rather than later. Maggie dearly loved Sally and her parents and leaving them would be heart-breaking but, she still had what she described as a magnetic pull to move to the other side of the world. She couldn't fully explain it. She only knew that she had to do it.

Chapter Thirty-Two

At eighteen both Sally and Maggie had secretarial jobs working at different firms and they would sometimes meet each other for lunch. They travelled eight miles on Ernie's bus into Maidstone every day for work. Maggie enjoyed working in an office environment but was unable to brush the guilt she felt in not working on the land as per her ancestral roots.

She knew her father would understand this but sometimes she felt that she had let him down. Although she had been an extremely young apprentice to him she was quite competent at the time in her knowledge. *Could I ever get that back?* she wondered. In the meantime, she was swept along in the day-to-day just like everyone else.

One afternoon as they were on the bus heading for home, Maggie decided to talk to Sally about how she was feeling.

"Sally, I like working in the office, the job is good and the people are lovely. But, it is as if I am being pulled in another direction, do you know what I mean?"

"No."

"I am thinking that I want to get back to the land, to learn how to fix machinery and all that..."

"Really?"

"Yes, really. Do you think I should have a word with the Squire and see if I can be an apprentice?"

"I know women worked in mechanics during the war but now it's over it's mostly men. I wouldn't want you to be disappointed as I'd imagine it would be difficult to get into I suppose, but you're serious aren't you?"

"Absolutely."

"Will it make you happy?"

"Yes, I think so."

"Well, that's it then." Sally grinned, "I'll come with you on Saturday and wait with Mrs Sutton while you see the Squire."

"Are you coming for support or to sample the goodies from Mrs Sutton's kitchen?" Maggie laughed.

"No comment," giggled Sally, as Maggie gently prodded her in the side nearly causing her to fall off the seat. Just then the bus slowed to a sluggish pace, jolted and stopped.

"Not again." They sighed and looked at each other.

"Sorry folks. Everyone off the bus," said Ernie apologetically as he looked at his passengers in the rear view mirror. They filed off the bus at what was locally known as 'Problem Hill'. It was actually Buttercup Hill but due to the endless problems the bus had in climbing it, the locals had renamed it accordingly. When filled to capacity, the poor old bus didn't have the power to climb. By lightening the load and with a firm push, the bus was able to climb successfully.

"Sorry again folks."

"It's all right Ernie," said one passenger, patting him on the shoulder. "We know what to do. Come on lads, get your backs into it."

"At least it isn't raining," said one woman.

"Amen to that," said another.

The following Saturday morning Maggie and Sally set out for the pleasant walk to the Manor. As directed by Mrs Sutton, Maggie went in search of the Squire in the walled garden while Sally stayed and kept her company. Maggie playfully rolled her eyes at Sally while she just smiled sweetly back and accepted the offer of a cup of tea and a scone with strawberry jam while she waited.

The Squire was delighted at Maggie's request and said that the estate would be honoured to have her as an apprentice mechanic. He was all for the modern times with women continuing these roles after the war. He said he would arrange all the details and after Maggie served her notice she would be on the payroll the following month.

"Your father would have been very proud Maggie, make no mistake," he assured her as he bade the girls farewell.

"Thank you Squire, I hope so. Bye Mrs Sutton and thanks for the cake," said Maggie holding up the cake tin. "We'll have this after dinner this evening."

Chapter Thirty-Three

Time seemed to fly by and over the following months the estate managed a bumper harvest of pears and apples. Even when the orchard workers were not picking the fruit there was plenty of preparation ahead for the next crop. In early September, Mr Dawson, the Primrose Estate Manager and his team, carried out some maintenance repairs on the hop-pickers huts prior to their arrival and were now on this warm sunny September morning awaiting the London train to pull in.

At the Manor, Mrs Sutton was clearing the breakfast table when Adam breezed into the dining room dressed in the finery of an English country gent.

"Good morning, Mrs Sutton," he said quite cheerily, which was completely out of character to how he usually was.

"Master Adam," she replied, as she noted that just recently he had stopped drinking again and had started to smarten himself up. He now looked quite presentable, clean-shaven and thankfully smelled pleasant for a change. But, they had been down this road many times before and she was sceptical as to the real reason for this sudden change of behaviour.

"I apologise Mrs Sutton, that I am late this morning, spent a little too long shaving I'm afraid. Am I too late for some tea and toast?" he asked politely, as he took a seat at the table and proceeded to read his father's newspaper.

"I'll bring you some, it won't take me long to make a fresh pot of tea," she said, making her way to the kitchen.

"Splendid, thank you very much," he said, when she returned with his breakfast. "Has my father left for the train already?"

"Yes, Master Adam, he left about a half an hour ago. He said there was something he needed to check on first."

"I'll finish this then and I'll make my way there too," he said, as Mrs Sutton raised her eyebrows in surprise.

"Why now? You have never taken an interest before…" she stopped abruptly, cringing slightly, awaiting a rebuke.

Adam stiffened on hearing what she'd said. *Stupid old witch,* he thought. However, aloud he calmly said, "No, I haven't Mrs Sutton but it's about time I started to take more responsibility around here." He took a small sip of tea, rose from the table and as he did, he knocked his teacup, spilling the contents over the crisp linen tablecloth. "So sorry, Mrs Sutton, how clumsy of me." He then bade her a good morning and waltzed out the dining room.

Mrs Sutton had no doubt that the spilt tea wasn't an accident but a response to her subtle scolding. "Well, I'll be," she whispered to herself, as she quickly wiped the table. "What are you up to now?"

Adam had decided a week ago to start cleaning up his act. He had an engagement to keep and a detailed plan in place. His first port of call was to his father's study when he knew the old man was out at a meeting in town and the kitchen woman was at a church meeting in the village.

He had carefully looked through his father's filing cabinet to check the families that had confirmed this year's hop-picking season and then which orchard and hut his father had allotted them. During his search he had found a silver hip flask tucked behind some files at the back of the cabinet.

"Sly 'ol bugger," Adam muttered, as he unscrewed the top and smelled the glorious whisky that caused his drinking senses to go into an almighty frenzy. "Holding out on me are you father?" he smiled and unconsciously licked his lips. He was extremely tempted to gulp the lot in one fair swoop but his inner advocate told him that what was coming was much sweeter than a few pleasurable seconds drinking his father's whisky.

He placed the flask back where he'd found it, handling it as delicately as he would a priceless heirloom, and quietly left the study. He walked down the hallway with a spring in his step that he hadn't had for many years. His willpower had been tested and he was proud that he had passed with flying colours.

At the train station, Adam frantically searched the noisy bustling crowd for Tommy Dunn. His heart and eyes filled with hate for unfinished business and a score to settle. How he had waited a whole damn year for this day to arrive. Then, suddenly his eyes caught sight of Vivien, Tommy's sister. She was even more beautiful than he remembered and in a split second an uncharacteristic beaming smile lit up his otherwise grim face.

Everyone else melted away into the background as if it was only the two of them alone together, in a different world. Adam had never felt this way before. He was overcome by an emotion that was totally foreign to him and it threw him into utter confusion.

His carefully thought out plan was suddenly in pieces. He spun around and walked back in the direction of the Manor trying to analyse what had gone so dreadfully wrong. Even before he arrived back at the Manor's gates he had convinced himself that he had completely overreacted to last year's events. *Tommy isn't so bad,* he thought, *after all it was my own stupid fault that caused the incident by being so drunk to begin with.*

For once in his life, Adam resolved he would take responsibility like a man. He would find Tommy and apologise for his unforgiveable behaviour. Tommy would then shake his hand and they would become the best of friends and then Tommy would practically beg him to court his sister.

When he entered the kitchen, his revised plan had begun to unfold.

"Mrs Sutton, any tea on the go?" he said cheerily, taking Mrs Sutton by surprise yet again.

"I was just about to make some Master Adam," she said, getting up to put the kettle on.

"You sit down and take it easy Mrs Sutton. Allow me to do the honours, it can't be that hard can it?"

"Master Adam?" she said quite bewildered.

"Mrs Sutton, it is long overdue believe me. Come on now, take a seat," he said, ushering her back to the kitchen table and gently guiding her to a seat. "If you don't mind me saying, you could do with a little help around the place, particularly around hopping season."

"Some help?"

"Yes, a little help. You have so many extra duties that I cannot believe why father hasn't addressed it before. Even for a few hours per week. I was just down at the station and happened to see Mr Dunn's daughter, Vivien. She'll be perfect. I remember hearing something somewhere that she has prior experience in managing household duties working with a well-to-do London family. Have you heard that?"

"Well..." said Mrs Sutton, trying to recall if she had heard this or not.

"Perhaps it was my father who mentioned it to me," Adam said, as he poured hot water into the teapot. "Well, that's splendid of you to agree to accept some help. I will clear this with father when he returns home later. Good day to you, Mrs Sutton."

"But your tea..." said a puzzled Mrs Sutton. Adam had totally thrown her off guard as she stared at the empty kitchen doorway hearing his footsteps echoing down the hall. What on earth had just happened?

A few days later, Vivien Dunn quietly knocked on the kitchen door. She was dressed in her finest to conjure up some confidence. She and her mother had spent ages deciding on what was best to wear without over or under-doing the occasion. They had brought with them plenty to see them through the six weeks but hadn't planned on catering for this type of occasion, so they decided on Vivien's Sunday best church outfit.

"Fer goodness sake, jus be yerself girl," said her father, the night before as they sat at dusk enjoying the peaceful summer evening.

"Oh, Dad. What if they don't like me?" she asked nervously.

"Then they don't deserve yer. Jus hold yer head up high, turn around and come back to us. But there's no reason why they will be like that. The Squire's a decent enough man and the Housekeeper seems a bit strict and uppity but seems a fair woman. Just look out for the Squire's son, don't trust him at all. He had a run-in with Tommy and his mates last year. A bad 'un that one. You mark my words. Stay clear."

These negative thoughts taunted Vivien as she waited for the door to open. She was extremely nervous and wished that she had stayed in the hop field with her kind and wasn't trying to be hoity toity at the Manor. She was just about to turn around to leave when the door opened and Vivien found herself looking at a very stern Mrs Sutton.

"Do come in girl, don't just stand there. My name is Mrs Sutton; address me accordingly. Know your place and we'll get on like a house on fire. Cup of tea?"

"Good morning, Mrs Sutton," stammered Vivien, as she walked into the most magnificent kitchen she had ever seen. She was somewhat taken aback by the woman's tone of voice, which was totally unexpected from what she had heard about her. Mrs Sutton, to be honest, was embarrassingly taken aback by her own gruffness.

She was still a little aggrieved that Master Adam, and the Squire too for that matter, had agreed that she could do with some help. She had gladly given decades of loyalty to run the Manor like clockwork. She didn't need any help but the decision had been made and there was nothing she could do about it.

She knew it wasn't Vivien's fault, but she couldn't help herself. She'd had a restless sleep the night before where she had tossed and turned as she heard every hour chime from the Grandfather clock downstairs in the hallway. She threw herself into a frenzy thinking that this was it; she was out on her ear. They would expect her to train up this new girl then the Squire would put her out to pasture, give her perhaps a few weeks extra pay for all her years of service and then she'd be forgotten and brushed under the carpet. Her eyes had watered and that had made her angrier and more frustrated. She would try to be pleasant to the girl in the morning and later she would speak to Mrs Collins about her thoughts. She liked Mrs Collins and respected her opinion. Yes, it would be better in the morning.

"What's the matter love?" a sleepy Mr Sutton had asked. "You've been tossing and turning for ages."

"Can't sleep, that's all. Go on back to sleep, no use in both of us being awake.

Now as Mrs Sutton looked at Vivien she thought what a pleasant girl she was. She was not arrogant or conceited but was mild-mannered and even a little timid. She was a beauty that was for sure, but she appeared unaware of the aura that she carried.

"I apologise for my abruptness Vivien, had a bit of a bumpy night. Please take a seat," she said, in a kinder tone. "We'll have some tea then I'll go through some of the duties required. How are your family?"

"Thank you, Mrs Sutton," said Vivien with a beaming smile, relaxing a little at Mrs Sutton's more friendly tone. "My family are..."

"And you must be Vivien," interrupted Adam, as he practically ran into the kitchen completely ignoring Mrs Sutton. Then trying his utmost to compose himself, he walked over to Vivien and delicately placed a butterfly kiss on the back of her hand while staring into her deep blue eyes.

"Come with me, my dear and I'll show you the grounds," he said, as he kept hold of Vivien's hand and linked her arm with his and guided them both out the back door. "You will adore the herb and topiary garden, it's surrounded by a most spectacular high brick wall with ornate archways. At this time of year the garden is abundant with the scent of mature rose bushes, the colours all told are quite exquisite."

Vivien glanced back towards Mrs Sutton who stood there open-mouthed unsure as to what had just happened. Vivien's expression was one of the same as she was led away. Then, Mrs Sutton gave a brief uncharacteristic laugh out loud. The penny dropped. It all made sense. *You silly old woman,* she chastised herself, as she poured a cup of tea and sat at the table with a warmed cheese scone. The smile never left her lips.

Rose Dunn dried her hands on her worn blue apron and embraced her daughter tightly. "Goodness, child," she said frantically, "I was worried about you, it's just on 6 o'clock and you should've been back hours ago."

"Oh Ma, I'm sorry, I've had an amazing day at the Manor. Mrs Sutton is the nicest lady and she showed me a little of the kitchen up there. And what a kitchen it is Ma. But mostly I was with Master Adam, he was so kind and showed me all around the grounds and made me some lunch and afternoon tea. I didn't get to meet the Squire, but I've seen him around the orchards. Come, Ma and I'll tell you all about it. Let's sit outside and I'll help you with supper.

"Tommy!" said Vivien excitedly, as her brother entered the hut much later in the evening. "Where have you been? I wanted to tell you about my day."

"I don't like it, you being there," he said gruffly, as he moodily chucked himself on to his bunk. "You keep away from the Squire's son, do you hear me? He ain't no good. STAY AWAY."

"Oh Tommy, he isn't so bad, he was very pleasant to me today…"

"I bet he was," Tommy said angrily, as he turned and eyed his sister closely. "Why do you have to go there anyway? You belong here. There is more than enough work here in the hop garden earning money for the family, so we can survive."

"Tommy, they are paying me and it's only going to be for ten hours a week, and they will pay me more than I am getting working on the hops for a full day's work. Now, if you don't mind I'm going to bed and stop being so beastly."

Tommy was taken aback by Vivien's remarks. He was used to guiding and protecting his sister, but he now felt that she was already slipping away from him. He knew she would break away one day and this turning point stung him more than any punch that he received in the ring. He couldn't help his need to protect her, he loved her truly and God help anyone who hurt her. He stared up at the ceiling. *For goodness sake,* he thought, *I've got five weeks of being on alert before we go back to the smoke. I need to sort this once and for all.*

He had stewed for a whole damn year on what Adam had said to him about Vivien. He knew Adam was drunk but what he said kept going round and round in his head and he couldn't let go. He had tried to exhaust his aggression in the ring but to no avail. If anything, it had become worse.

Tommy still felt sick thinking about what had happened just a few months ago. Mr Doherty, his trainer, had introduced him to Adam, a new sparring partner, and instantly, on *hearing* that name it had been like a red rag to a bull. When the bell had dinged two of Tommy's mates and Mr Doherty had to forcibly drag him off of Adam. Tommy had regretted his actions immediately. He couldn't tell anyone, except for Smithy, the reason for his enraged behaviour.

Tommy had received an almighty ear bashing from his trainer. "WHAT THE FUCK WAS THAT ABOUT?" blared Mr Doherty. The shocked trainer was so red in the face from anger that Tommy had thought he would burst a blood vessel.

"You disgust me. I trained you better than that and now you throw it all back in my face." His voice had grown louder as he got nearer to Tommy, prodding him with his fat tobacco stained digit where each syllable sent bits of white warm spittle flying all over Tommy's face. Tommy had desperately wanted to wipe it away but didn't dare move.

"You a big man?" Mr Doherty had hollered, pushing Tommy backwards. "You wanna street fight?" He pushed him again. "You wanna go bare-knuckle?" He pushed him for a third time. "Well, not on my time, not under my roof, do ya hear me? Do ya? Ah, get outta my sight you thug. You ain't nothing but a cheap two-a-penny fucking thug, you ain't what I thought you were. You ever come here again, I meself'll make sure that your boxing career will be permanently over jus like that poor kid in there. Clear ya locker and fuck the hell off my property before I cap yer."

Mr Doherty ended his rant by giving Tommy one final shove where the gym lockers broke his fall, the contents of which could be heard crashing to the floor. Mr Doherty marched out of the changing room and slammed the door so hard that the loose robe hook on the back jumped free of the screw and fell to the stone floor. The screw rolled away and twanged beside the metal spit bucket.

That was the last Tommy had heard or seen of his trainer. He had planned on going to see him when he got back from hopping, to apologise, and hope that Mr Doherty might take him back on a helping out basis until his suspension period was over. He missed the training and being in the ring and he missed all his mates. It had been a long few months.

Tommy had tried to make it up to the young boxer with the unfortunate name, but with a broken eye socket, busted jaw and severe concussion, his boxing days were well and truly over before they had begun. Tommy would live with the guilt that he had ruined the lad's promising career. He had tried twice to visit him in the hospital. The first time he had walked nervously through the corridor clutching a brown paper bag that contained an orange that he'd acquired at the docks from a consignment due for Covent Garden. But, the sight of a policeman stationed outside the ward had panicked Tommy who immediately fled.

The second attempt the following day caused more sorrow when he saw Adam's heartbroken mother crying by her son's bedside. Tommy had felt like a true shit.

Miraculously, the young boxer didn't want to press charges, much to the annoyance and frustration of his family. Tommy was suspended from boxing for six months and ordered to pay Adam five pounds in damages. That was almost the entirety of Tommy's life savings, but he gave it gladly. All his mindless stupidity caused because of a name. He needed to get his head and temper in control to begin and make amends.

He had heard on the grapevine that a gang of lads were out for him to take revenge for what he had done to their friend. He wasn't surprised, he'd be out for revenge too if it were one of his friends. He wasn't a coward either and would cross that bridge if and when. But, knowing this had made him a little more wary of his surroundings, particularly when walking down dark alleys and out and about at a late hour.

Albert Dunn was quiet and placid by nature but, on his return from work when he learned of his son's actions, he had grabbed Tommy forcibly by the upper arm and dragged him outside into their modest back garden. He had spun his son around and for the first time ever he hit Tommy with a right hook that sent him lunging backwards into the wall. The action winded Tommy, who slumped to the ground trying to catch his breath, while his father turned and walked away.

Rose was distraught as she witnessed the punishment through the kitchen window. She knew Tommy had to be punished but it was still hard to bear. Albert was a good father and he reprimanded as he saw fit and for that she would not interfere. It broke Albert's heart when he re-entered the kitchen and saw his wife crying. He knew they would talk it over later so he continued through to the parlour to cool off. Vivien had been oblivious to all that had taken place and he was thankful for that.

Motherly instinct made Rose run out into the garden to check on her son. He was embarrassed that she had seen him like this and when she reached out to console him he waved her away. He clambered unsteadily to his feet and clutched his jaw as he walked through the gate to the alleyway leading to the street to lick his wounds and take stock of his actions. The whole episode had taken place without a word being spoken. Rose just wanted to hold her son, she knew he was hurting mostly from pride, and she dabbed a tear with the corner of her housecoat.

Tommy went into hiding for a couple of days staying with Smithy who, like the true friend he was, didn't shun him like so many others had. Despite the short beating, Tommy respected his father and accepted his punishment. He hadn't even tried to block the punch that went against all his training. The irony was, Tommy thought, his quiet, placid father would've made one hell of a heavyweight.

As he now got ready for bed in the hop-pickers hut, Tommy inhaled deeply. The earthy and deep scent of hops calmed him but he still planned on getting the Squire's son alone one evening and out of sight of prying eyes so they could continue their chitchat. He deeply regretted his decision last year when he just walked away, believing he should've bashed Adam at the time. This, he believed, would've gotten the bastard out of his system and then that boxing incident with the other Adam wouldn't even have happened. So many lives would have been so different now if only he had dealt with the trouble at the outset instead of letting it fester into something bigger.

The next couple of days were somewhat trying for the Dunn family. Rose and Albert, although committed to their working holiday and involvement with orchard life with the other families managed to find a few private moments to discuss the changes in their children. They always knew Tommy was overly protective towards Vivien and that he was unhappy with her working at the Manor. Even though for them, the Squire's son was a concern, they were blissfully unaware of what Adam had said to Tommy in the orchard the year before. Surprisingly, they found the most significant change was from Vivien herself. This once shy, complying girl had almost overnight gained a fighting spirit. She started to speak up for herself, which Tommy was finding hard to accept. Although taken aback by the sudden change in their daughter they were pleased at her newly gained strength and confidence.

At tea break the next morning the workers sat down to a well-earned rest. The women kept an eye on the children and occasionally flicked the air with a tea cloth to deter any wasps that flew too near the youngsters who drank warm squash from beakers. The adults gathered around and drank cups of tea from chipped metal mugs. Some had a dunking contest to see whose biscuit would last the longest as they dipped their biscuit, trying their hardest to time it just right before it became too soggy, eroded and sank to the bottom of the mug. There was nothing worse than taking the final swig of tea only to get a mouthful of biscuity pulp.

Chapter Thirty-Four

Eric Collins was just entering the hop field on his morning rounds when he came across Albert.

"Albert, good morning to you," he said.

"Good morning Eric, how's tricks?"

"Good thanks. How are things with everyone today?"

"Ay, not bad. No complaints so that's good." He pondered a moment... "It probably isn't worth any breath..." he said, as he scratched his salt and pepper beard, "but was told that some townies were askin' questions in the Oak Pub as to the Squire's son last night."

"Townies, you say?"

"Ay, not hoppers. Some of me china's heard in the pub. Personal questions like, wanting the whereabouts of him."

"Trouble?" pondered Eric.

"Who's ter say, but got the feeling they weren't askin' for his wellbeing, so surmise it ain't no good. You know Vivien's working at the Manor? She likely to be involved with any trouble there? Need to know Eric, you understand that."

"Yes, I understand Albert. I know Adam was involved in a string of bad debts a while back that is why he came back to the village. But that's common knowledge and as I said, it was a while ago. Can't think of anything else. Besides, the Squire and Mrs Sutton wouldn't have any nonsense at the Manor. Your Vivien will be safe enough, it's not like..."

Albert raised his eyebrows. "Like living in London, you were going to say?"

"Sorry. You know what I mean. The country is different you know that, no offence 'ol man."

"Ay, none taken. Different worlds."

"I'll mention it this afternoon at our weekly meeting with the Squire though. That way there's no opening for taking things the wrong way. Between me and you Albert, I've never really taken to that son of his; don't trust him as far as I could pick him up if truth be told. How many men doing the asking?"

"Three, and from what I was told he had better watch his back because they meant business and wouldn't be surprised if they were carrying." As Albert lightly tapped his hip making Eric stare back at him with eyes widened. Different world's indeed.

"Thanks Albert. I'll keep you posted and please not a word to anyone. Something like this can be blown out of all proportion."

"No more said, bid you good day," Albert said, tipping his cap in farewell before he went on his way to morning tea.

Eric mulled it over all morning as to what Albert had said and arrived at the Manor's office shortly after two, greeted by Pat Dawson. Eric had liked Pat right from the start. He was a decent man and a good manager and Eric knew that William would have approved. Pat had fitted well into the estate and Primrose Cottage with his family and shortly afterwards he had asked Eric to be his second-in-command to which Eric had accepted much to the delight of the Squire.

On the table before them, underneath muslin cloth to keep out the flies, was a china plate of freshly prepared tomato sandwiches. Mrs Sutton had delivered them to the office alongside a tall glass jug of homemade blackcurrant squash and four upturned glasses before she cycled into the village to get some supplies.

"Good afternoon Squire, Adam," said Pat and Eric as they stood waiting for the Squire to sit.

"Pat, Eric," acknowledged the Squire. Adam ignored the men and started to eat the sandwiches like he hadn't eaten for days.

"What's the latest on production Pat? Are we on schedule?" asked the Squire as he side-glanced disapprovingly at Adam for his lack of manners.

"Actually, we are just ahead on production Squire," reported Pat, which caused the Squire to smile.

"Splendid, splendid, that's good news. You have it all under control. There was nothing else pressing really, just wanted an update..."

"Pardon me Squire," said Eric "but I've heard that there were three townies in The Oak Pub last night asking questions regarding Master Adam. I have it on good authority that they mean business. I just wanted you all to be aware of this. So, as there is no more pressing estate business, we will leave you to discuss." Eric tipped his cap at the Squire and quickly ushered himself and Pat out of the office. The Squire then continued to stare at Adam who stopped chewing as the blood drained from his face.

"Sorry about that Pat," said Eric as the men walked across the courtyard, "but thought it best that we left. I don't think it will be pretty in there."

"Understandably 'ol man," said Pat, as he offered Eric a toffee from a small bag as they made their way to the workshop.

"CHRIST ADAM, NOW WHAT?" blared the Squire, as he thumped his fist hard on the table causing Mrs Sutton's blackcurrant glasses to rattle in protest.

"There's nothing more father, I promise you," said Adam in

shock. It was rare to hear his father swear and knew that he had finally pushed him to breaking point. "I haven't gambled and have no outstanding debts, I'm in the clear. Honestly."

"Apparently not," said the Squire as he paced the room.

"I am, I am. That's all behind me now, you know that."

"I stupidly thought this was all behind us," the Squire said quietly as he composed himself. "Let me make this perfectly clear, son. As much as I support you, let it be known that if you so much as bring a whisker of trouble to my door after all that we have been through to make it right, I will personally throw you out for good.

"No coming back. No excuses. You stand on your own two feet and sort this mess out. Think long and hard as to what it might be and put it right as your whole future, your independence and your inheritance depends on it. Is this clear?" The Squire's eyes locked sternly with his son's and in that moment, Adam was scared.

"Clear father." He bowed his head feeling like a reprimanded schoolboy. He genuinely did not have a clue as to what this latest trouble was about.

"Good. Now get out there." The Squire pointed toward the door. "Find it before it finds you. I vow, that if I hear of any trouble on the estate it will be YOUR head that rolls. I suggest you start with The Oak Pub and speak to Mr Vinter."

How strange, thought Mrs Sutton as she approached the turnoff to Foxden Orchard on her way back from the village store. Three tall men stood across the lane blocking her way. "Can I help you?" she called out as she brought her bicycle to a stop and dismounted.

"That depends, grandma," said the first man as he slowly approached her.

"Don't you 'grandma' me, young man. Who are you?" she

demanded, forcing herself to sound strong while inside she was very scared. The men were menacing with their gaunt faces and all dressed in black. They looked like vultures intimidating their prey.

For one confused moment she thought they may be Germans and that she would be taken prisoner. But the war was well and truly over. If they were not Germans then, who were they?

"We'll ask the questions, grandma," said the second man, who had a huge scar down his cheek, as he too approached her. They all had thick greased back hair and their unshaven faces, somewhat crumpled jackets together with whiffs of body odour suggested that they had slept out in the open for a couple of days at least.

"Are you the old bird who resides at the Manor?" asked the third man menacingly as he leered at her. His breath was rancid like he had eaten rotten cabbage and the foul smell and his knowledge of who she was, shocked her.

"What's your business?" she said defensively. How dare these upstarts try and frighten her. She'd seen off many a ragamuffin in the past. But her instincts told her to beware. These men were dangerous.

"Feisty eh?" laughed the first, "just like my 'ol ma. Right, enough is enough Duchess. No more fooling. We're after Adam Marsh. Tell us where he is and you'll not get hurt."

Her eyes followed his movements as he opened his jacket to reveal a pistol. Her reflexed gasp added to the thugs' pleasure. Rifles were a way of life living on the estate but this was something much more sinister. As much as she detested Master Adam, she did not want him dead.

Moving closer still, their stance blocked out the sunlight leaving her in a cool shadow. She was intimidated and hated herself for it.

She felt weak and helpless when one of them rummaged through her wicker basket and slowly but deliberately dropped each package to the ground, eyeing her for a reaction. The first to go was a bag of flour, then a bag of sugar closely followed by a packet of butter.

"STOP IT. STOP IT," shouted an angered Mrs Sutton while at the same time frantically ringing her bicycle bell. The thought of precious produce being wasted enraged her so much that it overtook her fear. Her voice carried such volume and venom that it caused the grocery vandal to take a step backwards in amazement.

"Harry?" the one with the scar questioned.

"No names, you idiot," came Harry's angry reply, as he quickly covered Mrs Sutton's hand with his own to snuff the bell. Mrs Sutton winced in pain as her tiny thumb was forced into the metal bell lever. "Listen grandma, no more fooling, tell us or we'll have no problem hurting you. We have ways of getting information that won't be so pleasant. Do we have an understanding?" he said, bending over to match Mrs Sutton's height and looking her directly in the eyes. Mrs Sutton was just about to reply when...

"Oi," came a loud shout from out of nowhere. The thugs spun around looking for the source. Mrs Sutton gave a brief smile of relief and wiped away a solitary teardrop.

"What's going on? Get away from her," shouted the lone voice that seemed to carry on for miles. "Smithy, get the coppers, Pete you go with him and get the other men from the orchard." Tommy Dunn stepped up and over the orchard gate and walked towards Mrs Sutton.

"Just a misunderstanding son," said Harry, as the men backed away from Mrs Sutton. "See you grandma, come on lads let's go." And with that the three men turned and walked back towards the village. Another opportunity would present itself. It always did.

"You alright Mrs?" asked Tommy as he tried to retrieve some of the groceries.

"Thank you," said a relieved Mrs Sutton holding onto the handlebars tightly to stop herself from shaking. "You're Tommy Dunn, aren't you? Vivien's brother?"

"Yes, Mrs. What was that about then?"

"Oh, please catch up with your friends," said Mrs Sutton in alarm as she pointed to the hedgerow, "Stop them from going to the authorities. There is no need now, I won't report it. Thank you, to all of you. I am just so pleased you came along at the right time."

"Well, it's just me really, Mrs. I made that bit up, but it did the trick didn't it?" Tommy laughed and shrugged his shoulders. He was relieved that his bluff had paid off as he wasn't too sure that he would've been able to take on all three men.

Mrs Sutton was shocked at this but admired Tommy's quick thinking. She decided she wouldn't tell him about the pistol that she had seen. And likewise, Tommy wasn't about to reveal that he had heard most of the conversation. He had been taking a rest and was lying down on the other side of the hedge. He now knew that Adam was in big trouble for some reason. To have hired muscle looking for him meant that even bigger fish were out for him. But what had he done?

"Not much harm done, Mrs," said Tommy as he inspected the produce and put it back in the basket. "You shouldn't have any more trouble from those apes, but I'll walk back to the Manor with you." Tommy started to push the bicycle and held out his arm to which Mrs Sutton gladly took for support. She still felt a bit shaky.

"Thank you Tommy. I'll make you a nice cup of tea when we get there. I think we could both do with it!"

Later that evening, Tommy looked dapper in his best togs and despite still feeling hatred for Adam, he also felt a tad optimistic about the future.

He was twenty-one, good-looking even with his flattened boxer's nose. He always received admiring glances from pretty lasses of all ages and his ample charm meant that he was never far from female attention. As he walked out of the orchard and down the lane towards the village he reflected that today had been unusual but very productive and he was looking forward to having a pint or two with his mates.

To round off the perfect evening he might even get a kiss or two, or maybe more, with Maggie Harris who was living at the pub and had more than caught his eye recently. *The poor girl, she doesn't stand a chance against my almighty charisma,* he thought with a playful smile. He had known Maggie since they were children and they had more or less grown up together through the hop seasons when the villagers and Londoners came together. But this year was different. At eighteen, Maggie certainly wasn't a child anymore and the few flirting glances over the bar told Tommy that Maggie liked him too.

As dusk approached, the sky was awash with vivid pinks and deep apricots and by shepherds delight it would be another unusually warm autumn day tomorrow. He smiled to himself as he thought more about Maggie. He gently kicked a loose stone along the lane avoiding the potholes towards an imaginary goal post. He kicked, he scored and when he threw his arms in the air to celebrate he couldn't believe his luck. Lo and behold as if by magic, he saw Adam walking down towards the village also. *What good fortune,* he thought.

Adam's mind was on finding the three men who were looking

for him and cleaning up this mess from his doorstep. He had just started to get his life together, had met a beautiful girl he was sweet on and was finally getting his relationship with his father back on track. Before he had left earlier he grabbed a wad of money that he had saved and was confident that he could pay the thugs off and, more importantly, learn who had sent them and why. He had searched his brain all afternoon trying to think what the hell it could be about.

There was only one thing that he thought he had gotten away with. But that was so many years ago he genuinely doubted it could be that. His head had been in a really bad place back then and she had sworn she wouldn't go to the police. He had made damn sure she wouldn't by bashing her to within an inch of her life. Stupid whore. But that was years ago and he had turned over a new leaf. He was a changed man who deserved a second chance. Vivien, at seventeen years of age, had changed everything and suddenly, after all these years, life was finally worth living.

Generations of excellent education and refinement showed in his stance as he swaggered down the lane. At twenty-eight he was a relatively young man but his receding hairline aged him more than it should. His physique was powerful and on the outset he was quite handsome to women. Although, after a short time, most women found that his aloofness, sparse personality and clandestine heinous conduct meant that he didn't date the same woman for very long.

Once, he had confronted a woman who had dared to turn down a second date to ask the reason why. Her brutally honest response had struck a nerve and temporarily wounded him. He had silenced her with a swift backhand when she explained that a woman's built-in sense triggered when they were near dangerous or creepy men. "By the way," he had spat, as he winched her up by the throat and looked into petrified eyes. "Your sense works." He slapped her brutally again and calmly walked away, leaving her heaped and unconscious on the floor.

He was, however, a red-blooded male with what he thought were normal needs and desires. What he couldn't get for free with a bit of coercing or force he would frequently pay for. In the old days these specialities had cost him dearly, or rather, had cost his unknowing father.

He had been a relentless rogue in the past; some would say a heartless bastard. Yes, he had given his father a hard time. Yes, he had done many things he was not proud of and regretted. Yes, yes, yes to all of them. But in a short space of time, Vivien had changed his whole world for the better. She had opened up his mind to see everything from newborn eyes. He felt he had been given a second chance and he would do his utmost to make amends to everyone he had wronged. It was time to stop blaming everyone else and to take full responsibility for his actions, to be decent and to move on.

It was crazy but he knew he truly loved Vivien and, more importantly, he sensed that Vivien felt the same in their short sweet courtship.

This delightful, beautiful woman had rescued him and he was not going to let her down. The eleven-year age gap didn't bother them and for once in his life, Adam actually respected another human being. He knew he would never harm her; he genuinely loved her. Even his secret desires about getting revenge on her brother absconded and that was something he never in his wildest dreams believed could happen.

Vivien would be going back to London very soon and he

desperately wanted her to stay. He couldn't bear waiting a whole year until he saw her again and knew that her parents, her father and her brother in particular, would put a stop to Vivien seeing him.

Tommy spotted Adam walking towards him just as the three townies were leaving the pub. They too spotted the pair and ran towards them as they approached the fork in the road.

Tommy's boxer's instinct kicked in immediately and he sprinted as fast as he could towards Adam. In one fair swoop whilst still running he grabbed a handful of Adam's shirt by the shoulder and dragged him backwards. Adam's arms flung about like a drunk windmill as he tried to stay balanced much to the townies' confusion.

"It seems all four of us are after you, you bastard," Tommy hissed in Adam's ear. "We'll do this my way. Don't argue, hand over all your money, NOW!"

"What are you talking about?" he stammered.

"Look, there's no time," said Tommy urgently blocking the men's view of the situation, "hand over whatever loot you have. You're mine son, I haven't wasted a whole fucking year so others can take this away from me. No way."

The men didn't see Adam hand over his wallet that Tommy pocketed quick as lightening. Tommy then let go of Adam's shirt and turned around shielding Adam from the men who were now upon them.

"Well, well, well." Cabbage breath smirked, as he looked Tommy up and down. "It seems gentlemen that Mr Do-gooder here crosses our path once again. Isn't rescuing little old ladies enough for you for one day?"

"Small world ain't it?" said Scarface, stepping forward. The nasty scar down the left side of his face ran from his protruding ear to his stubbly chin giving him a menacing look. Tommy hadn't noticed this earlier and was now starting to regret what he had run into.

"Yes, gentlemen," said Tommy putting on his best apologetic smile. "This morning was different. It's not right three big men like yourselves bullying a little old lady, and you know it. What if she was your 'ol granny? Wouldn't like it would ya? Now, it's different again. You see it's like this..." said Tommy as he stepped closer to the men and gently lead them away from Adam's earshot. "We have a slight problem here gentlemen to which there is a simple answer and an all-round win solution that's satisfactory to all," he said in a conspiring whisper engaging all three men who were quite intrigued as to what this young oik had to say for himself.

"What's 'e on about 'Arry?" asked Scarface in confusion.

"What'd I tell you before about using names? Now shut the fuck up and let me sort it," snapped Harry. "Now, oik. You are once again in my face," leered Harry, "And if you are in my face, your face will get smashed. Get it? Now, this is all good unexpected entertainment and the boss didn't say that we couldn't have some fun along the way. Believe me that nothing would give me more pleasure than to rough up that pretty boy face, but time's money. Get out of our way and poke your nose in someone else's business or end up brown bread. Your choice son…"

"And what slight problem is that then?" interrupted Cabbage breath hoping to get to the bottom of the whole matter as he leaned in closer.

Tommy quickly went into his plot hoping that these planks bought his story. They were obviously the employed muscle and it didn't look like they possessed a brain cell between them. Yes, this was turning out to be a very good day indeed and he didn't plan on being brown bread for many years to come.

"Look gentlemen, we're obviously after the same man,"Tommy said. "I am also after this gentry bastard. I've invested a whole year, a whole damn fucking year tracking him down, can you believe that? He did the dirty on my sister and he's gonna pay big time. Believe me, I intend to make him pay. Now you wouldn't begrudge a fella for doing the right thing by his sister would ya? What if she were your sister mate? How'd you feel? You know I'm doing the right thing don'tcha?"

All three nodded in agreement and Tommy knew that he had them eating out of his hand. Time to wrap this thing up.

"I'm gonna have this bastard singing by the balls,"Tommy said gleefully "By the end of closing time, believe me gentlemen, he's gonna squeal like a pig on heat when I put his meat and two veg through the vice. You understand?" said Tommy, pointing towards his trouser department with cutting movements making the men cringe.

"Look, mate," said Harry who was obviously the leader, "I understand your predicament, but we have a job to do or it's *our* balls in the vice." He opened his jacket to reveal the piece inside, which sent shivers down Tommy's spine. He now knew that he was in over his head.

"Shit, that for real?" he said without thinking "Look, whatever he's done, it's between him and you, but I want him too. How about we strike a deal?"

"Like what?" said Harry.

"Money. Gentlemen. Money. It makes the whole world go sweetly round so they say. Save your bullet for another day. Take the cash and walk away. Tell the boss man you've sorted it. Have a good time and treat the ladies."Tommy opened up Adam's wallet and was shocked to see the wad of fivers inside. He'd never seen so much money together in one place. There was an audible gasp from the trio who never would have thought that an oik would possess such money, let alone carry it in broad daylight.

"Who'd ya rob for that then?" leered Scarface.

"Good honest labour gentlemen, good honest labour. There are fifty big ones," he said as he counted each note before them, "I plead to your better nature as I've waited a long time for this. What yer say?" Tommy held the cash and his breath and hoped that his ace card would seal the deal.

Cabbage breath stepped forward and snatched the fifty and the expensive leather wallet from Tommy's hand and stuffed them into his pocket while Harry leaned forward and gently tapped Tommy twice on the cheek with his calloused hand. Then they turned and walked back towards the pub. Both Tommy and Adam watched as the men got into their black car and drove off without even giving a clue about why they were after Adam.

Adam ran up to Tommy with a smile and relief on his face. His recent judgement had been right, Tommy was a good man. Although hugely out of pocket and still none the wiser about which particular past indiscretion had caught up with him, he was grateful for the rescue.

"Thank you Tommy. I don't know what I would have done if you had not come along," he said with his hand outstretched.

"What?" exclaimed Tommy as he looked at Adam's hand in disgust as if he had just pulled it out of a steaming cowpat. Adam didn't even see the punch coming and the next thing he knew he was on the ground nursing a painful jaw. "You think that because I saved you from those apes that you're off the hook? Far from it, we've unfinished business. I hate you with a vengeance that you wouldn't believe you thick bastard, I was never gonna let them have you.

"Come, we've a lot to chat about..." he said, as he dragged Adam off the ground and led him back down the lane towards the quieter side of Foxden Orchard with the large apple tree where it all began one year before.

Chapter Thirty-Five

The full moon made it easy to navigate through the orchard. There was silence all around. It was nothing like the city, it was too quiet. *The country is a weird place,* Tommy thought.

He guided Adam to a spot in the far west corner where conveniently there were two upturned apple logs placed opposite one another. Tommy forced Adam to sit. It was a perfect place to have a private talk without interruptions.

"It's been a long time coming," began Tommy as he looked at Adam's worried and confused face.

"I have put a lot of thought into this myself," said Adam as he looked over his right shoulder at the very tree where he'd been tied up. This was where he'd ranted and drunkenly raged his tirade at Tommy and his friend, and he now shuddered at the thought of what he had said about Vivien. He looked back to Tommy.

"And what did you come up with I am interested to know?" said Tommy, as he also eyed the tree. He pulled a flick knife from his pocket and pressed the catch. The blade caught the moon and reflected a piercing light into Adam's eyes. Tommy picked up a small fallen branch and began to whittle.

"To be honest with you," said Adam, as he glanced at the knife wondering *how much worse this day was going to get*. "I imagined it to be straight forward fisticuffs with no talking. I know that's all you Londoners understand..." he said unthinkingly and immediately regretted it, fully aware of the flick knife and Tommy's mood.

"That's the problem with you toffs," said Tommy as he pointed the knife in Adam's direction, "you believe us 'commoners' are the scum of the earth. What's all this 'fisticuffs' private schoolboy horseshit? I am a boxer, with discipline," he cringed as he thought of his recent behaviour, "I am not proud of the way I am thinking right now and I do not know why I am explaining myself. You bring out the worst in me, you posh prick." Tommy grew more angry. "Just because you were born with a silver spoon stuck up your arse you believe you have the right to look down on me like you stepped into a bucket of warm shit. A man, a real man, earns respect in this life and you have earned Jack. Get it? You piss me off beyond belief that you treat the 'not so privileged people' like dirt and when you made that remark last year about my sister I saw red. You don't know us, we're good people earning an honest quid. And you? You take, take, and take.

"You spend Daddy's money, that would take my family a lifetime to earn, and you take for granted what's in front of your stupid pathetic face. Well, I know about you, your background and you are a bad un and no doubt deserved a good kicking from those thugs. You have no loving home, have no mother and were passed from pillar to post as a kid. The poor little rich boy that nobody wanted or loved. Just an outcast with nothing more than a huge chip on his shoulder.

"Well, I've no pot to piss in. But, what I have you cannot buy, which makes me far richer than you'll ever be. You hear me?" Tommy was shaking from temper and when after a few moments of silence he looked up from his carving, he saw a glisten of a tear in Adam's eyes. He knew that he had hurt Adam more than a bullet or going ten rounds in the ring. Tommy felt a sudden release from his yearlong torture. This had turned out better than he'd ever imagined. Perhaps he would now be free to move on. The revelation almost made Tommy cry too.

"You're right," said Adam. "You're perfectly right and for that I am truly sorry believe it or not. I did not envisage this turn out either, I thought we'd be locked into a bloodied fight. I was wrong to say that about Vivien and I am truly sorry..."

"Don't you dare say her name," Tommy spat rising to his feet, "you are not worthy to even think about my sister."

"But, I thought..."

"You thought nothing. Nothing has changed. I accept your apology for what it's worth. We were both angry but you are not to see my sister anymore. The damage has been done. We are all going back to the smoke soon and you'll never see her again. She will not come down next year."

Rising, an angered Adam said, "Don't you think that is Vivien's choice, not yours?"

"She'll do as she is told." Tommy once again pointed the knife in Adam's direction.

"You are not her parent and Vivien has a mind of her own. We are good together, if only you could see that. I have changed Tommy; your wonderful sister has changed me for the better. I have a lot to offer her. We could have a good and happy life together..."

"You'll end this now or I will end you tonight."

"Are you threatening me?" Adam squared up to Tommy.

"Call it what you like. This is between the three of us. You, me, and my little friend here." He wagged the knife in front of Adam's eyes.

"This is getting us nowhere," said Adam as he sat back down hoping to take the heat out of the situation. "We were beginning to make a little progress. Look, it all stemmed from me being stupidly drunk last year and knocking your friend's beer. I was in the wrong; I admit it and I want to put everything right. I spoke without thinking last year. My head was in a bad place. You were right, I didn't know you or your family and I had no right to speak of Vivien in that way.

"Please understand that at the time I just wanted to hurt you, but no more. I was angry at being tied up, angry at you and your friends escorting me out of the pub. I was seriously out-numbered, you lot threw beer over me, marched me here, tied me up and left me. Words were all the ammunition I had. Can't you see that? And for that I now apologise to you.

"I was tied up all bloody night, I was in a right state. My legs and arms ached beyond belief, I was bitten to hell by gnats, I threw up three times and pissed myself too. I stank to bloody high heaven."

Tommy laughed.

"Glad you are amused," whispered Adam. "I was untied at dawn by a young sniggering farm-hand and to make sure the story didn't go around the village like wild-fire I paid him five pounds. Next to me he was the richest bloody person in the village and whenever I see him he just smirks like he has one over on me and there is nothing I can do about it. Look, can't we let bygones be bygones and move on?"

"It's too late for that, damage has been done. You will never be good enough for my sister."

"Be honest with yourself, Tommy. In your opinion, no man will ever be good enough for your sister and you know it."

"Anyone but you," he spat back.

"You know it." Adam held Tommy's stare.

"Stay away," Tommy said calmly "I have ended one man's career and I have no problem with ending another."

"You know I'm right, you just can't admit it can you? It's not natural you feeling like that. Not natural." Adam watched Tommy's face closely. "Anyone would think that *you* had *feelings* for her. Is that it? Is that what's tearing you apart?"

"I don't have to listen to any more of your bullshit, you arrogant prick. Stay away from Vivien or I will kill you in a blink of an eye and that 'ol son, is a given."

"What do you think Vivien would say if she could hear you talking like this?"

"That about sums you up, you are not a man. That's little schoolboy stuff, running telling tales and twisting things. This is between us. End it gently or I will catch up with you and Daddy won't recognise you, you hear?"

Adam didn't bother to reply. He knew he wasn't going to get through to Tommy tonight. He turned around and slowly walked out of the orchard. Tommy was shaking with anger at Adam and at himself by being out of control. After a couple of minutes he walked a few paces towards the hedgerow and at a particular spot kicked his foot sideways, which made a metal sound confirming that the crow bar was still in place.

Suddenly, Tommy was consumed by an overwhelming rage. He bent down and retrieved the crowbar in one quick snatch feeling the comforting heavyweight in his hand, ignoring the sudden sharp pain from the stinging nettles. He sprinted through the orchard that was now awash with shadows courtesy of roaming clouds and a sudden southerly wind.

Tommy's head was suddenly over-powered by thousands of inner voices all demanding his full attention. They were as loud as the audiences at one of his boxing matches: *Hunt him down, make him pay, kill the bastard once and for all.*

He picked up pace as adrenalin spurred him on faster and faster, he was near the end of the orchard and had to get to Adam before he reached the road. This was his only chance, he had to run faster. Then rounding a slight bend as he saw Adam's shadow a little way ahead, his boot caught the rim of a rusty bicycle wheel. With the speed he was travelling, Tommy fell hard to the ground as if a giant had come up behind him and swot him like a fly. He was winded for a quite a while and forced himself to stay still while he assessed possible injury. He was relieved he hadn't banged his head but the pain coming from his collarbone revealed that he'd landed on the head of the crowbar. There was no blood but there would be an almighty bruise and he'd know soon enough if he had broken or fractured a bone.

After a few minutes Tommy managed to sit up and as he inspected the cause for his untimely tumble he gave a brief laugh that brought him back to his senses. The old bicycle wheel minus the rubber tubing was weighed down with apples and he recalled that he'd seen the children play pretend shops at that spot that very afternoon.

What a difference a few hours could make. That afternoon the orchard had been busy with laughing children and adults going about their day's work and now it was dark and menacing. It so easily could have been an ugly murderous scene, which would have ended the life of two men, one dead and the other spending the rest of his life in prison through one moment of madness.

"I need a beer," said Tommy as he gingerly rose and placed the crow bar against a tree and slowly made his way to the village before last orders. "Bugger that," he corrected, "I need a whisky."

"Tommy 'ol son," cheered Smithy as Tommy walked into The Oak pub. "What'll it be?"

"Whisky for me Smithy and I'm paying."

"What on earth happened to you?" said Smithy, as he looked Tommy up and down. "Looks like you've been in the wars."

"Very funny lad. Had a bit of a run in with a bicycle wheel when I was out rabbiting," laughed Tommy. "Long story, not worth the effort to tell. Come on where's this drink? A man could die of thirst around here."

"Gentlemen," said Mr Vinter, "What'll it be?"

"Mr Vinter, one pint of your finest and a whisky if you please," said Smithy.

"Someone's pushing the boat out tonight," remarked Mr Vinter as he reached down a whisky glass and, after offering it up to the light, decided to give the inside a quick wipe with his barman's apron. "Not many calls for this nowadays," he said. "Special occasion, birthday perhaps?"

"Yes, I've a feeling it's going to be a very good birthday," said Tommy as he winked at Maggie behind the bar whilst at the same time stepping heavily on Smithy's foot before he gave the game away. Tommy knocked back the whisky in one and felt the fire travel all the way down to his stomach. "Oh, that's good. Pity I can only afford one, but tonight is going to be special. I can feel it in me water Smithy." He slapped Smithy on the back. "Another drink?"

"Steady on son, I've still got most of my pint. You're in a funny mood tonight, everything alright?"

"Couldn't be better. And, to top it off, tonight is going to be her lucky night," whispered Tommy, as he smiled in Maggie's direction.

"You reckon do you?" laughed Smithy. "Out of your league son, I've seen her knock back a fair few fellas in 'ere. You won't get past knicker elastic, you mark my words. Oh how'd I love to get beyond her or any knicker elastic," said Smithy as he downed the rest of his pint in a hazy lustful dream.

"It's all show Smithy, she's definitely interested. I'll be way beyond knicker elastic before closing time I guarantee it."

"You're bad," laughed Smithy. "Can I watch?"

"Go and get me a pint, and no you cannot watch you bloody pervert. But, be warned, if I get an inkling you are near I will personally cut off your little man with a blunt pen-knife and feed it to the foxes." Tommy laughed as he pushed Smithy back to the bar.

Whilst Smithy was ordering and keeping Mr Vinter engaged in conversation, Tommy led Maggie further down the bar and out of earshot and whatever he was whispering in her ear was obviously working from the quick glances Smithy could see.

After about ten minutes when Tommy finished his pint he got up and slapped Smithy on the back. "See you tomorrow son, don't wait up. Now, I want you to remember three little words. Blunt knife, foxes."

"Sure thing Tommy, whatever you say you 'ol beggar."

"Night Smithy," said Tommy smiling as he left the pub. Smithy looked around and Maggie was nowhere to be seen. *How does he do it?* he thought, as he walked over to a group of men to join the conversation.

Chapter Thirty-Six

"Come on, this way," ushered Tommy as he led Maggie by the hand through the orchard. The night was still warm and the light breeze danced all around them.

"What are we doing here?" she giggled. The excitement of being here alone with Tommy sent shivers down her spine and the butterflies in her stomach were going nineteen to the dozen.

"Shhh," he said quietly as he brought them to a close embrace where Maggie closed her eyes in anticipation as she tilted her head upwards to him. Suddenly, she gasped as Tommy began kissing her neck tenderly. *How can this be?* she thought. It was a warm evening and yet she had goose bumps. Sensation travelled along her arms down to her knees and ankles. The over-powering sensation was almost torturous. She groaned softly, she wanted more.

Tommy broke away from his kisses and smiled, noticing not for the first time, that Maggie had grown into a beautiful young woman. He knew tonight would be special.

"What are you smiling at?" she asked as she looked into his eyes.

"Just enjoying being here with you, Maggie," he whispered, "you are so beautiful, like a porcelain doll." He had a deep urge to kiss her passionately but it was important to wait, the time would come, but not yet.

"Thank you Tommy, that's lovely." She had never felt more alive and at this moment truly believed she was beautiful and desirable.

She let go of his hands and, still holding his gaze, she reached up and ran her hands tenderly down the side of his face, neck and strong, solid chest until they came to rest on his braces to which she playfully pulled and let go with a twang. They both laughed. Then she grasped them again and pulled him towards her.

Maggie was petite and the thought of being with this handsome, big strong boy consumed her completely. She had never experienced this sort of strong physical attraction before. Her upbringing reinforced that you didn't have sex before marriage but, contrary to her beliefs, she felt ready to take that next step, which both confused and excited her.

Tommy took her hand and led her further into the orchard.

"Where are we going?"

"Come on, this way." They ran towards 'Gentry's tree' as Tommy had so aptly named the tree to which he had tied Adam last year. "Now, young Miss where were we?" he said, as they looked at one another slightly out of breath from their short run.

"Please kiss me before I burst," she said, as he leant down and wrapped his strong arms around the small of her back pulling her towards him even closer and kissing her gently and slowly. She felt as if she was melting as she ploughed her delicate fingers through his thick dark hair.

Tommy could feel the effect his kisses were having on her. *It never fails,* he thought. He liked to tease, to break down defence barriers before he moved in for the kill. These moves always got him beyond knicker elastic, if only Smithy knew – he'd have a few more notches on his bedpost. But, tonight was different, Tommy knew. He felt a deep attraction to Maggie, they had a connection, she was not some quick cheap thrill.

Tommy didn't want to push too far too soon but he was

gradually getting beyond the point of no return. His inner demons that were so alive and powerful earlier in the evening with rage had now been replaced by a deep sexual wanting for the beautiful young woman in front of him. Right here, right now.

"What if somebody sees us?" Maggie asked, suddenly aware of the openness of their surroundings as she looked from side to side scanning the orchard.

"Shhh," he consoled not taking his eyes off her as he tilted her chin so she was once again looking at him. "There's nobody here but us, trust me. We are the only two people in the world right now." He slowly lowered his braces and let them hang by his sides.

Then he swiftly lifted his shirt up and over his head without undoing the buttons and let it drop to the ground. Maggie was breath taken. His bare chest was smooth and powerful and the thought of being embraced by his bare muscles made her tingle even more.

Still testing the waters, he gently kissed her as he slowly pulled down the zip of her summer dress. The straps slipped from her shoulders and rested just above her elbows that only enhanced her ample cleavage even more. He knew at this point that she wasn't wearing a brassiere and broke away briefly from his kisses to admire her.

"Don't think badly of me," she said almost apologetically, "this dress fits so much better without one."

"Oh, I can see that," he winked at her. "You are a truly beautiful woman Maggie, enough to make any man weak at the knees."

"Touch me," she said softly, "I want you to touch me."

Now Tommy had the go ahead he was determined not to rush things, but the ache he felt was gradually becoming too much to bear as he tried his utmost to take it slow. If he spent now he'd never forgive himself. He broke away briefly before it was too late.

"Wait there," he said.

She looked on puzzled as he picked up his shirt and secured it by tying the sleeves together around the trunk of the apple tree about four feet from the ground.

"Now, where were we?" he smiled as he began to slowly remove her dress. She breathed faster in anticipation of what was about to happen. Tommy found this deeply erotic and with one gentle tug her breasts bounced free and the dress fell to the ground. Her body was electrified by tingles she had never experienced before as he cupped her breasts in his hands. He could feel the hardness of her nipples as they pressed against his palms.

"God, you're gorgeous Maggie, I'm a lucky boy," he said breathlessly then kissed her again as he playfully squeezed her nipples with his thumb and index fingers.

Maggie's body was consumed with desire as his arms then wrapped around her and as she stood on tip toe to meet his kiss the sensation as her breasts rubbed against his chest was electrifying. "You're a little over-dressed," she playfully whispered.

"It's soon sorted." He laughed as he whipped off his trousers as they stood before one another.

"Are you laughing at my underwear," he joked, "or are you laughing for the state in which you have got me in?"

"The latter," she said, pleased at the effect that she had on him.

"I'll show you mine, if you'll show me yours," he said with a twinkle in his eye as he stripped off completely. The freedom of being naked in the warm evening air was exhilarating.

"If you want me," she said as she slowly backed up against his shirt so that the bark did not scratch, and raised her arms above her head, "then you'll have to rid me of mine."

"Anything you say Miss," he grinned placing his hands on top of hers then traced them slowly down her body lingering lovingly over her breasts and stomach. Then his hands moved round to her pert bottom where he gave small delicate pinches, all the while delighting in watching Maggie's pleasure. Her head was slightly tilted back against the tree, her eyes were closed and her mouth slightly open as she breathed in short expectant gasps.

Anticipation at being touched in her most vulnerable and desired place was almost too much for Maggie to bear, but Tommy knew what he was doing. Over the top of her panties he teased her, gently stroking then making circling movements everywhere but. She moaned in pure bliss as his fingers finally encircled her most tender spot for a few brief seconds.

He gently removed her panties and continued to drive her wild by circling once again before sweeping her up in his strong arms. With her legs wrapped around his waist, arms loosely around his neck and her back supported by the tree, he kissed and teased with his tongue each breast and as the moonlight reflected on her erect wet nipples they kissed passionately as he entered her and they became one.

Chapter Thirty-Seven

It was the morning that the hop-pickers were due to return to London and the huts were a hive of activity with small children running about in excitement at the train journey ahead. The dew was all but surrendering to the morning sun and it promised to be another fine day.

"Tommy, love. Go an' meet Vivien would you?" asked his mother "She is at the Manor saying her farewells but I thought she'd be back by now and I need her help here."

"Sure Ma," said Tommy as he ran from the hut. "Be back before you know it." Tommy was annoyed that Vivien was at the Manor but told himself that she was saying her goodbyes to Mrs Sutton, as she had grown very fond of the woman over these last few weeks.

"Hey Smithy!" shouted Tommy as he waved to his friend in the next orchard. "See ya next week at The Arms for a pint back at the smoke."

"Sure thing Tommy, see ya then," waved Smithy, who seemed to be laden with various bags from his hut, ready for the journey.

Tommy thought he was ready to go back to the smoke. Although it was hard work, he had enjoyed his break down in Kent. Plus, he had really enjoyed his time with Maggie last night. It had been very special indeed.

"Tommy!" called Maggie, her heart ran aflutter as she ran up to him.

"Hey, good morning Maggie," he beamed. "How are you today?"

"Wonderful, just wonderful. I really enjoyed our time together and was wondering when I would see you again?"

"I would love to see you again soon," he said as he drew her in closer and kissed her passionately. Again, Maggie's knees melted as she yearned for a repeat of the evening before. When they parted, Maggie was suddenly conscious that they were in the street where they had caught the attention of a few passers-by. Simon Dwyer had also seen them from the Post Office window and felt an awkward stab of jealousy that was to dampen his day.

"I need to fetch Vivien or she'll miss the train. I will be here for a couple more days as I have some business in town. Don't tell anyone, but I will be bunked up in the hut at Foxden to keep expenses down. Perhaps you would like to join me tonight, say at seven, and we can sizzle some more?" he said, with a glint in his eye. Maggie nearly melted on the spot. How could she possibly wait until seven?

"Say bye to Vivien from me and I will gladly sizzle with you at seven Tommy," she whispered as she squeezed his hand. She walked back inside the pub as if she was walking on air.

Before he knew it, Tommy was almost at the Manor, and apart from the bustle of the farmhands helping the hop-pickers on their way, it seemed like a normal day in the country. From a distance as he cut through the woodland at the back of the Manor, he could see Mrs Sutton hanging out some tea towels on the washing line and when he moved round a little further he could just see inside the kitchen. He couldn't see Vivien there so he decided to move round a little further.

To Tommy's astonishment, through the garden wall's open archway, he saw Vivien and Adam in a passionate embrace in the herb garden. There they were, bold as brass, in a lover's clinch. Tommy's anger shot to a new high as he sprinted through the woods and leapt the stile to the plush lawns of the Manor. He dodged perfectly pruned rose bushes and through the arch into the herb garden.

Adam and Vivien's perfect mid-morning ended abruptly as Adam was brutally swept off his feet to land heavily on his back. Before he knew what was going on he was being dragged to his feet only to receive what felt like a blacksmith's anvil slamming into his jaw as he again fell to the ground.

Vivien couldn't believe her eyes as her brother acted like a man possessed. "TOMMY, STOP IT!" she shouted hysterically, as she went to Adam's aid helping him to his feet.

"Get your things," Tommy hissed at Vivien. "You're coming with me. Ma wants your help, we're leaving soon."

"I won't leave like this," she said ferociously, as she glared at her brother causing him to take a small step back. No one had ever looked at him like that. Not even in the ring. He was momentarily taken off guard. Or was it that the venomous look had come from his sister, his loving, timid little sister?

"You'll come with me now or I'll finish him off for good, do you hear? And that's a promise," he said, trying to regain control.

Vivien turned away from her brother and slowly guided Adam to the wooden bench by the wall. He appeared groggy and disorientated.

"You really hurt him," admonished Vivien. "And for that you have really hurt me and I will never forgive you." She held Tommy's stare and he instantly knew that he had lost his sister for good. The adrenaline was wearing off and his knuckles throbbed to hell.

"We're leaving," he said gruffly. "Get your stuff."

"Give me a few minutes, you owe me that at least," she said.

"I'll be out front." Tommy turned to leave. "And if you're not there in five minutes, I'm coming back."

"Adam, can you hear me? I am so sorry. My brother has got it in for you very badly and I do not know why."

"It's all right Vivien, I will be fine," said Adam, as he recovered somewhat and tenderly brushed away a tear from Vivien's cheek. "Hey, none of those," he smiled. "It's fine. He's just being protective, he'll come around. I just wish he was a librarian compared to a boxer," Adam said, rubbing his already swollen jaw making Vivien laugh briefly.

"Tommy knows that I was a bad egg and he's looking out for you, we've talked about that haven't we? You know all there is to know about me and that is the way I want things now, all out in the open. We have a future Vivien, a brilliant future. You are my future and I want to be with you always. Tommy wants the best for you, as do I and when he gets to know me better things will be brighter."

"I can't leave you like this," she said, as she lovingly looked at him. "We'd had such a lovely morning and now I must go under these horrible circumstances. I love you Adam and I will be back, I promise. You know that don't you?"

"Yes I do. I love you too. Very much. Now the sooner you go, the sooner you will be back and everything will have righted itself."

They sat in a deep embrace for a precious few minutes before Vivien turned and hurriedly ran through the herb garden and to the clothesline where she gave Mrs Sutton a brief hug and a light kiss on the cheek.

"Goodbye Mrs Sutton and thank you for everything," beamed Vivien with watery eyes. "I can't believe what my idiot brother has against Adam and to hit him like that is like he has hit us both. Tommy has no idea how I feel. Please look after Adam for me. I will be back."

"Goodbye Vivien," smiled Mrs Sutton. "I have really enjoyed your company. I will go and see Master Adam, don't you fret. Until we meet again." They briefly hugged once more then Vivien ran down the side of the Manor and out by the front garden scrunching gravel underfoot to meet her deadline with Tommy.

"How dare you," she spat angrily, as they walked down Honeysuckle Lane. "You had no right to barge in there like that. This is my life and if you cannot accept that Adam and I love each other deeply and have a future together then you, dear brother, have no further part in my life."

"How can you say that?" Tommy said in astonishment. "You've only known him five minutes," he turned to face her, to make her see sense. "And what do you know of love? You're young, you don't know what love is and what it involves, you're just a girl with a schoolgirl crush that will pass."

"Is that so?" She raised her eyebrows, put her hands on her hips and again held his stare in defiance. "And what right have you to solely own that statement of what love involves… What it really involves?…" as she let that linger. Tommy was unable to speak for several moments while he tried to comprehend this awful information. It was like he had been winded in the boxing ring and needed time to recover as the realisation of what Vivien was saying dawned on him.

"How could you?" said Tommy, as he looked at his beloved sister. "How could you? How could he? You're just a child. I'll string him up by the balls and kill the bastard for taking advantage of my little sister. He forced you didn't he?"

"I am most definitely not a child, I am practically eighteen you know that. And no, he most certainly did not force me. We have something special and we have a future together. The plan is to talk to mother and father to tell them how we feel then I want to come back down here to stay."

"You're worlds apart, it wouldn't work. Them and the likes of us, you know that deep down. You are a silly dreaming girl."

"Oh, but that's where you are wrong Tommy," she said calmly. "I'm not a little girl any longer. That's maybe hard for you to accept but it's true. Anybody listening to this would assume that you were my father, not my brother. Let it go Tommy, just let it go. You are stepping into a parent's role when you have no business being there.

"To my brother, I say this," she taunted. "Adam and I love one another and we both enjoy the lustful pleasures of our union that is truly beautiful."

"You're mad," spat Tommy. "He's too old for you. How could you? You are on the brink of becoming nothing more than a common slut."

"How many lovers have you had Tommy?" Vivien asked calmly not rising to further argument. "Quite numerous from what I've heard. Why is it that you are 'Jack the lad' with numerous lovers and for me, the only lover I have makes me a common slut?"

Tommy just looked at his sister in stunned silence as she continued. "From all accounts we both know who the 'common slut' is here, don't we?" And with that she turned on her heel with her head held high and walked back to Foxden alone, as Tommy stared on in disbelief.

For the next few hours Tommy was nowhere to be seen. Earlier that afternoon Vivien was somewhat surprised to learn from her mother that Tommy wouldn't be travelling home with them as he had some boxing business in town and would catch a train within the next day or so. Vivien knew this was for the best, as the journey back wouldn't have been a pleasant one. It would also give her a chance to speak to her parents in private.

Chapter Thirty-Eight

It was just approaching dusk when Tommy walked silently along the village lane towards Foxden when he realised for the first time what village life was all about. The last six weeks were abuzz with the dozens of hop-pickers and families together with the village residents and now the Londoners had left there was almost a deafening silence all around. A silence that Tommy had never known living in the hustle of London.

How on earth can anyone hope to sleep in this silence, he wondered?

All day Maggie had been unable to concentrate on anything except Tommy and had waited impatiently for the evening to arrive. Sally picked up on her mood and overall manner and decided that it must definitely be about a boy, but Maggie wasn't giving too much away.

"I may be late home this evening or maybe not at all," she finally told Sally excitedly. "Please don't be worried and please cover for me with your parents. I'd rather they didn't know."

"Of course, Maggie. Come on tell me, who is he? I know you want to and I'm not letting you out of the pub until you tell me," Sally said eagerly as she tried to stare Maggie down.

"Tommy Dunn, and don't say anything," Maggie blurted.

"Thought they went home today?" Sally said surprised. "Tommy Dunn eh? You lucky girl. He is totally gorgeous. All those muscles. Wow, Tommy Dunn!"

"Yes, wow, Tommy Dunn, he makes me tingle all over."

"I imagine he does," Sally swooned. "When did all this happen?"

"Just recently. Pity that we'd wasted all the weeks they were here though."

"Do you think you'll still see him when he's gone back to London?"

"I certainly hope so, we haven't discussed anything about it yet. Blimey Sally, he makes my heart race."

"Wouldn't mind a bit of heart race myself," said Sally as she led Maggie through to her room, so they could talk more in private.

"When are you seeing that Edward from your office next," said Maggie, "thought he was taking you out to the movies this weekend?"

"Yes, he was, but I made an excuse and said I felt like I was coming down with a cold and wanted to rest up."

"You said you liked him. I thought he was gorgeous when you introduced us the other week."

"Yes, he is attractive, but it was on our last date when he kissed me…"

"Kissing you is a problem? Sally, he obviously likes you enough to invite you out again, what's the problem then?"

"His name is Edward."

"Sorry, you've lost me."

"Dad's name is Edward…"

"Oh, I see. That's a pity."

"Yes it is."

"I say we get a cold squash," said Maggie, "and listen to some music, then we'll style our hair and paint our toenails like we used to do. Let's have a Sally and Maggie afternoon."

"Knock, knock, anyone home?" called Maggie eagerly as she approached the hut's door. Tommy called out to her and when she spun around she saw him leaning against a tree smiling at her. He looked breathtaking wearing a blue short-sleeved shirt beneath his braces. Again her body tingled in anticipation of his touch as she ran and leapt into his arms. She wrapped her legs around his waist as he spun her around kissing her deeply.

"Well, good evening," said Tommy as he gazed into Maggie's eyes. "Fancy seeing you here."

"I had nothing else better do to," she said, as their lips barely parted then they kissed some more as Tommy carried Maggie to the hut's door then closed it behind them. When inside, she was pleasantly overwhelmed to see that there was a gas lamp aglow on the shelf. Tommy had moved the bunks to one side of the hut and had made a makeshift bed by placing all the single mattresses from the bunks together on the floor and had covered them with a clean sheet that he had sprinkled with pink rose petals. The feint petal aroma was on a losing battle with the hop vine garland that was suspended from the ceiling. Beside the bed was a bottle of red wine and two glasses.

"Tommy, this is so romantic."

Tommy was pleased with her reaction as he had enjoyed putting it all together. It helped him take his mind off of Vivien and Adam.

"You deserve the best Maggie and this is the best that I can manage at this time," he said handing her a glass of wine.

"It's perfect. I shall never forget this moment." They sat on the bed and sipped their wine while keeping eye contact and savouring the moment. "Tommy, you are gorgeous," she said, not caring if it sounded daft or not.

"And you are beyond beautiful Maggie," he replied, as he put their glasses to one side then he quickly turned off the gas lamp, then they knelt facing each other, their eyes locking as the subtle moonlight embraced them from the hut's windows. She slowly slid off his braces and rid him of his shirt and Maggie was again in awe at just how beautifully toned he was. Likewise, Tommy slowly unzipped Maggie's peach dress that complimented her figure and long brunette curls perfectly and once more had to contain himself when it fell to her waist. She then briefly stepped up and out of her dress and then lay down. Tommy rid himself of his trousers and lay gently beside her as they kissed passionately.

They were both so consumed with each other that they didn't hear the men approaching the hut until they spoke. "Just this last one to check Pat then we can call it a night."

Maggie broke the kiss and froze knowing it was the voice of Eric Collins. Tommy and Maggie looked at one another fully aware that they were naked and wondering if they were going to be caught.

"Righto Eric," said Pat, "or, how about we just lock up now and come back early tomorrow to check everything in daylight? It'll be easier, it's getting dark fast."

Maggie and Tommy heard the distinct sound of a padlock being fastened to the hut door followed by it being rattled from side to side to make sure that it was securely locked.

"Sounds ideal. Fancy a quick tipple before we go?" said Eric as he produced a hip flask from his pocket.

"Sounds good to me, a few minutes won't do any harm," said Pat as Tommy and Maggie heard the men shuffle to get comfortable as they perched on apple logs against the hut wall barely inches from where Maggie and Tommy were lying.

The lovers knew that if they kept quiet they were safe, but it was scary and exciting knowing someone was within touching distance. Tommy couldn't resist planting several small kisses all over Maggie's body before whispering in her ear, "While they're having a tipple, how about I have a playful nibble of your nipple, Miss?"

Maggie had to bite her lip to stop from bursting out laughing as she fought the tingling sensation as Tommy continued to kiss her all over. Soon they heard the sound of retreating footsteps as the men made their way home.

Early the next morning, Tommy helped a giggling Maggie climb through the hut's window. Being small, it wasn't easy as she had to balance on some apple boxes to get her body through and Tommy helped her from the outside as he supported her from under her arms. The process wasn't glamorous but they ran laughing all the way through Foxden as if they didn't have a care in the world. At the edge of the orchard Tommy cupped Maggie's face in his hands and drank in her beauty. "Sorry that this is it for now Maggie, I really enjoyed being with you these last two nights."

"And I you, Tommy Dunn. I hope we can see each other soon after you finish in town and before you go back to London."

"I'd like that very much. You are very special Maggie."

They embraced for a final time.

Early that evening Eric Collins came into the pub.

"Mr Collins." Maggie blushed as she poured him a pint. She couldn't help but remember the previous evening. "How are you and Mrs Collins, Pete and Billy? Haven't seen you all in a while."

"Aye, we're doing okay Maggie." He smiled. "And how are you?"

"All going very well, thank you."

"That's good. Oh, by the way, I found this earlier down at one of the Foxden huts..."

He gently placed a small flowered brooch on the counter. "Recognised it as yours, from your grandma I believe?" He turned around and took his beer over to one of the tables and sat down and when Maggie met his eye he gave a slight wink. She blushed more heavily, said thank you and quickly left the bar where she broke into fits of laughter. Eric could hear her from where he was and laughed as well. He must've seen all the set up in the hut, the bed, the wine and glasses.

He knew it was her but not who she was with, how embarrassing.

Chapter Thirty-Nine

Tommy stopped by the Manor's kitchen that afternoon.

"I want no trouble Tommy, do you hear?" said Mrs Sutton sternly on opening the door and crossing her arms as she stood in front of him. "You tore Vivien's heart out, that poor girl," she reprimanded. "Adam can look after himself, but your own sister, Tommy?"

Tommy tried to look as sorry as he could. He took a small step forward and took Mrs Sutton's hands in his and looked her straight in the eye. "Mrs Sutton, Vivien is so very lucky to have a friend in you, to look out for her. I have come to apologise for my bad behaviour and ask for your forgiveness. I will speak to Vivien later but for now, if you can find it in your heart to forgive me, I promise that I will make it up to you all."

Mrs Sutton saw the sincerity in Tommy's face and his words and quietly stepped aside allowing him into the kitchen.

"Thank you" he said, as he sat in response to Mrs Sutton's gesture towards the table. As soon as he sat Adam walked into the kitchen and froze on the spot. Tommy was the last person he expected to see.

"Adam, I am sorry," said Tommy as he stood. "I was out of line and it won't happen again."

Mrs Sutton's radar was way up and she tried to be as inconspicuous as possible standing in the corner of the kitchen drying a cup that was already bone dry. She was fully aware that there were men out in the workshop that she could call upon if needed.

Adam glared at Tommy through his good eye, the other was still shut from yesterday's beating, and the swelling looked like it wasn't going away anytime soon. He had insisted Mrs Sutton get him a steak to place over it to alleviate the swelling, but it hadn't done as well as he had hoped.

Mrs Sutton had confessed to Mr Sutton that it was scandalous to use such an expensive and luxurious commodity. Not being one for wastage she had cooked and served that very steak for Adam for his supper. He was oblivious to this and had chomped away like it was his last ever meal.

For all the times he had frightened her in the past and when he was abusive and rude to them all and for everything he had put his father through, Mrs Sutton did not feel guilty at all about the steak.

"Good on you 'ol girl," Mr Sutton had said, "that's the spirit."

To try and make amends Tommy said that he had business in Maidstone before he was to get the train back to London the following morning and would like it if Adam were to join him. They could spend a little time together and get to know one another a little better. They had had a rocky start, but if they could let bygones be bygones it would make Vivien very happy. Adam wasn't keen at all regarding going into town with Tommy but on hearing that Vivien would be happy, he agreed and said he would drive them that afternoon.

The journey into town was a little frosty at first but soon the conversation flowed. Tommy talked about Vivien as a child and of their upbringing and family members. Tommy could tell that Adam thought highly of his sister but he was still incensed about the man. Damn, his mind just wouldn't let up on this vendetta he had. Tommy genuinely tried to like him; it was just proving to be much harder than he thought.

Tommy led them straight to a bar he knew where the landlord wasn't too strict on opening hours. As the liquor flowed, so did the conversation and Adam informed Tommy that he had plans to marry Vivien. He wanted Vivien to move to the Manor.

"I swear, she will be looked after Tommy, and one day, she'll even become the lady of the Manor. Of course, you would be welcome to stay whenever you wanted and your parents too."

All Tommy could hear was noise, meaningless noise. He supposed Vivien could have a good life living at the Manor – just not with this man. Any man apart from Adam. Tommy's judgement, already a little fuzzy from the booze, suggested that they make a move to a more discreet little place he knew.

It was the early hours when they emerged both a little worse for wear. They were quite near the train station so Tommy guided Adam to a platform bench to sleep it off while he staggered into the park next door to relieve himself. Then unwittingly he fell asleep. A loud noise awoke him some time later. He relieved himself again, then took the time to steady himself as he gingerly walked back to the station, all the while his head was spinning.

The loud noise was a train pulling into the station where stern looking men holding clipboards and shouting at the top of their voices ushered groups of noisy young men aboard. Then the train departed.

Tommy looked around in confusion. Adam was nowhere in sight.

"Looks like you missed it son," said the train guard, as he approached Tommy with a broom.

"Sorry?" said Tommy croakily, not quite comprehending what the train guard was saying.

"The train to London then they're heading off up North." He

stopped when he saw confusion on Tommy's face. "National Service lad, for a two-year stint? There was another lad in the same state as you, passed out on a bench he was. Took three of them to drag him onto the train. You'll be in trouble I expect, from missing it. Good luck son." He continued sweeping along the platform.

What the bloody hell have I done? thought Tommy, as he quickly sobered up. He panicked as he tried to remember what he had done last night. He and Adam had obviously had a skinful, but there was something else. Tommy sat on the bench with his head in his hands desperately searching his memory but nothing was forthcoming. Eventually, he got up and bought a one-way ticket back to the smoke.

Just as he left the ticket office he stopped, frozen in his tracks. The blood seemed to drain from his face as he remembered where else they had frequented last night. The stark shocking realisation of what he had done was beyond frightening.

He knew that the train would terminate in London and they would have to board another for the North. The ticket guard said Tommy's train would get into London around an hour and a half behind the previous train so Tommy realised he wouldn't be able to find Adam there.

But, as he reasoned with himself, Adam was a big boy, he would've sobered up by then and would get off the train in London and get another one back to Kent.

So, problem solved.

Adam's train was filled with raucous young men. Pushing, shoving and general disorderliness was rife in all carriages. The only exception was when the corporals wielding batons descended through the train. Adam was easy pickings to some of his fellow travellers in his drunken state and it looked like he had already gone through the mill as it was. Soon his pockets were being felt and every item pilfered; car keys and documents were flung out of the window. Before long, he was completely unidentifiable.

Chapter Forty

A few weeks after the Dunn family arrived back home Vivien was shocked to learn that she was pregnant. She was almost eighteen, unmarried and very concerned that she hadn't heard from Adam as promised. She was at a complete loss what to do.

When the family where she worked was away for the day, she took it upon herself to telephone the Manor knowing that Mrs Sutton would answer. She didn't like taking liberties like this at work but she didn't know what else to do.

After a few rings, Mrs Sutton did indeed answer. "Vivien!" she exclaimed, "how lovely to hear from you."

"Likewise Mrs Sutton, I hope that you are very well. Is it possible to speak to Adam please?" The short silence scared her and she thought for a moment that they had been disconnected. "Mrs Sutton, are you still there?" she asked nervously.

"Yes, Vivien, I am here. Not sure how to say this really but Master Adam hasn't been seen since he went into town with Tommy the day after you all left. We assumed that he just wanted some time to himself and with past behaviour… as he has done this quite often. I am sure there is nothing to concern yourself about. Did Tommy arrive home safely?"

"Yes, Tommy is home," Vivien said quietly, trying to process the information.

"There you are then."

"May I come and see you Mrs Sutton? Please. I really need to speak to you."

Mrs Sutton detected the urgency in Vivien's voice and said that she was welcome anytime.

That evening, Vivien made sure she was alone with Tommy and asked him if anything had happened between him and Adam the day he came home.

"How do you mean?" he asked a little nervously.

"I spoke to Mrs Sutton today. She said that Adam hadn't been home since you both left for town. What did you both do? Did he say anything about not going back to the village?"

Inwardly, Tommy panicked. He was so cocksure that Adam had sobered up when he arrived in London and went straight back to Kent, that it never even occurred to him to check.

He could see how worried Vivien was and could only assume that Adam had ended up in the North after all, or had alighted in London. Tommy knew he had to be careful about what he said. "We drove into town, parked and went to the pub to get to know one another better," he started. "Yes, I admit, we both had a skinful but that's just how things were. Then we went to the station's platform to sleep it off before we went our separate ways home. Look, while I took a leak in the park, a train came in and the station guard said that someone helped Adam onto the train, obviously thinking he intended to board. He would've sobered up on the journey and alighted when he got to the smoke and then made his way home." As Tommy told this story he almost convinced himself that it was that simple.

Vivien was horrified. "Why didn't you say this before?" she shouted, as she pushed him backwards.

"Didn't give it a thought really. Took it for granted that he was at home. He's a big boy, he can take care of himself. From what I gather, he's been drunk so many times before that he probably sobers up in no time." Tommy genuinely felt this was a perfectly reasonable assumption.

"I need to go back to the Manor," Vivien said. "I will tell Mum and Dad that I spoke to Mrs Sutton to catch up on news and that she kindly invited me to tea and I am welcome to spend the night and catch the next train home. They won't have a problem with this I am sure. And YOU will back me up if I need it. AND you will give me the money for the return fare because YOU are an idiot Tommy Dunn."

Over tea the following afternoon, Vivien looked Mrs Sutton in the eye. "I am pregnant Mrs Sutton. You are the only one who knows. Adam is missing and I do not know what to do and I do not want to tell my parents. Well, not yet."

Mrs Sutton's heart skipped a beat and it took her three attempts to align her cup in the rim of the saucer. She took Vivien's shaking hands in her equally shaking hands. "Goodness me child, don't mind me, I am temporarily off kilter but I will be back on track soon." She took a sip of her tea and this time her hand was as steady as a rock. "Firstly, we have to find Adam."

Vivien smiled, knowing she was right to tell Mrs Sutton, she would know what to do.

The Squire was in London on business so Mrs Sutton telephoned his office and passed on the information that Tommy had told Vivien. The Squire was relieved that they had a little more information to work with. He said that he would begin to make enquiries and would keep in touch.

Before Vivien left the following afternoon a plan had been

devised. Vivien would return to the Manor when the baby started to show. They would say that Mrs Sutton required Vivien's permanent help. Then, when the baby was born, they would decide what to do next. They realised that the plan was not ideal and they prayed that Adam would be back home well before the birth, so they could organise a wedding on his return.

Christmas and New Year came and went and still there was no word from Adam. Vivien was starting to show so Mrs Sutton wrote to the Dunn's as per their plan requesting her help.

The Squire was delighted for Vivien to stay at the Manor as a helper to Mrs Sutton as he knew how much Adam loved her. During the hopping season they had had a very rare father-son conversation when Adam had told his father of his true feelings and love for Vivien and that he hoped that one-day they would marry. But in saying this, Adam had been missing for three months now. Apart from Tommy's beating at the end of the hop season, Adam had seemed blissfully happy. Despite his unreliability in the past, his disappearance at this time did not make any sense at all.

In the coming months, it became perfectly clear to all at the Manor that Vivien was expecting. The Squire was shocked at first then absolutely delighted with the news. He already regarded Vivien as a daughter-in-law and commended Mrs Sutton highly for all that she had done. "Mrs Sutton, I am concerned that Vivien's family doesn't know about her 'condition'. It's only right that we should tell them."

"Oh no, Squire. Please, not yet," Mrs Sutton implored. "Let's wait until we find Master Adam. I am sure that would be easier for everyone, especially young Vivien."

The Squire reluctantly conceded, only because of his fondness for Vivien and not wishing to cause the girl any further embarrassment.

Chapter Forty-One

When Adam had arrived at the army barracks in a beaten up, drunken state he had been sent immediately to the hospital wing while he sobered up and the commanding officer decided what to do with him. The corporals on the train journey had been severely reprimanded for their tardiness and demoted as they had delivered one man too many. The man was not on their inventory and had no papers or identification.

The senior doctor immediately discovered and reported an unfortunate tattoo on the mystery man, and because it was obviously new and raw, the doctor dressed it to avoid infection, but most of all, to avoid any further trouble. The man had also suffered a minor head wound and seemed confused and disorientated that was not alcohol related. It was obvious that he was unaware of his tattoo and foul play was suspected. The commanding officer gave the doctor strict instruction that *the wound* was to be bandaged and concealed until further notice and that no one was to see it.

As time went on the commanding officer felt that they would become a laughing stock for enlisting an unnamed recruit who wasn't even on the register. So, rather than reporting the man straight away to the local constabulary, as he should have done, he decided to keep the mistake in-house. Overall, he thought he would be doing the man a favour by letting him complete his National Service.

Adam recovered. He tried to give his details and his father's contact details, but no one wanted to help or take him seriously. The corporals who had been demoted, gave him a hard time because it was his fault that they lost their stripes. He was sent to solitary for picking a fight and was labelled as a troublemaker. In solitary there was no provision for communication at all with the outside world.

When the allotted solitary period was over, his superiors deemed it relatively safe enough for Adam to be assigned a billet, although he was still instructed to keep his wound covered. Much to Adam's annoyance, he was still denied any outside contact. He did not understand how this could continue and ranted and raved about how it was all a mistake and that he shouldn't have been there at all. Being under pressure, he resorted to his old ways of trying to bully the people around him: he was wealthy, educated, and thought himself 'better' than the people around him.

His bullying attitude and intimidation won him no friends and his constant requests to contact his father repeatedly fell on deaf ears. One day, while visiting the hospital wing to have his bandage changed, the senior doctor angrily warned, "I've heard you are causing all kinds of trouble. If I were you, I would stop being such an arrogant prick and play nice."

"Excuse me?" Adam said defiantly, "just who the bloody hell do you think you are to talk to me that way?"

"Someone who has saved you from getting the shit kicked out of you ever since you arrived, that's who I am," retorted the doctor, as he slowly un-bandaged Adam's upper arm revealing the tattoo. "Just so you know. The word is out. I am not pleased that someone here has broken confidentiality but there is nothing I can do about that now." And with that he left Adam to come to terms with the pending consequences.

Three hours later, Adam was found hanging in the toilet block. His upper arm was cut to shreds where he had obliterated the tattoo. The discarded bloodied razor blade lay innocently on the spattered floor.

Chapter Forty-Two

It had been three months since Vivien had left London and even though she had regularly been in contact with her parents and brother, Tommy was missing his sister. As a surprise he decided to visit her at the Manor, hoping that she had forgiven him for their differences about Adam.

There were moments when Tommy felt guilty that Adam was still missing. Whenever he felt responsible he reminded himself that Adam had regularly gone missing for periods of time in the past so it was not completely out of character. At this point in time though, it was a little concerning due to how Adam had said he felt about Vivien.

When Tommy arrived at the Manor he walked into the kitchen hoping to surprise Vivien but it was he who was surprised. Vivien was heavily pregnant and Tommy was stunned beyond belief.

"Please don't tell Mum and Dad, Tommy, promise me you won't?"

"I won't, I swear," he said dumbfounded as he sat at the kitchen table.

That evening, Mrs Sutton left the siblings alone while Vivien poured her heart out telling Tommy about the love she shared with Adam. "We'd even talked about getting married," she sobbed. "I know he loves me, he really does, but where is he?"

Tommy's heart broke to see his sister so upset. He needed to think and clear his head. He left Vivien and walked to The Crown pub, deliberately avoiding The Oak, where he could easily bump into Maggie. He needed some space and planned to see Maggie some other time. He ended up having too much to drink and slept it off in Foxden Orchard.

The next morning he returned to find absolute chaos at the Manor. The reasons why Adam had disappeared started to fall into place. The village constable had arrived at the Manor to break some devastating news. They had received a telephone call earlier from the commanding officer at the National Service base. Adam was dead. Suicide. No reason was given as to how or why he had ended up at the base, just that he had been serving his country there. Upon hearing all this, Vivien collapsed and went into premature labour.

The Squire demanded an immediate investigation be opened and planned to visit the commanding officer although it would take time for the coroner's report to be released. He was incensed that it had taken this long for information to come through and he was frustrated at the sheer incompetence from all the authorities involved.

Tommy's guilt was more than he could bear. He knew that his stupidity was probably the cause of Adam's death. "Do you know *why* he did it?" Tommy asked the constable waiting by the police car in the Manor's courtyard.

"It's early days," he replied, "and there is an investigation underway."

"Is that all you know?"

The policeman could tell that Tommy was upset. "Look, not sure I should say really, I heard that his upper arm was cut to pieces."

When Tommy heard this, he knew for sure that Adam's death was his fault. His stupidity, jealously and hatred had caused the death of the man his sister loved and now her child, his niece or nephew, would be without a father.

If only he hadn't taken Adam to the tattoo place. The tattooist wasn't too picky that they had arrived drunk and Tommy had given him a five-pound note from Adam's wallet. It had taken five more to persuade him to ink the word RAPIST on Adam's upper arm.

Within a couple of days Vivien's condition stabilised and the Squire insisted that she stay at the Manor to rest for the baby's sake and for hers. They all hoped it would be another couple of months before the baby was born and the Squire knew that he would dote on the child. He vowed to love his grandchild and make up for all the mistakes that he had made with Adam. He contacted Mr and Mrs Dunn and invited them to the Manor. They were shocked about Adam's death and astounded by Vivien's condition but once over the initial shock they were delighted about the baby.

The day after, Eric Collins made the gruesome discovery as Tommy Dunn's body was found hanging in the Squire's barn adjacent to the Manor. He had left a letter addressed to Vivien that simply said: *Forgive me.*

Word soon swept through the village about the tragic deaths of Adam Marsh and Tommy Dunn and, as a mark of respect, some of the Manor's employees went to the pub that evening to raise a glass.

As soon as Eric Collins entered The Oak Pub he caught Maggie's eye and he knew from that moment that it was Tommy that Maggie had been with that night not so long ago. He held his arms open as Maggie rushed to him and sobbed her heart out.

Chapter Forty-Three

Over the next four years Maggie threw herself into her work where she continued as an apprentice mechanic on the estate. She was now more than capable of stripping and rebuilding every kind of farm equipment. She also helped out in the stables and obtained exemplary horsemanship skills.

Unbeknown to anyone, she often went and ate her lunch in the Squire's old creaky barn among the bales of hay and reminisced about Tommy as she lost herself in her memories: the first time they had met when they were children, when she was around five years old and he was a lovable rascal of eight; his smile and those twinkling sky-blue eyes; then, years later when they were older and their attraction had sizzled, goose bumps prickled up and down her arms just thinking about their passion. *Such a waste,* she thought. *He was a beautiful young man we may even have had a future together.*

Maggie felt total peace at the Manor and loved working there as did her father. She smiled recalling a time when she was small and he had hoisted her up onto his shoulders as he ran into the barn to avoid a downpour and she nearly clanked his ears as the lunch boxes she carried swayed wildly as he ran. Then as they sat, he motioned her to be quiet, so they could hear the scurrying all around them as the mice took cover from the sudden inclement weather.

Beautiful memories. But, the time had come to move along. She was preparing to sail to Australia next week. Slowly, she inhaled the old familiar aroma of hay, apples and hops. Although winter, it was still prominent, but not as stuffy and heady as summertime. This was to be the last time she would sit here.

Not for the first time she wondered: *Would all this be happening if not for that four-penny stamp all those years ago?*

Maggie was excited to learn that the Squire was holding a farewell party for her at the Manor and it seemed as if the whole village had accepted the invitation. Early December was normally much too early for Christmas celebrations, but the Squire had decided that this year would be a special exception, plus it would be an added treat for his grandson George.

Mr and Mrs Sutton had arranged for the Manor to be decorated in its Christmas finery just like in the old days and were delighted when Maggie said she wanted to help. They also involved Sally and her parents to help take their minds off the fact that Maggie would be leaving. They all wanted to do their utmost to give her the send-off she truly deserved.

Six days before departure, Mrs Sutton invited Maggie to accompany her around the grounds to select the best Christmas tree. It was the ultimate compliment, the Squire had informed, because for nigh on decades, Mrs Sutton had always achieved this yuletide task alone.

The two women were rugged up tightly as they strolled through the woodland to select the tree when Mrs Sutton stopped suddenly and turned. "We want you to have this, Maggie." She pulled off her mitten and delved into the pocket of her woollen winter coat. "Goodness, it's cold today, I imagine my nose is redder than Rudolph's."

Maggie gave a small chuckle at the thought. "No redder than mine, Mrs Sutton."

Mrs Sutton retrieved a small wrapped item, no bigger than a matchbox and placed it gently into Maggie's hand. "Just a little something to remember us all by. It's for you to open on Christmas Day, out there on the ocean somewhere, wherever that may be. Safe journey and think of us often. I wanted you to have this today so you can pack it away as you'll have enough to contend with over the following week." Mrs Sutton's eyes glistened.

Maggie clenched her hand gently around the gift and leaned in and kissed her on the cheek, then she embraced the woman who she had known all her life. "Thank you, Mrs Sutton. That is more than kind of you. You've taken me by surprise I'm not sure what to say."

"Your thank you covers it perfectly well. Goodness look at us standing out here freezing our boots off. Our tears will turn to icicles if we're not careful. Now, let's find that tree..."

Five days before departure, Maggie received her final letter from McKinnley Station. After all the years of corresponding they were excited to finally be meeting her. They wished her a safe journey and said that they would be seeing her soon. They informed her that Mrs Heppler, McKinnley Station's housekeeper and all-rounder, would be waiting when the ship docked in Fremantle.

It was all becoming very exciting and frighteningly real to Maggie. Her cases were more-or-less packed and she had bestowed most of her possessions on Sally, who was doing her utmost to be brave. They spent as much time together as they could and enjoyed the rest of the day helping out at the Manor preparing for the party.

Four days before departure, Maggie and Sally boarded the bus into Maidstone for a final look around the shops.

"All the best to you Maggie," said Ernie the bus driver as he waved the girls by, not taking their fare. "You are quite the local talking point at the moment. Most of us have never known anyone to venture out of Kent before, let alone to the other side of the world."

"That's kind of you Ernie, thank you. I will miss everyone."

"Yes, thanks Ernie, appreciate that," said Sally as the girls took a seat and placed the blanket over their laps that Ernie left on the seats to keep his passengers warm on brisk days.

The journey was jolly and everyone who boarded wished Maggie a safe journey and not to forget them. Mrs Sharp, who boarded at Kitts Corner decided to sing a Christmas carol medley much to the delight of almost everyone. Mr Knox who had travelled on Ernie's bus ever since he could remember said to Mr Bryant on the next seat that he was grateful to be partially deaf. Mr Bryant cringed slightly as Mr Knox spoke rather too loudly for what he said to be a whisper. Mrs Sharp ignored this as she upped the volume, specially for Mr Knox's benefit, and the girls laughed and joined the other passengers in the medley.

Once in town, Maggie and Sally went to the photographer's shop in the high street for professional pictures to be taken. They posed for one single picture each and two of them together. While the pictures were being developed, Maggie treated Sally to tea and cake in the Department store. Next, they went to a jeweller where Maggie purchased a gold-plated locket and delicate chain. The jeweller helped Maggie to place the Koala stamp inside the locket and listened with delight as she explained the significance.

After they had walked the entire length of the high street they continued up towards the park and saw that the town pigeons had taken refuge in the bandstand that provided a little shelter. When the hour was up they ventured back to collect their photographs in good time to catch Ernie's last bus home and prayed that the bus would make it up 'Problem Hill' without any problem today. The last thing they fancied doing was getting out to push.

It was now only three days until departure and time was flying way too fast. That afternoon Maggie said that she wanted a little time alone to mentally say goodbye to the village and to have a last walk around. Sally understood saying that she would make them a special tea on her return. Maggie raised her eyebrows where Sally said no, she wouldn't be dropping any more ingredients on the floor and they both rolled up laughing at the memory.

Maggie wrapped up and took a leisurely stroll around the village being careful in her footing as it was still quite frosty. She walked down Honeysuckle Lane and stopped outside Primrose Cottage where she seemed to spend ages staring nostalgically at the little cottage with its pale-yellow painted door and window frames. The cottage had been her home for seven happy years and in her heart, it would always be home to her.

Happy memories played before her: from her father making daisy chains, when she fed the chickens as they scrambled around her wellied feet and the time when she was so proud of herself for mastering the lavatory chain, to bouncing down the stairs on her bottom whenever she could get away with it and most of all, the endless treasured and cherished stories her father had told her.

Her various expressions depicted the type of memories she was recalling, but then thoughts turned to the morning that she had come down for breakfast to be met by her sobbing mother and a distraught Mr and Mrs Collins. That was the day her whole world fell apart. The day she became an orphan as such. She shook her head slightly to rid herself of the memory.

She knew Pat Dawson and his family were out at work, so with no one around, she walked up the garden path where over the years she had ran, skipped, jumped and even tripped over one small stone paver that her father said he'd fix but never got around to it. It protruded only a whisker, but from time to time, Maggie's feet seemed to find it. Mr Collins joked that she could trip over thin air.

She now unfolded a piece of paper from her pocket and carefully placed it over the embossed Primrose Cottage tile. With a chunky red crayon she etched gently to and fro as the sign imprinted onto the paper. She planned to keep it with her always as a cherished memento.

Maggie bade a sad silent farewell to Primrose Cottage and made her way back through the village and up to her grandma's house on the hill. At this moment she would gladly give her last sixpence to go back in time for a little while, to see her grandma sitting on the porch and for all the times there was laughter and music when she, Sally and grandma had sing-a-longs or danced. She also thought back to that rare occasion her mother brought her here when she was a small child, when the air raid caused her grandma to have snow in her hair.

"Goodbye grandma," she whispered softly. "I love you."

Chapter Forty-Four

Knowing she needed to do it, Maggie walked almost begrudgingly on to her mother's cottage. Her last visit had been a couple of weeks ago. It hadn't been pleasant, but she knew that she had to come here today. She was taut as she opened the garden gate knowing that the hinge would still protest and squeak from lack of oiling. She always felt tense and on edge whenever she came here as she never knew what kind of reception awaited.

On a few occasions her mother had been too blind drunk completely unaware that she had visited at all. On another occasion her mother had pushed her out of the house shouting that she wasn't to visit again. "I TOLD YOU NOOOOOOOOOO," she had screamed in Maggie's face, as she dragged her daughter by the arm down the garden path.

Maggie took a deep breath and knocked on the door.

"Oh. It's you," Iris said disappointedly.

Maggie was hopeful, this was the best greeting she'd had in ages. Her mother looked appalling, unkempt and dressed in only her under slip. It was actually colder inside the house than it was out, but it seemed the liquor and blanket on the sofa were keeping Iris nice and toasty as she scuttled back and climbed under her blanket. Maggie side-stepped the mail on the mat and entered the living room and wasn't surprised to see how untidy and dirty the living room still was.

"What do you want this time?" asked Iris, obviously inconvenienced.

"I've come to say goodbye. I will be leaving in a few days and just wanted to stop by," she said, trying to maintain eye contact.

"Just wanted to stop by did you? Well, isn't that just grand."

"How did we come to this mother?" Maggie sighed, not really expecting a reply.

"YOU, MAGGIE," bellowed her mother, as she pointed viciously towards her daughter. "You is how we came to. If it hadn't been for YOU then none of this would have happened. You know it's your fault, don't you? You killed your father. Did you know that? You are nothing but a cold-blooded murderer."

Maggie staggered backwards slightly, thankful for the wall to support her. "You're drunk and don't know what you are saying. He was killed because of the bomb in the village, you know that."

"He was taking eggs to Mrs Mews to thank her for the cardigan she knitted you. If he wasn't there he would still be alive today."

Maggie couldn't believe what she was hearing. She knew her father was taking eggs to Mrs Mews but even so, that was not her fault.

This was the final straw.

For years she had taken so much from her mother but she would not be made to feel guilty or take responsibility for her father's death. She was just days away from leaving and she wasn't going to take this guilt-ridden baggage with her.

It was about time her mother heard a few home truths.

"If you seriously believe that, then you are more stupid than I thought," she said to Iris. "You're just lashing out to make excuses. To clear your conscience, if you have one, for being a cold-hearted, unloving wife and mother. You were completely heartless, you left me alone for days on end without food while you were out gallivanting with your lover."

"Again, Maggie? Again? This is soooooo boring," Iris slurred, then more calmly she lit another cigarette and blew a plume of smoke towards the nicotine stained ceiling. "Tediously boring. We've been over this a million times. All I am hearing is whine, whine, whine. GROW UP CHILD."

"Then give me an explanation, you know that's all I've ever wanted. Offer some reasoning to your unmaternal ways. Tell me *why* you feel the way you do. *Make me understand,*" Maggie said, as she cleared some magazines off of the dining room chair and sat down.

"What's to understand?" Iris flicked ash onto the carpet. "You don't like my parenting, so bugger off. Oh, that's right, you are." She laughed. "Bye bye."

"Don't like your parenting? Is that honestly the best you can offer?"

"It's as good as it gets. What's the point? You're leaving, so off you go, don't let me stop you."

"These last few years I've tried to understand why you act like you do and what went wrong between us after father was killed. It's perfectly clear that you should never have had a child, we both know that's true. Even though you came from an abusive childhood, you were too damn stupid, stubborn and ignorant to see that when you married my father your life was beginning for the better."

Maggie stood up. "You are lazy and self-centred. Well, good for you; look where that has got you." She swept her arm across the room. "You live in a shit-heap, you look bedraggled and pathetic, and you'll die a lonely, bitter and twisted old woman. Is this what you really want? No one has any time for you anymore and what on earth possessed you to throw away a great friendship with Betty?"

"Ah, Betty." Iris shook her head pitifully. "Friendships don't last Maggie, remember that. It ran its course. It happens when one side is inferior to the other."

"Oh, don't put yourself down mother."

Iris waved off the insult like she was swotting a fly, then leaned over and picked up her glass of whisky that had a fresh clump of ash floating on the top and gulped the lot, ash and all. "If you've come here for an argument you can leave now. I'm too tired for this, it's old ground Maggie and don't attempt to steer away from the fact that your father's death is on YOUR shoulders."

Maggie angrily pointed to her mother. "I'm not responsible for my father's death, you only mourned him because you are a parasite and didn't have him to feed off anymore." Then, more calmly, she added, "Grandma had you summed up from the start and she was spot on. I thank God I take after my father. He was a decent loving man who deserved so much better."

"Finished now?" garbled Iris as she angrily stubbed out the cigarette on the blackened wooden arm rest and flicked it into the empty glass and dropped it onto the floor where the carpet prevented the glass from shattering as it tipped over and rolled away. She sat back up and slow clapped mockingly at her daughter. "Make little Maggie feel better did it? I never want to see your sorry ass ever again.

"YOU ARE DEAD TO ME, DO YOU HEAR?" Iris's anger mounted with her voice full of venom. "You have been dead to me for years, do you hear?" She looked her daughter in the eye.

"I wish you had never been born."

"You're jealous!" Maggie said, as the revelation suddenly occurred to her.

"Of what. YOU? Don't make me laugh."

"That's it! You couldn't bear the father-daughter relationship I had with my father because you never had one with yours. You've said over the years what a bastard he was and for what it's worth, I am sorry…"

"Don't you dare pity me, child. I'm not jealous of YOU. Who the hell do you think you are?"

"I'm right," Maggie continued. "You didn't have that bond, so you punished us for it because it was what you wanted the most but couldn't have."

"Really? If that's what you want to believe, then good for you. I'm not going to agree just to make you feel better. Leave me alone. ALL I HAVE EVER WANTED IS TO BE LEFT ALONE. You suffocate me, you both suffocated me. I want you gone. I don't need anyone. You cease to exist. GO AWAY."

"The saddest thing of all," said Maggie, not rising to any bait, "is that we could have been the best of friends if you had forgone your bitterness. Do you understand that?

"We could have been the best of friends. Think about that."

"Close the door on your way out." Iris slowly slipped further under the blanket and turned her back on her daughter.

Inside, Maggie was seething. She fought hard against the desire to slam the door off its hinges, but instead shut the door with a gentle click. Shaking with rage at her mother's harsh words and brutal dismissal, but knowing that she hadn't held back either, she walked down the garden path. After a few tears Maggie told herself that she wouldn't waste any more tears over this woman ever again. She had a chance at a fresh start and she was going to grasp it with both hands.

Chapter Forty-Five

It was Saturday 6 December 1958, two days until departure. Sally and Maggie had rushed back from the Manor that afternoon, having completed the final preparations for the party, and had spent the late afternoon and early evening dressing in their best Christmas clothing as they prepared for the evening.

Much to everyone's surprise, as they left The Oak Pub and Mr Vinter was locking up, Mr Sutton pulled up in the Squire's best car ready to chauffeur the guest of honour and her friends back to the Manor in style.

"Thank you Mr Sutton, mighty appreciated," said Mr Vinter, as he helped his wife get into the car.

"Mr Sutton," said Maggie, "Sally and I are wearing heels, you're a lifesaver."

"All part of the service Maggie. Alright everyone, here we go."

Soon the Christmas party atmosphere at the Manor was in full swing and all the guests were having a great evening by catching up with friends, dancing, drinking and eating.

Before it was too busy, the Squire linked Maggie's arm through his and patted her hand. "A moment of your time Maggie, if you please." He led her out of the Great Hall and down to his study.

Maggie hadn't seen this part of the Manor and as she marvelled at the oil paintings and luxurious furnishings, the Squire poured them both a small sherry from the ornate crystal decanter.

"To your very good health," he said, as they gently clinked the tulip shaped glasses. "Your father would be very proud of you Maggie, as we all are." He ushered her to the fireside chairs.

"Thank you Squire, that means a lot. I still miss him very much," she said as they both sat.

"I know you do. We all do. But, it is time for a new chapter in your life Maggie. Things may be tough for a while, but you are strong. You have made the right decision. To that I am certain."

"Thank you, that's comforting to hear."

"Remember. Be safe, be smart and be wise. Trust your judgement Maggie, it won't let you down. If ever you wonder if you are doing the right thing, think of your father. Think what he would do and what he would advise you to do.

"We all know that your father was supportive of your dream, even when you were very small. I remember him telling me about Mr Dwyer giving you that four penny stamp and ever since then you had wanted to go to Australia. We would talk often about it and he glowed with pride at your determination.

"Goodness." He smiled. "They do sound like a lively bunch of characters on McKinnley Station, and that Mrs Heppler, sounds like the Australian version of Mrs Sutton, doesn't she? Now don't you go saying that to Mrs Sutton." He continued to laugh. "I have enough to contend with one let alone two!"

Maggie giggled. "I will let you know in my letters to you, in code, of course." They both laughed.

"I'll look forward to it. I know I'm not your father, but I still look out for you and all I wanted to say is that he trusted you Maggie. Never forget that. Wherever you may be in the world, you will have your father's blessing. And in his absence, the knowledge of that alone should be very powerful indeed. It will carry you through whenever things may be a little tough. It will help you and I pray that it will give you peace."

"Thank you Squire, I really appreciate that and thank you for everything that you have done for me." They finished their sherry and stood.

"Now, are you totally sure you don't want me to drive you to the Docks? It's no trouble at all, you know that."

"Thank you, I know and really appreciate that, but I want to remember everyone in their normal surroundings going about their usual day. I want to do this on my own, if you don't mind."

"I understand and respect your wishes. Right, back to the Great Hall before Mrs Sutton sends out a search party."

The Great Hall in its festive finery always reminded Maggie of that special magical Christmas Eve when she was a child: of the carols on the lawn, Mr Collins appearing to majestically float over the lake while playing the accordion, the male voiced choir that included her father as they held lanterns, the tiny flames from the lanterns dancing in the breeze. It had been one of those special occasions that she would forever treasure.

She now watched as Mrs Sutton weaved in and out carrying trays of cakes, sausage rolls and a multitude of delicious finger food. She was now in her early eighties but she looked as sprightly as always and in her element organising activities at the Manor. Mr Sutton was allotted his usual fireside duties and Vivien was handing out small trays of sherry with Master George by her side. At three years of age he was the image of his father and everyone adored him.

After Mr Dunn's death that summer, Mrs Dunn was warmly invited to live at the Manor to be with her daughter and grandson and she and Mrs Sutton got along like a house on fire and shared the duties between them while Vivien looked after George. Mr Sutton had made George his very own vegetable patch where the youngster enjoyed digging but enjoyed getting muddy more so.

It seemed there was an endless string of partners wanting to farewell Maggie with a dance and as the night went on she thought she had never danced so much in her life. "Are you going to show me up once more with your exemplary dancing Simon?" she laughed, as Simon continued to twirl her around.

"Couldn't resist it Maggie. Goodness, you need the practice girl."

"I must say this before I go, Simon," as they moved around the floor, "Sally likes you and I believe you would make a lovely couple."

When they came up to the final spin, Simon kissed Maggie on the cheek.

"Ask her out," as they looked at each other.

"I will." He smiled back as the prospect uplifted his soul. "Take good care of yourself Maggie and don't forget to write. You will be missed." Then he was gone, swallowed by the crowd.

Next in line was Sally. "If you can't beat them, join them, as the saying goes. It seems this is the only way I will get to spend some time with you at the party. Come on let's dance."

Last to twirl Maggie around the dance floor was Pete Collins. The twins were both now married with children of their own but they had come down to the village specially to farewell their childhood friend.

"All the best to you Maggie," said Pete with a hug.

"Cheers, Pete and likewise."

"We'll miss you, Maggie," said Eric Collins as he gave her a hug. "Be safe and remember us."

"Bye Mr Collins, there's so much I wanted to say..."

"No need, Maggie," said Mrs Collins as she hugged her also. "We know, love. There will always be a special bond between us. We consider you the daughter we never had. Enjoy your life, you are doing the right thing. Your father would be proud."

"Thanks Mrs Collins, that means a lot. I am so sorry how things worked out between you and my mother..."

"No need to apologise when it is not your doing. What's done is done." She hugged Maggie again.

"We always regarded you as a little sister," said Billy, as he hugged Maggie for the last time.

"And I shall miss my big brothers," said Maggie. She wiped away a tear. "You taught me good life skills, and you never know when I may need to use a catapult," she exclaimed and they all laughed. "Did you ever give your mother back the elastic?"

"Elastic?" queried Betty. She eyed the twins who towered above her. "You mean that catapult *elastic* that mysteriously disappeared from a certain pair of trousers back in 1941 give or take?"

"You knew?" asked the twins in unison.

Betty winked at her sons. "Completely transparent. A mother knows everything..." She kissed Maggie on the cheek. "Safe journey love, we will miss you." She escorted her husband and sons away leaving Maggie to the next group of well-wishers.

"Isn't this a great party? Everyone seems to be having a good time," Maggie said to Sally.

"Think we wish that time could stop for just a moment," said Sally, "Make it at least this time last week. No, make it this time two weeks ago or even three..."

"How many sherry's have you had?"

"Only three." Giggled Sally. We'll wait till my folks are asleep and then sneak a couple more, like in the old days."

Maggie was just about to agree, when…

"I always knew." Mr Vinter was standing behind his daughter laughing.

Sally was just about to reply when Mrs Sutton came by with a platter.

"Cheesy sticks anyone?" she enquired.

Sally and Maggie burst into laughter, bordering on hysterics, at Mrs Sutton's perfect timing. They dashed through the crowd leaving Mr Vinter and Mrs Sutton looking puzzled.

"I'll never understand those two," he said, as he scooped up a couple of cheesy sticks.

"It's the young," said Mrs Sutton, as if that explained everything.

All too soon the party came to an end. Mr Sutton drove Maggie and the Vinters home with Maggie waving frantically out the back window to everyone until they were out of sight.

Chapter Forty-Six

Maggie and Sally spent their final day together trying to make it seem like just another day. It wasn't possible. They rugged up and took a stroll down Foxden Orchard where hundreds of memories flooded Maggie from when she was a small child riding in her little seat on the back of her mother's bicycle to playing with all her friends and to sitting with all the grown-ups at morning break.

Her heart quickened when they approached that special tree where she and Tommy had been and she remembered their sizzling time together. They bypassed the hop-pickers hut that he had decorated out for her. She smiled and thought about telling Sally how she and Tommy had nearly been caught by Mr Dawson and Mr Collins.

"You okay Maggie?" enquired Sally, "you seem flushed."

"Fine Sally, just remembering things. Lots of memories down here. Let's say we head back for a cuppa, my feet are freezing, how about yours?"

"Yes, it's a bit fresh today, isn't it? Come on." They linked arms. "Let's go and sit by the fire and toast some bread then put on enough butter so it ooooozes down our chins like when we were kids."

"Now you're talking," said Maggie as they headed back to the pub trying to avoid all the frozen ruts in the orchard.

That evening Mr and Mrs Vinter cooked a special meal. It was an extraordinary cross between happy and sad, celebration and farewell. Over the years Mr and Mrs Vinter had naturally become like Maggie's second parents and they were finding it hard to accept that she would be leaving for good. To brighten up the conversation Mr Vinter asked, "What is it with you girls and cheesy sticks? Every time they are in the picture you two are consumed by giggles."

Before Maggie and Sally stopped laughing, Mr Vinter said, "See, Gwen, it wasn't my imagination, I told you – cheesy sticks. There, that proves it, they're off again…"

"Oh Dad, please stop, my stomach hurts." Sally reached for a handkerchief to wipe her eyes.

"It all goes back to the Coronation…" said Maggie, as she dabbed her eyes with her hankie also.

"But that was five years ago," said Mrs Vinter as she started to laugh too.

"Why you are laughing Gwen?" asked Mr Vinter.

"It's infectious," was all that Mrs Vinter could offer.

"At the Coronation," Maggie went on, "Sally and I were making cheesy sticks when the block of cheese sort of ended up on the floor… well, twice actually. We were going to get rid of the bits but Mrs Vinter walked in and Sally sort of, well before we knew it, she just…"

"I panicked, not sure why but I did. I sort of plonked the cheese into the mix and hence the mix was a mix of gritty bits."

Mr Vinter burst into a bellow of a laugh as the mystery was finally solved. "I can still recall eating one of those sticks and it had a gritty texture." He took a long swig of beer as if to wash away the taste.

"Sorry, Dad." Sally smiled.

"Sorry, Mr Vinter." Maggie was grinning.

"Well, you both need to work on your sorrys! That was said with lack of feeling," he said. They all burst out laughing together.

"Maggie," said Mrs Vinter, "you are like another daughter to us, you know that and you two will always be sisters. I know we'll see you in the morning, but we won't prolong the painful goodbye. We love you Maggie, always remember us, we'll always remember you, and be safe. We will look forward to all of your news from Sally."

Mr Vinter nodded in agreement as he and his wife embraced Maggie with tears in their eyes.

"I will miss you so much," said Maggie, "all of you. You have been so kind taking me in and treating me like your family, you will always be family to me. I love you all too."

They left the girls to spend the last remaining hours together where they were awake most of the night reminiscing over all the memories that they had shared. They knew they wouldn't see each other ever again and they cried between their laughter.

The girls awoke at dawn. All their words to each other had been spoken and they treasured their last precious moments together in a serene comfortable silence. Mr Vinter carried Maggie's two suitcases downstairs and Maggie took in the pub for the final time. She visualised the pub bursting at the seams during the crowded hopping season on balmy evenings and she remembered the sound of the harmless banter between the city and country folk. Her heart fluttered as she remembered when Tommy had sweet-talked her out behind the bar and also when Mr Collins had brought back her missing brooch, then the awful memory when she knew that Tommy had died.

She embraced all the Vinters quickly through a stream of tears then picked up her suitcases and shoulder bag and without looking back (for fear of running back!) she walked across the road to the Post Office.

The Squire and Mr Dwyer had worked together, with Maggie's permission as they arranged for the majority of Maggie's savings to be wired into an account set up for her with the same bank used by McKinnley Station and this prevented Maggie from having to travel with a huge sum of money.

A few days prior, Mr Dwyer had also handed Maggie some cash from her savings to tie her over for the journey and had also added some of his own in case there were any emergencies and to help her settle in when she arrived.

"Hello Maggie," said Mr Dwyer and she smiled at the familiar 'ding' of the bell over the door "Just wondering how different your life would have been if you hadn't taken such a liking to that stamp all those years ago, when you were only knee high to a grasshopper?"

"I wonder too, Mr Dwyer. It's funny how something as small as a stamp has got me where I am today." She hugged him warmly.

"Indeed. But, it is through your hard work and determination that has gotten yourself where you are today young lady. Don't you forget that. You are extremely fortunate as not everyone has a chance to pursue and live their dream. Life is very interesting at times. Do you still have the stamp?"

She smiled and unbuttoned the top of her coat. "Sally and I went into town the other day and I bought this," she said, as she showed Mr Dwyer her new gold-plated pendant. She carefully opened the hinge to reveal the koala stamp affixed inside. "It's my talisman. Do you like it?" she beamed.

"I think it is just perfect Maggie and after all these years it will shortly have completed the round-trip home. I hope Australia will be a good home for you too."

"Thank you for everything Mr Dwyer, you are a good friend. Speaking of good friends, where is Simon, is he here?"

"Alas, no. He hoped you would understand and sends his good wishes for a safe journey."

"I understand, Mr Dwyer. I'll telephone when I reach Tilbury Docks and I will write again when I arrive in Fremantle to let you all know I've arrived safely.

"Good bye, Mr Dwyer and thank you again for everything."

"I'll await your call and will pass on all news. Take good care of yourself and have a safe journey."

He opened the door as Maggie picked up her suitcases and stepped out of the Post Office for the last time. The air was still crisp, and the morning sun hadn't yet melted all the frost covering the grass on the village green.

She knew that Sally would be looking through the upstairs net curtain, so she put down one case and blew a kiss at her window. The curtain twitched in response as Sally returned the gesture. She tearfully watched as her best friend in all the world walked down the street and out of sight forever.

Maggie handed her ticket to the stationmaster as he bade her a safe journey. She recalled the first time she went to the platform with her parents to greet the hop-pickers. It had been a noisy hub of activity then. Today, she was the sole person waiting for the London train. She walked over to the Marden station sign near the waiting room and with a warm smile she slowly brushed her hand over the red painted sign as each of her fingers gently felt in and out of the embossed letters.

When the train arrived she found a carriage all to herself and sat staring out the window as her beloved countryside and home swept passed for the last time. After a while she unwrapped the small packed lunch inside her shoulder bag and found a note in Sally's familiar handwriting, she missed her friend so much already. The note said to look after herself and to stay safe and she hoped that she enjoyed her lunch. She also reminded Maggie that she wasn't abandoning her father, grandma or Tommy and said that as long as they were in her heart they would be with her forever. She ended with a PS: 'I promise, no grit' and when Maggie unwrapped further she found a small batch of cheesy sticks that caused her to laugh and tear up a little.

Then there was a PPS as Sally referred to their first day at school where she informed her that no old decrepit rulers were required in which to make special friends, Maggie just had to be herself for people to love her unconditionally.

Chapter Forty-Seven

Maggie was one of a vast number of British subjects known as 'Ten Pound Poms' due to the ten pound fare set by the Government. Because she had an offer letter of employment from McKinnley Station, together with a certificate stating her mechanical qualification, the Australian authorities agreed that this was adequate to bypass hostel accommodation and she would be eligible to apply for citizenship after one year's residence.

Maggie's head was buzzing with all kinds of thoughts, memories and people as she travelled up to London then boarded another train onward to Tilbury Docks. When she arrived, she realised she wasn't prepared for the sheer scale of the ship. She had known it would be big but this surpassed her imagination. The dock was abuzz with passengers, crew and the dock workers as they prepared the ship for the journey.

The process for boarding went by in a blur. She was overwhelmed and felt quite scared and excited all rolled up with a mixture of doubt and insecurity. There were a few occasions when, if she could have, she would have bolted back home. Her head was crammed with so many different emotions that she now regretted not having anyone with her.

The Squire would have calmed her down and thinking of this helped her through the afternoon. She remembered his advice and thought of her father and she knew that he would tell her to take a deep breath and be reassured that she was doing the right thing and to make the most of her new adventure. Thinking this gave her the strength she needed as she took a deep breath, held her head high and proceeded to board.

It was December 8 1958, and this ship would be her home for the next four weeks.

The crew were very helpful and once her paperwork was all in order she found her cabin. Small was indeed the word for it, but what had she expected? It had everything she needed, a bed, chair, small wardrobe and a small table.

There were ample shared facilities down the deck and Maggie was grateful for what she had, especially when she learned that not all ships catered for single cabins and some only had dormitory accommodation.

As she unpacked a few things she discovered that Sally had somehow sneaked a small batch of letters into her suitcase with strict instructions on each envelope to open them at various stages of the journey. It was extremely tempting to open the lot in one go, but she maintained some self-control and opened the first envelop only.

'Letter one, open on first boarding' it was titled. Maggie sat on the bed and read: 'Welcome aboard Maggie!' She grinned from ear to ear, it was as if Sally was with her. 'Unpack, then go and explore your new home. Meet as many people as you can, you are all in the same boat – literally!!! Take care and enjoy day one of your adventure. Love you lots xx'

How thoughtful of Sally. Maggie headed towards the upper decks and detected the smell of salt in the air. She navigated her way to the dining hall that was abuzz with people milling around as they found their table. She was guided to a table that had one seat remaining.

"Hello,' she said, smiling at the seven other occupants who were introducing themselves to each other and shaking hands as they greeted her warmly, 'I'm Maggie, pleased to meet you all."

Everyone took their seats and proceeded to talk about their boarding stories and to tell their fellow passengers a little about themselves. Maggie felt herself relax and she enjoyed the meal and the company.

There was a young family of four who were immigrating to be with other family in Perth, the two boys reminded Maggie of Pete and Billy as youngsters. The other three passengers were an older couple who were going to live with their son who had immigrated a few years back and one other single lady passenger like herself. Her name was Nicola and she was a qualified nurse who had obtained a posting at a hospital in Perth. Maggie liked her instantly. Nicola was a little older than she and a good head taller and she had hazel eyes and long auburn hair.

"I cannot tell you how excited I am, Maggie," said Nicola, "I have been working towards this for a few years, I now have my qualification and am finally on my way! How about you?"

"I am going to an outback sheep station. I have a qualification in mechanics and hope to be of some use out there. I've been corresponding with the family there for many years and feel like I know them already!"

"That sounds much more exciting than what I'm doing," laughed Nicola, "You seem lovely, I'd love for us to talk more about how we came to being here. Don't think me rude, but I had always intended to use this journey time as study time and I plan on hijacking the ship's library for the duration. Perhaps we can sit together at meals if you wish?"

"Completely understand. Yes, we'll catch up meal times."

The conversations that followed were a mix of tales and adventures from their fellow travellers until it was time to retire for the night.

Over the next few days, Maggie's outgoing nature helped make new friends wherever she went. She found it comforting to know that there were a number of passengers travelling alone and most people were friendly and helpful. Although she felt safe, for her peace of mind each night she secured a chair under the cabin doorknob before she went to sleep.

She discovered early on that she wasn't a natural born sailor. Even the slightest rocking motion caused her to feel queasy. She tried lots of things to take her mind off of it but nothing seemed to work. Even all the old wives remedies that her fellow travellers were so eager to share didn't help alleviate the sickness. So, whenever she felt queasy she retreated to her cabin and sought solace in reading with the comfort of knowing there was a bucket in the corner if she needed it.

This is all part of the adventure, Maggie reminded herself. *I need to embrace the lows as well as the highs. But, when your new best friend is a bucket…*

She lay on her bunk and eyed one of Sally's letters and knew that it was time to open the envelope titled 'Iffy Tummy'. As she started to read, her insides were going up and down in time with the motion of the ship. Sally had written:

'Sorry it got to the point where you had to open this letter Maggie, I hope it isn't too rough for you. I don't think on this occasion that I will be of any help and to be honest, I feel a little queasy just writing about it, but that's not helping you at all so sorry for that! Try and sleep it off if you can, big hug. Yes, I know that this letter is absolutely useless, and I'm hoping you never have to read it, so I don't feel too silly.

Love you lots, take care xxx'

Maggie didn't know whether to laugh or cry at this. Typical Sally, trying her utmost to make her feel better. She would heed Sally's advice and try and sleep it off.

On good days, Maggie walked numerous circuits around the decks and spent as much time up on the top deck as she could. She joined in card games, general knowledge quizzes, bingo and other games organised by the crew. The ship had a decent library that she visited often and enjoyed immersing herself in stories.

She tried to keep a daily diary and knew that one day it would be good to look back and re-live the experience. It was important to write how she felt and the voyage gave her more than enough time to think about things.

At this stage she felt it was fair to say that she was not really enjoying her new adventure. She had wobbled on more than a few occasions wondering if she had made the right decision. She hadn't been away long but missed everyone terribly and she put a big part of her feelings down to not feeling well and more than a little homesick. Ever the optimist she hoped that she would think back to these times in the future and take comfort that she had indeed made the right decision.

"You okay Maggie?" said Nicola as they walked around the top deck, "you look a little forlorn today."

"Just a bit down that's all. Missing everyone, probably the same for everyone I know. It's the adjusting, it will take some time to get used to a new routine." Maggie breathed in the sea air. It was a glorious sunny day and the weather was getting warmer.

"Yes, that's the hard part Maggie," said Nicola, she gently shoulder bumped Maggie in solidarity as they weaved around children playing on the deck. "Missing friends and family is all part and par, but we'll be okay. Nurse Nicola says that it is normal to expect down days, and a glass of wine with your dinner is the best medicine I can prescribe."

"You are the best nurse I know," laughed Maggie, "isn't that sea just spectacular? I've never seen a more vivid crystal blue, truly beautiful." Maggie peered over the rail and then continued their stroll.

Chapter Forty-Eight

Maggie found comfort in clutching her pendant whenever she questioned her reasons for leaving and found that it gave her the strength to carry on. She opened another of Sally's letters, titled 'Wobbles'.

'Dearest Maggie,

You will probably wobble, I would definitely wobble. Wobbling is natural, it's who we are. All my letters are silly, I know that. I wobbled writing about wobbles! I believe that wobbles are nature's way of keeping your emotions and decisions in check. It's like a safety device. You will be okay and I sincerely hope that the only wobbles you get are caused from the swaying of the ship, nothing else!

Love you xx'

The crew made a special effort over Christmas and New Year as they decorated the common areas with beautiful decorations and assembled a large artificial tree in the foyer near the concert hall. On Christmas Eve the passengers joined in with the crew at the carol concert and as the ocean was calm Maggie was delighted to join in.

Early next morning she thought she was dreaming when she heard bagpipes. When she stirred, she realised the sound was coming closer and closer and as she poked her head out of her cabin door she saw the lone piper turn down the end of the corridor and disappear. It was Christmas Day and she was in the middle of the ocean. She rushed to the table and sat looking at the two gifts waiting for her.

First, she opened the one that had been given to her from Mrs Sutton when they chose the Christmas tree for the Manor. The matchbox size was intriguing as she slowly unwrapped to find a small silver brooch. Maggie clutched it tenderly to her chest as she teared up a little. It was one of the best presents she could have asked for and so very poignant – a silver primrose, such a thoughtful gift.

She held the other gift from Sally, savouring to make it last as she took her time to unwrap. It was a delicate silver bracelet with silver primroses attached and Maggie couldn't help but laugh out loud at the wonderful gifts. Inside the box Sally had written a small note that wished her a Happy Christmas and that yes, Mrs Sutton and she had gone to the same jeweller in town!

She then opened up the letter from Sally marked 'Christmas Day!' and gleefully read as Sally wished her a Happy Christmas and said that the whole village would raise a glass to her wherever she may be. Maggie hoped that Sally had loved her Christmas gift too as she had left it with Mrs Vinter. Ironically, she had bought Sally a silver pendant from the same jeweller that she had purchased her pendant and chain from.

It had been just days before Maggie was leaving that the two girls had gone into town. It had been tricky to distract Sally so Maggie had quickly handed a little written note and money to the jeweller asking for his discretion in helping her purchase an item. He had been a good sport and had briefly gone to his storeroom on the ruse of selecting a suitable box for Maggie's pendant whereas he was really wrapping Sally's gift.

The waiters served a traditional Christmas meal with all the trimmings and after it was over, Maggie and her fellow diners stood and sang more carols with the crew as they toasted Christmas day on the ocean. It wasn't quite the same as Christmas at the Manor, but it was still a lot of fun.

A few days later, just prior to dusk, the ship entered rough seas. At the onset, Maggie coped quite well as Nicola had taught her some breathing techniques that had helped considerably. They sat at a small table in the dance hall and watched with much amusement as couples tried their best to dance the Quick Step.

Everyone watching and everyone participating were laughing as the couples tried their hardest to dance correctly. Even the musicians were amused as a wave would tilt the ship and cause the dancers to all head towards one side of the floor then the other.

At one point, the trumpet player blew a hilariously high-pitched note as he burst into laughter while playing and watching the couples stagger all over the dance floor. Afterwards, the Quick Step was renamed as the Quick, Quick, Double Quick, Quick Step.

Maggie recorded in her diary that they had sailed down the Mediterranean and she was mesmerised by the sheer blue of the sea, as clear as a blue summer sky. When she was on the top deck looking out toward the horizon, it was as if the sky and sea were as one, completely merged, making it difficult to know where one started and the other stopped.

When they passed Egypt she joined a brief tour with her fellow diners who had all bonded well to see some of the pyramids. They even went on a camel ride. She had written a huge pile of letters to Sally describing her visits to these exotic places and she planned on posting them all when the ship docked in Fremantle. When she described the colour of the sea and sky to Sally, she ended the letter saying that it would be a very difficult jigsaw puzzle!

Days of sailing flew by with brief ports of call in Yemen, Ceylon and Bombay and soon they were completing the final leg to Fremantle. The ship docked before sunrise and Maggie was up and dressed and felt refreshed. She was more than ready to meet Mrs Heppler who would be waiting for her dockside.

The time had come to open Sally's final letter. Maggie wondered what delight Sally would have come up with this time.

'Dearest Maggie,

My one true best friend. You have now arrived at Fremantle after a long time at sea and hope that you can start to walk in a straight line again! As you have been good and opened this letter on your final day at sea (I hope you didn't cheat and open when you first boarded!) this is to say best of luck, I miss you already and I will write very soon to you at McKinnley Station.

I leave you with this fond memory from the days of the week rhyme from our early days in school…

Thursday's Child has far to go…

You made it, Maggie!

Love you lots xx'

Maggie held the letter to her heart and shed a tear. She missed her best friend but she also felt pride and joy. Her dream had come true, she was here! It was still scary, but she knew she would be okay. From here it was onwards and upwards and she couldn't wait to get started.

Acknowledgements

My heartfelt thanks, Stephen and Annette for recommending Brolga Publishing and added gratitude to you Annette for reading my first draft and encouraging me to submit my manuscript. Thank you, Mark Zocchi, Julie Capaldo and Elly Cridland at Brolga Publishing, for believing in my story and for your expert advice, editing, typesetting, designing and guidance through the whole publishing process.

To my great circle of friends, family and colleagues both in Australia and England. I appreciate your never-ending encouragement, support, fabulous stories, memories and character influence! In particular Debbie, Peter and Frances *who all live at the real Primrose Cottages*, Aunty Brenda, Tracy, Hazel, Elaine and Russell, Pat, Sue, Mel and Ian, Trina and Mark, Alex and Gareth, Yvette and Grant, Kim, Kathy, Warren, Chitra, Russell, Olga, Gail, Julie and Margaret. Space dictates, so immense appreciation to those I have not mentioned as you all made a huge difference just by asking how things were going every time we met – you all walked alongside me and kept me company as I pursued my dream.

Thank you, dad, for keeping a space on your bookshelf for many years awaiting this moment. Please clear a little more room as book two is approaching! Your childhood memories and stories of actual events gave me a better understanding of the village during the war and allowed me to build a better picture of that time. Your endless love and support have always meant the world to me as we are two peas in a pod.

I thank and acknowledge you, mum, as your influence has enhanced my character writing. I thank you because you were able to bring out my best creativity that I believe would not have happened under different circumstances. Childhood memories of yesteryear and village stories gave me a better insight to capture my characters in the era.

Debbie, you are still my best friend - even though you ratted on me during an English class some forty-five years ago causing me to lose three house-points… *still not over it!* Seriously Deb, I am blessed to have your lifelong friendship with endless happy memories. Thank you for your valued feedback as you read my first draft as we re-lived some of our school antics through Maggie and Sally. Distance does not diminish a true friendship as we live on opposite sides of the world. I dearly miss catching up for a coffee and a cake or three.

To my son, Matt and daughter, Kelly thank you for your encouragement, pep talks and for making me endless cups of coffee, particularly when accompanied by incentive goodies so I could continue writing. You listened to ideas and gave valuable input and helped when I came across a sticky situation that I had to write my way out of. Thanks also, Kelly, for reading my first draft and for great character discussions. To you both, I will forever be in your debt for your infinite tech support where you saved the day on many occasions. I will always be a very proud mum.

Lastly, to my wonderful husband, Wayne. I cannot thank you enough for your endless support during this pleasantly challenging, rewarding and roller coaster journey to achieve my dream. Of the hundreds of hours where I commandeered the dining room table with endless pieces of paper and for cooking more than your fair share of dinners, although we all know that your dinners are way better than mine! You listened to plot ideas and gave valuable input. You kept the house and its occupants ticking over while also working hard so I could complete one more chapter, then another. This year marks our 30th wedding anniversary, so thank you as always for being nothing less than supportive. We are a fab team. You are an inspiration, my rock and my soulmate.

My dream was to see *Thursday's Child* on my bookshelf. So, collectively, I send each and every one of you my sincere gratitude because I could not have achieved this without you all. Thank you.

from Orchards to Outback

The compelling sequel to ***Thursday's Child***

Ten Pound Pom Maggie Harris arrives in Fremantle Australia, eager to begin her new life on McKinnley Sheep Station. This is the country she has been fantasising about since she was a little girl and saw a koala on a postage stamp.

From the moment Maggie arrives at the station (in a blaze of dust and barking kelpies) she knows Australia is the place for her. Life in outback Australia is very different to life in the English countryside. Maggie soon realises even though the landscape may look foreign, people world-wide are the same; there are good and bad, kind and cruel.

The McKinnley family welcomes Maggie into their lives but other difficulties arise and threaten her stay.

The chemistry between her and the station owner's son Jack, is undeniable. But Jack is engaged to Kara, a dangerous, unbalanced young woman, and Maggie knows she must keep her true feelings to herself for the well-being of all concerned.

But can she? Will true love find a way or will Maggie be destined to watch as the man she loves is deceived and she is threatened with deportation from the country that she has grown to love and has become her home?

ORDER

Thursday's Child

Tracey Friday

ISBN: 9780987639004			Qty
	RRP	AU$24.99	.....
Postage within Australia		AU$5.00	.....
		TOTAL* $________	
		* All prices include GST	

Name: ....

Address: ....

....

Phone: ....

Email: ....

Payment: [ ] Money Order [ ] Cheque [ ] MasterCard [ ]Visa

Cardholder's Name: ....

Credit Card Number: ....

Signature: ....

Expiry Date: ....

Allow 7 days for delivery.

Payment to: Marzocco Consultancy (ABN 14 067 257 390)
PO Box 12544
A'Beckett Street, Melbourne, 8006
Victoria, Australia
admin@brolgapublishing.com.au

Be Published